Love
Follows
THE *Heart*

JUNE MASTERS
BACHER

HARVEST HOUSE PUBLISHERS
Eugene, Oregon 97402

LOVE FOLLOWS THE HEART

Copyright © 1990 by Harvest House Publishers
Eugene, Oregon 97402

Bacher, June Masters.
    Love follows the heart / June Masters Bacher.
        ISBN 0-89081-748-0 (Trade Paper)
        ISBN 1-56507-248-0 (Mass Paper)
        I. Title.
    PS3552.A257L67   1990   89-27077
    813'.54—dc20   CIP

Printed in the United States of America.

To
The Wilsons and the Bachers,
Family of My Husband, George Wilson Bacher,
Who Are Vital Links Of
Oregon's Pioneer History
In the Fields of Railroading, Agriculture, and Medicine

Contents

The kindgom of God is not meat and drink, but righteousness and peace and joy.... Let us therefore follow after the things which make for peace, and things wherewith one may edify another.

—Romans 14:17,19

It is astonishing how little one feels poverty when one loves.

—Bulwer

1

Wedding with a Vow
"To Keep"

Alone, in the still of the night, True North pressed a warm cheek against the age-smoothed gallery post. It was cool and comforting. Motionless, face lifted to the stars, she breathed in the mystic fragrance of the June night. Something tugged at her senses. Some small demon of apprehension which had no right to be there clawed at her inner peace as if in effort to destroy her joy.

"Go away!" she commanded. "You are unwelcome—uninvited—"

And then the slender, blonde girl laughed at herself. Why should there be a sense of fear or dread, or even the tiniest molecule of uneasiness? After all, it was not as if she were marching to the gallows tomorrow! She was marching down the stairs of "Turn-Around Inn," where she and Young Wil had spent so many childhood hours—straight into his waiting arms. And with her would be . . .

Happiness flooded her being again, rendering her incapable of completing the thought which, in some strange way, might be the culprit disturbing her tranquility. Nothing, *nothing*, was going to spoil the perfection of her wedding day. Up, up, up through the golden glory of the heavens her spirit climbed to God.

"Please, Lord," she prayed, "let me be the right wife for this wonderful man You have chosen for me. Together let us work always for the highest and the best, because we have lived it with Your help—"

The prayer would have included Marty and Midgie, who were so fragile in their fledgling faith, had there been no interruption. But the soft twitterings of nightbirds broke the sacred silence of the dark, their tender flute-notes an undeniable "Amen."

Surprisingly, True slept late. The sun was peeking into her bedroom window inquiringly, reminding her to rush. Food was out of the question, although a tempting aroma of coffee trailed up the stairs. Any minute now Aunt Chrissy and the twins would be here, meaning well but actually being more hindrance than help. She smiled tenderly as she stepped out of the long nightgown. Always she would remember her aunt and Grandma Mollie's attention to detail during the prenuptial shopping. How Aunt Chrissy had shocked the saleslady with her disdain of the flower-splashed silk material which the woman had tried to lure her into purchasing, parading the length of Centerville's Ladies' Best Apparel Shop! Rolling her eyes ceilingward with practiced skill, the enterprising lady had clasped her hands, their nails highly buffed, as she paraded before them draped in an entire bolt of the cloth. This dress, she declared to her obviously "classy" customer, would rekindle her husband's interest and outshine the bridal gown—to which Aunt Chrissy had answered coolly, "My husband's interest needs no rekindling. It is the flame of love we hope to pass on to our daughter, whom I have no desire to outshine!"

A lift of her hand to smooth the widening gray streak that striped the midnight black of her right temple had settled the matter. The clerk sighed and brought back the navy crepe de Chine. Christen Elizabeth North nodded and joined Miss Mollie in search for the proper fabric for the grandmother-of-the-bride gown.

Heart aching with love for the two women who had shaped her life, True had watched Grandma Mollie (Malone O'Higgin), hair now whiter than the winter snows atop Mount Hood, select patterns for the event which rounded out their dreams. God bless them! Their definition of love cut a pattern for her to follow which was far more important than the dresses which their clever fingers would design.

And their sentimentality was an added trim. "I would settle for a barn, horses as witnesses," Young Wil had laughed. "But I will go along with *anything* that makes them happy and enables me to claim one Miss Trumary North as my bride!"

From inside the circle of his arms, True agreed, knowing that he would have preferred the third-generation "Big House," where he had grown up as the namesake of his uncle, Dr. Wilson North. True herself might have preferred a church wedding. But they were little more than consulted. The wedding was to take place at Turn-Around Inn, once a home-away-from-home when stagecoaches instead of trains were the means of transportation in the Oregon Country.

Trains! True leaped to her feet, moving with the sense of urgency to finish dressing as if she were chasing the last coach of a rapidly disappearing freight train. Thank goodness, there was no question as to what *she* would wear, for Aunt Chrissy and Grandma Mollie had taken care of that matter too: her aunt's wedding gown, of course (and Miss Mollie's before her). Midgie, bride-to-be of True's adopted brother, Marty, would wear the pale-blue gown that Evangeline, True's natural mother, had worn when the sisters had a double wedding.

Dressed now, she stood before the mirror, molten-gold curls caught up in a snood until the moment Aunt Chrissy would adjust her veil. Both girls would carry nosegays of sweet-scented wood violets. There would be few jewels (Midgie wearing Grandma Mollie's only jewelry of value, a single-strand pearl necklace), and True's only adornment would be the sapphire-and-diamond brooch around which so much of the family history would remain forever in orbit.

The girl in the looking glass twisted and smiled. Her lips made no movement. But from somewhere True heard the greeting loud and clear: *Hello, Mrs. Wil North.* The sweetest words this side of heaven . . . the words she had waited for all her 20-year life . . .

And that was the last clear memory she preserved of the preparations other than Aunt Chrissy's slipping a pair of white gloves over the ones that True was wearing to keep them as spotless as her vows. As unblemished and undefiled as the sweet virginity of body and soul, the most precious gift a bride could offer her husband. True understood the symbolic gesture. She had been conceived out of wedlock and marveled now at her aunt's ability to bring her sister's daughter up so genteelly while preserving the memory of "Angel Mother" so beautifully. Her delicate, childlike mother was blameless, Aunt Chrissy explained. That was how God worked—when one asked His forgiveness.

True and Midgie, daughter of Conductor Callison (True's self-appointed guardian in her West-to-East trek in search of her identity), now "given" by their fathers, stood side by side—two near-identical Dresden-china beauties, trembling like aspen leaves in a gentle breeze. But there the resemblance ended. True's violet eyes, now cast downward behind her veil, gave vulnerability to her face. But even her maidenly blush did not deny the courage of the rounded jaw jutted out ever so slightly. By contrast, Midgie looked uncertain, almost afraid.

And that is how their eyes met those of their respective husbands. True, adoringly. Midgie, imploringly.

The timelessly beautiful vows were made: "to have...
to *keep*..." There was a fractional pause when Marty
claimed a brother's right to kiss the other bride, the
words "to keep" lingering. It was as if somehow True had
pledged herself to two men.

2

Departure and Return

There followed a flurry of good wishes and congratulations. Somebody was pumping away at the old organ,
and guests had to shout above it. The smiling clergyman,
in futile effort to quiet the jubilant guests in order to
introduce the newlyweds with proper dignity, upset Miss
Mollie's improvised altar, so carefully woven with bright
flowers and wood ferns, causing a new pattern of wrinkles across her face. The Reverend Mr. Brewster raised an
apologetic hand, erasing the pucker from Miss Mollie's
brow. After all, a beginning minister could be forgiven a
few transgressions.

Where had the man gone in this hour of crisis? *"O'Higgin!"*

The surrounding hills had no more than ceased to
echo the summons in Miss Mollie's voice when there
followed a stream of words. "Oh, no, you don't! Get that
tin can off'n the mare's tail! Want the newlyweds to be
spilt before the honeymoon gets goin'? That mare's spirited 'nuf as is—always in th' lead. An' stop laughin'— it
ain't funny, O'Higgin. Be gittin' in here to hep!"

Laughter filled the vast rooms. The long diningroom

table, presided over by a subdued O'Higgin, creaked and groaned with its burden of food. It was a miracle, everybody said, that the North twins managed to bring in the enormous wedding cake without stumbling.

True heard herself addressed the first time as "Mrs. North." A surge of pride, then something akin to laughter, resulted. Had anybody counted the number of women who bore that title? Across the table Midgie was responding to it now. "Such a pathetic little waif," Miss Mollie had called the girl who was now Marty's wife. "You'll always be lookin' after her—but then you're used to that, lookin' after Marty th' way you did.

Grandma Mollie was right. Although the two of them were the same age, True had always been more mature. She remembered with a pang the bitter disillusionment which Marty's scrimmage with the law had brought to the family. Of course, Midgie Callison was only a description then—the "little girl lost" in Portland, according to her worried father, motherless and left alone while the conductor made his back-and-forth runs between Portland and San Francisco. Marty needed a mothering wife. Young Wil disagreed: A wife who depended on him for strength would give him a sense of worth. But what about Midgie? A wife had a right to become her own person. Thankful that she herself had a near-perfect husband, True's heart filled up with prayer for the other couple. Life had hurt Midgie enough already. Marty must bruise her no further. She was so trusting, as easily amused as a child, and so grateful for small kindnesses. True doubted if Marty could do anything she would not forgive. If only he would be open and honest with her . . . he owed her that.

"You are a beautiful bride, my darling," Uncle Wil, a more mature version of his nephew (and still as handsome as ever), said softly.

Before she could reply, Young Wil came to claim his

bride. "They want the four of us to cut the cake," he whispered. "Then we will make our getaway. I love you—brat!"

"Wil North!" True began, then stopped short. They had an audience. And the playful gleam of triumph in his dark eyes dared her to forget that he had the advantage. Just because he was ten years older and her idol did not mean that he was to continue his bossiness.

"Stop playing the heavy-handed husband," she warned between clenched teeth as they smiled and waved the crowd toward the diningroom.

His hand closed over hers as she and Midgie prepared to cut the first slice of cake, and her silly heart began to thud. Her fixed smile melted under his warm gaze and all else was forgotten. *Oh, Wil, Wil, wonderful Wil!*

"Come on, you two, stop dillydallying," Miss Mollie said, blowing her nose. "You got the rest of your life t' be starin' moon-eyed at each other 'crost th' breakfast table!"

A twitter of giggles brought the rosy-cheeked bride back to earth. It was good luck for the newlyweds to feed the multitudes, Grandma Mollie had coached. So the two couples moved about the room, greeting their guests and hand-feeding each with a tidbit of the fluffy, white, 14-egg wedding cake. Chris Beth stood in the shadows of the O'Higgins' new brocade drapes until all others were fed—smiling, though her dark eyes were misty.

When she stepped into the light True dropped the plate onto the nearest table with a clatter. "Oh, Aunt Chrissy—*Mother!* It was lovely!" Then they were in each other's arms, laughing and crying.

It was Chris Beth who let go. Holding her sister's daughter at arm's length, she looked deep into the steady blue, blue eyes (so like Vangie's), noting the carriage of the head, the character and tenderness of the lovely mouth, the determination of the finely chiseled chin (so uniquely her own). "I am so proud," she whispered.

The three-day honeymoon was all that a honeymoon is supposed to be—only shorter than planned. It began with laughter as the new husbands helped their lovely brides into the two-seated buggy while attempting to dodge a barrage of rice. More laughter followed as the horses galloped across the countryside, paint buckets and old shoes clattering behind them. It had always been like this, even when Young Wil had to be cross with little True after she and Marty tampered with his botany collections. Marty would cry, but True would make faces that caused Young Wil to burst into laughter. Even then she had been in love with him, knowing with women's intuition that they would be married. Now they could do anything, absolutely *anything,* together—with the help of the Lord. And, just as she had known that Wil was for her, she knew that the Lord had plans for them together. Who knew but what one day they could even teach Marty how to laugh?

The hotel suite was the best that Portland had to offer—not that True would have cared. What mattered was their being together, registered as Mr. and Mrs. Wilson North. In a dream, she slipped into the white velveteen robe that Aunt Chrissy had folded so carefully, and then brushed her golden hair until it was even more golden. One hundred strokes...101...102...5... 10...until a rap at the door reminded that she was working overtime. "I'm seeking a bride!"

With a bubble of laughter True opened the door. "Wil! You—"

The expression on his handsome face stopped her. Wil was studying her face as if he had never seen it before, his eyes widening in admiration. "Any regrets?" he whispered huskily. "I'm just a poor—"

"Don't tease me—not tonight," True whispered, then rushed into his arms where she belonged as he turned out the lights...

The next morning the telegram came.

3

It Is Always Today

The air in the quaint old hotel diningroom was bright with sunlight and gaiety before the telegram came. Every eye was on the center table awaiting arrival of the two sets of newlyweds. The balding manager, who talked as if his tongue were oiled, saw to it that the rumor spread. Everybody enjoyed watching young couples in love, and to be sure it was good for business! And 'twas mighty rare when a groom was as cooperative as this Mr. North—standing that sign up in the middle of the table: HAPPILY MARRIED. No hen-husband, that one. The other one—hum-mm, must be a brother, the name being North too—left doubt in the mind. Sort of unsure of himself, maybe even a little shifty-eyed. Could be a "shotgun weddin' "...oh, here the four of them came down the unstable stairs, stopping on the one that squeaked.

At the caretaker's signal, the other diners (just plain folks like himself) burst into vociferous song:

"Here comes th' bride,
Big, fat, 'n wide—
See how she wobbles
From side-to-side—"

16

"Enough a'ready!" the little man said, adjusting his nose-glasses uncertainly. Those log-rollers and fur trappers sang like their pipes were rusty. Might be embarrassing to his classier guests.

Wilson North waved good-naturedly. Marty tugged at Midgie's arm almost dragging her to the table. True, in keeping with Chris Beth's training, carried the situation off with becoming dignity, managing a small smile and nod in spite of what she considered a breach of good manners. But once at the table, seated with her back to the well-wishers, she turned flashing eyes toward her husband's face "Wil North, you are impossible—you—you—"

"—wonderful man," he finished, eyes adoring her. "You loved it just as you love me. Shall we kiss and make up?"

"Don't you dare!"

She was saved further embarrassment by the arrival of a breakfast obviously intended for a dozen hay-balers, all of them starving: sourdough biscuits, almost as tasty as Grandma Mollie's fried potatoes, eggs (sunny-side up), and sage sausage swimming in cream gravy.

Wil reached out his hands to indicate linking them with his wife and the other members of the family. True took his hand without hesitation and waited until Marty and Midgie overcame their confusion and completed the circle. Young Wil's voice was low with reverence.

"Lord, we praise You for each other. Erase our yesterdays and take care of our tomorrows. But remind us that today belongs to You—for the miracle of our marriage is that it is *always* today."

A lump rose from True's heart to her throat, threatening tears. Then, like sunshine after a shower, it spread over her soul. *Oh, dear Lord, how I love this man!* She squeezed his hand so hard that it hurt her own. Young Wil answered with a lovelit glance and seemed about to say something when the keeper was back, wearing a look of importance mixed with curiosity, to deliver the yellow envelope, the color which could only spell out "Telegram!"

How strange—it was addressed to the four of them. Wil accepted the telegram and thanked his host with a "Thank you" in a dismissal tone. Then the four of them pushed aside the "Happily Married" sign and leaned forward in a huddle in effort to achieve a measure of privacy.

"Shall I do the honors?" Wil asked, already reaching for the flap.

Wordlessly, True, Marty, and Midgie nodded.

The message was brief: TAKE CARE OF BUSINESS AND COME HOME. The command was signed simply "O'Higgin."

All was silent at the table, causing a silence to fall over the other diners. Young Wil was first to speak. "O'Higgin would have been last on my list of guesses as to the sender." There was perplexity in his lowered voice. Marty and Midgie's eyes were question-mark blank.

True bit her lower lip, trying to ease the queasiness which the mountains of food caused in her middle. "Something must be wrong with Grandma Mollie—no, O'Higgin would have managed it. Oh," she said breathlessly as fear clutched her heart, "could it be Aunt Chrissy—Daddy Wil, the twins?"

"Let's not borrow trouble, darling," Young Wil said, touching her hand reassuringly. "Note that he said to take care of business, so that hardly means a matter of life and death."

Marty had not spoken. But Midgie, disappointment filling her childish voice, almost whimpered. Raising the gray-green eyes that slanted appealingly upward at the corners, she touched her near-perfect upswept hair. For the first time True noted in some far-off corner of her mind that Conductor Callison had used up the miles between Portland and San Francisco describing his Midgie —referring always to her "dark hair, done up fancy-like." Fancy it was, but dark it was not. The girl must have had it bleached—something only the more daring young ladies would do. And her next words confirmed it.

"I needed to have my hair done—and wanted to see a stage play—and shop. Daddy always wanted me to shop—"

"You will have time, Midgie," Marty began, then stopped. "Or will she? How long do we have, Wil?"

"How long will it take? is the question. We can return then and get the mysterious matter all settled." He attempted a smile which in True's mind did not quite come off. "I can close my office, such as it is—about the size of my clientele—"

"No criticizing my husband, you! He will be the finest doctor in the Northwest, and," caught up in her dream, True talked on as was her lifelong habit when she was alone, "we will build ourselves a nest and—"

"Careful—it's too soon to feather it," Young Wil laughed.

True blushed but went on unabashed. "You'll love the role of Father Bird—being so bossy by nature!"

"I should paddle you here and now like I used to when you were naughty."

The crisis-to-come forgotten in their banter, True turned to Midgie. "The man was always a bully. He took every advantage of being ten years older than Marty and me—"

"Eleven," Young Wil interrupted, "just missing by two months."

True wrinkled her nose at him. "If you measure your medicine the way you estimate birthdays, you will lose the few patients you have."

"I do not dole out pills. You married a pathologist—remember?"

"But you will be both once you put in an internship with Daddy Wil—become the greatest doctor in the valley—make that the world!"

Her sudden mood swing brought Wil's rich, throaty laugh—beautiful, the kind that caused her heart to jog, at the same time arousing her ire. What an interesting life they were going to have! They would live in the little house across the creek where the sisters, her mother and aunt, used to live...close to her doctor-uncle and aunt...while Marty and Midgie—well, where *would* they live? For that matter, what would Marty do to support a family? He had never stuck with a job, and now it was harder to find one if a prospective employer knew his background—

"I don't have much to do—just see a few people—" Marty traced a pattern on the red-checked tablecloth, his eyes cast down.

"Then you can help *me*," Young Wil briefed as if it were important that his brother's time be spent profitably.

In the end True and Midgie helped too. True was delighted, Midgie disappointed. But, she admitted, she was familiar with Young Wil's filing system, having helped him before. That was before meeting Marty.

As if reading her thoughts, Midgie stopped, putting a slender finger in the *M* folder as a placeholder. "This is Marty's file, started when he had an earache. Complete medical background, but nothing about family history—you know, diseases that run in the family—I hardly know who I am. I guess," she said slowly, "I never did."

True dusted her hands while searching for the right words. "I understand, Midgie, having lost my own mother—and never knowing my father. At least you had Mr. Callison—"

"But who am I *now*? What is my real name?"

"It is North, Midgie, just as my name is—"

"Before marriage and after," the other girl said impatiently. "What are you holding back? What are *all* of you keeping from me?"

True felt her spine tighten with surprise. "Nothing— actually, I supposed you knew, that Marty had explained our wonderful family." *And*, she wanted to add, *it hurts a bit that it should matter so much—providing you are in love with your husband.*

Instead, she suggested a break, sinking gratefully into one of the worn black-leather chairs. "Aunt Chrissy will tell you anything Marty has left out." It occurred to her then that included everything. She explained briefly: "We know very little except that his parents, a very young and struggling couple by the name of Martin, were drowned in a terrible flood and by miracle the baby, Marty, was saved—thanks to Daddy Wil's expertise.

"And adopted by my Uncle Joe, Wilson North's lifelong friend—closer than a brother. Known and loved by the entire valley as Brother Joe—he was a minister, you know—" she hurried on after a pause.

"A *minister*? A *friend*? But the name," Midgie groped.

"It *is* confusing," True said. "Uncle Joe's name was Joseph Craig and he married Aunt Chrissy, Christen Elizabeth Kelly—after Marty was born."

"Marty's name was Martin—then Craig—I would have thought Wilson North was the stepfather—why didn't the doctor take him?"

"Daddy Wil was raising Young Wil, his nephew— and," she inhaled, determined to leave nothing untold, "planned to marry my natural mother, Aunt Chrissy's half-sister. It was a double wedding like ours, but with a more complicated plot. You see, Midgie, my mother, Mary Evangeline Stein, was," she raised her head proudly, "pregnant with me."

Midgie's eyes widened. "You mean—oh, me and my big mouth—"

"Never mind, it's no secret. And you are family, Midgie."

"But North? How can all of you have the same name?"

"When my mother died of consumption—" she swallowed hard, a faint memory of the fragile beauty of 'Angel Mother's' face floating before her, "dear Aunt Chrissy took me to her heart just as she had taken your Marty. Both of us leaned on Young Wil—he was so wise—and I guess we learned more how to love Jesus through him than through Uncle Joe's sermons. And then—and then—my heart broke again when dear Uncle Joe was killed in a senseless accident. Had it not been for Daddy Wil, the family would never have survived. We *wanted* his name—begged for it—"

"I'm so sorry," Midgie said uncomfortably, "I—I'm no good at trying to say things right, something consoling. Nobody taught me."

"There is no need for consolation, darling. God did that through Young Wil a long time ago. Oh, Midgie, I all but worship him!"

For the first time, her brother's wife grinned. "I wouldn't have guessed! Are you mad at me?"

True laughed. "Now, why would I be angry? You have a right to know—and to know that there is a strong tie between us in ways that are harder to count than the stars. Uncle Joe baptized us children, you know, when we accepted Christ with the same unquestioning love that all these loving people accepted us. We are so blest, so blest. Now," she said practically, "any more questions?" Then she remembered the twins.

Midgie hesitated. "Jerome and Kearby were born to Daddy Wil and Aunt Chrissy when, after years of loneliness, they were married," True said.

"And none of you are jealous of the younger ones, the twins?"

"We adore them! Being jealous of them would be like jealousy of ourselves. I would like a family *filled* with twins, just to put those two through what they have put us through—and what we put Young Wil through in our growing-up years. And now shall we make ourselves beautiful for our new husbands? They—I see a question in your eyes. So?"

"I still wonder about the Martins—and you never knew your father?"

"I never saw him alive—Michael St. John helped me find the tomb."

Immediately True regretted mention of his name. He, like her father, belonged to the past. Fearing another question, she said quickly, "I have built a strongbox and locked my heartaches and troubles there. I share them with nobody except the Lord. When I try to go back and look at the contents, He has taken them away. That's how He works!"

Midgie considered the words. "I hope He will take mine—about—well, everything in the future—maybe what we'll find wrong at the Inn—"

True tucked her own concerns away. "He will. He gave us *today!*"

4

Home—
Forever Home!

Homeward bound, the carriage topped a familiar knoll, allowing a first glimpse of True's beloved valley. The sylvan setting belied the hustle and bustle of the city. Abounding in the thick, shadow-filled woods and sunny groves where furry creatures and sunbeams played together, and dotted with orchards of unforbidden fruit, it was the land flowing with the biblical "milk and honey," Young Wil so often remarked. To True it would forever remain her secret "Sugarplum Valley"—a place to dream and to make those dreams a reality, a land she could never, *never* leave behind for new horizons. True smiled now, remembering that her fertile imagination of childhood years led her to confide to him that she was a sylphid, a young diminutive creature of the air, created to keep watch over the unbelievable beauty of the valley and its people, to see that they never changed, but just remained tucked away from the woes of the world outside its realms, where life was simple and needs were few. She would tell God—

Young Wil stopped such thinking in short order. "Sylphids grow up to be slender and graceful sylphs, little lady, *but* if they existed—which they don't!—sylphs would be mortal, and have no soul!"

That time True had cried instead of arguing. And he had ended up comforting her, reassuring her that she possessed the sylvan beauty of body and the far greater beauty of a God-given soul. And now she knew that the entire valley was one giant soul, bound together forever.

Delighted shrieks, punctuated by welcoming barks, broke into True's reverie. In moments the carriage was surrounded by swarms of children and dogs.

"Dog Star had puppies!" Jerome yelled above the others. "Daddy helped her, and I helped *him*!" There was pride in the little-boy face.

"We have 'em named already—and saved the best of the litter for you!" Kearby, the twin sister, beamed as they ran alongside the buggy the remaining short distance to Turn-Around Inn.

Both panting, the children interrupted each other in their haste to tell the news. "Tonsils' for True and Wil... got his name 'cause he can't bark yet... and Lucy Lungs' for Marty and Midgie...she barks *too* much... like Kearby sings too much and so loud she drowns out all the others in the church choir!"

The grown-ups came flying from the house, separating the children, hugging both couples until they were breathless, and everybody talking with speed that matched the children's.

"See what I told you?" True managed to whisper in Midgie's ear. And to her surprise she saw that the girl was crying—crying when she should be laughing at the crazy names the twins had hung on the helpless puppies. Tonsil and Lung indeed! That could mean only one thing: Midgie had spent more time in tears than laughter. And she was starved for love. She hoped that Marty knew.

And then all was bedlam. Valley folk swarmed from the great rambling house, beating pots and pans in wild sharps and flats of welcome. Then True too found herself crying, partly because of the genuine goodness and caring of these wonderful people with whom she fully expected to spend the rest of her earthly life, and partly from an overwhelming gratefulness to God for hearing her prayers. Nothing could be seriously wrong—not with this kind of earth-shattering welcome! Nothing mattered now...

5

Gifts with Condition

The quiet in the room so recently filled with a Tower-of-Babel happiness was now subtly portentous. Where was everybody? True wondered as she entered the enormous livingroom of Turn-Around Inn. Only Irish O'Higgin was waiting for his guests, his giant presence seeming to fill up the room. Omitting his usual blarney, the big Irishman motioned her with a finger to a nearby chair without lifting his red head from arms crossed and extended almost the full length of the mantel, where a few withering sweetbrier vines remained from the wedding.

"What are you doing—fire-worshiping in midsummer?" True tried to make her voice light, although she felt that she was speaking to a stranger.

"Where be the others?" O'Higgin asked, removing his arms from the mantel and thrusting hairy, hamlike hands deep into his pockets.

"I was about to ask you the same question."

"I asked me wife t'be makin' herself scarce—this bein' a soul-searchin' matter, a matter of me heart. Ever' man 'as 'is weak joint, 'n Miss Mollie be mine. That woman, a jewel she be, could change me thinkin', 'n me 'n the Lord's got it all figgered, we 'ave."

27

This was a different O'Higgin than True had known. What he had to say was a secret to all except himself, she supposed, since Aunt Chrissy and Daddy Wil were unaware of the telegram until they heard of it last night through Young Wil, herself, Marty, and Midgie.

Daddy Wil had brushed it away with a wave of his hand. "Probably just a whim," he smiled affectionately. "I have never known a human being to love a family in the way he loves all of you—and that includes Miss Mollie's brood."

"They have a family?" Midgie had ventured. "Somehow I thought—"

"That we were their only family?" Aunt Chrissy had laughed. "That man has a heart so big it can house us all—with room to spare. And, of course, he *is* lonely since all the other children are gone."

"That's another complicated story, Midgie, so complicated that even I get bogged down in an explanation. You fill Midgie in, Marty," True suggested.

"You're doing fine," Marty said shortly.

Fine? She had not begun. What was the matter with him? She glanced at her sister-in-law, hoping that she had failed to note Marty's attitude. Her red face said otherwise.

True covered the awkward moment with a brief explanation of how Miss Mollie had married a Mr. Malone, a widower with seven—wasn't it?—children. How his death left the wonderful lady alone to support them. And how happy everybody had been when the widowed Mollie Malone said "Yes" to Irish O'Higgin's flamboyant "beholdin'. " "So, you see, Midgie," she ended softly, "we pay little attention to bloodline here. Love takes its place."

True realized that her wandering thoughts had kept her from responding as to the whereabouts of Young Wil, Marty, and Midgie. And now they answered for themselves. The tuneful, vibrant whistle of her husband filled the hall, flooding her heart with joy, pride—and relief. The dirgelike atmosphere faded. Young Wil could handle any problem their beloved friend needed to share, and O'Higgin knew that. Yet it *was* puzzling just where Marty and Midgie fitted in.

All too soon she was to find out.

The question then would become: "But what has this to do with Wil and me?" She would find that out, too.

At sight of O'Higgin's troubled face, Young Wil stopped until the others seated themselves and the echo of his whistle trailed upstairs.

"Something is wrong." Wil's words were a statement, not a question.

O'Higgin's bushy brows drew closer together. The twinkle in his usually merry blue eyes was gone. And his voice was unsteady when at last he spoke.

" 'Tis no easy matter tellin' of me folly. And 'twould be breakin' me Mollie's bonnie heart should she come t'know. An movin' the likes o'her from Turn-Around—" O'Higgin stopped. Not a sound except the ticking of the clock as the silence lengthened into minutes.

The gravity in the ever-jolly man's voice unnerved True. She sought Young Wil's eyes, but they were focused on the pattern of the rug—lids narrowed as they had a way of doing when he was thinking.

"But I thought—" she began, then faltered. What *had* she thought? That trouble could never touch them? That they would go on forever like the wide river hugging the valley? Just for her security?

"That we be well off, lassie? Time was when 'twas so. But it takes a heap o'money-raisin' and educatin' a family—be it known there be no regrets now that they've all of 'em paired off and settled most proper. But the inn— oh, me achin' heart! 'Tis mortgaged to th' rooftop. Me 'n me Mollie ain't ones t'be askin' charity, but—"

The big Scotch-Irishman turned to face the four he had summoned while his wife was away at a quilting bee. His haggard eyes would haunt her forever, True thought, unless there was some way to help.

Young Wil spoke for her. "So it's money you need?"

O'Higgin's high color receded to its natural ruddiness. But his voice was strained with humiliation. "Shure'n it is—then shure'n it ain't. Meanin' I got meself some cash—" O'Higgin paused to pat the breast pocket of his plaid cotton shirt. "But—with condition."

Young Wil chuckled, a welcome sound in the tension-filled room. "So far, if you'll pardon my saying so, you've made no sense, kind sir. Care to explain just what we're talking about? *Condition?*"

"On condition Marty here'll cooperate—and 'tis a man-sized job."

"Me?" Marty's lips whitened. The startled question brought Marty North to his feet. "I have no money—no job—"

The older man's lips twisted into something that would pass for a smile. And all the while he was carefully scrutinizing the boy.

"Then 'tis likely the condition will be meetin' a need. Now, no ragin' 'fore ye be hearin' th' story. 'Tis a bit o'mystery—and was I 20 or 30 years younger, me lad, 'twould be me Mollie and meself who'd take this adventuresome trail 'stead o'ye an' yore lassie."

As if warned by a sudden flare of fire in O'Higgin's fading eyes, Marty dropped back into his chair, his deeper blue eyes smoldering as he listened to the incredible story.

True became so engrossed that she took no notice of Midgie, who strained forward, white-knuckled hands laced together around the floor-length sweep of her shepherd-checked voile skirt. True's first impression of the girl was that she feared the world and its inhabitants. Yet now her eyes, darting between Marty and O'Higgin, held a flare of hope. She looked excited and then uneasy, and a closer look would have revealed a tremble to the rounded chin. Only once did True glance her direction. That was when she unclenched her small fists and raised an uncertain hand like a child in need of "being excused" during a history lesson.

"Don't interrupt, Midgie!" Marty had said curtly. Half-frightened, half-defiant, the slight figure perched on the edge of the chair, her red lips clamped shut.

Still listening intently to O'Higgin, some far corner of True's mind longed to reach out to Midgie, to still her fears, to reassure her that nobody was going to hurt her. But from that same corner came a denial as if from Midgie's own lips. "I want to believe you—and I do *almost*. But not all people are kind like you. Sometimes they abandon you...ignore you...even put you in prison—like they did Marty...I had to learn in the orphanage what Marty learned in real life...a girl had to look out for herself...sometimes she can trust... sometimes not."

True shook off the illusion and gave full attention to O'Higgin, the trusted family friend, and his story, too incredible to be true, while too incredible not to be! Nobody could put together such fiction—and, most certainly, not O'Higgin, a devout man who firmly believed that God walked beside him every step of the way—sometimes taking his arm when his arthritic knee refused to support his weight—

"None o'ye knew I had a brother," his story had begun. True, very true. Nobody knew, or cared, about the good man's background. The gentle folk in this valley took newcomers at face value. No questions. No prying. They simply offered hands from every side to widen the "family circle." "Name was Artemis—smooth-haired, smooth-faced, smooth-talkin' one, Artie. Talked 'is way right into th' heart o'me Uncle Art afore 'im, sweet-talked 'is way, he did, right into steerin' Uncle Art's financial ship 'n sunk 'er—so I be thinkin' all these years. Never knowed much 'bout me good mother's brother—never liked 'im much, but th' ole coot musta been smarter'n I be thinkin', holdin' a wee somethin' back like he done fer me. Th' Lord works mysterious-like. Maybe all th' time He be teachin' ole Uncle Art t'be aware o'dogs like th' Good Book tells us mortals. Guess He 'ad a hand in lookin' out fer th' likes o'me—givin' me sweet Mollie—an' now this—yep, He did all right, all right—"

At that point, O'Higgin obviously began to enjoy himself, licking his lips from time to time as if he had finished a crisp-fried drumstick and was reaching for another.

Which, where words were concerned, he was. He had his audience in his hand and he knew it. "Know anything 'bout how t'ride, rope, round up cattle, Marty? How t'tell th' difference 'twixt wheat 'n chaff? Ever work 'til ye be fallin' stiff 'n sore on a bunk with yore boots still on? Know about work, boy—*real* work?" O'Higgin interrupted his own story to question. "Now, don' go talkin' when ye elders be speakin'—jest nod 'Yea' or 'Nay.' Ye hear?"

Marty, jaws tightened, eyes smoldering, nodded his head.

"Sooooo—why *you*? Well, a boy has t'become a man sometime. Gone 'n took yerself a wife—not a boy's job, ye best be knowin'. There be a *house* t'build an' little mouths t'feed. So here be yore chance. Here's yore chance t'hep yoresef 'n yore Gran'ma Mollie, well as please yore family 'n th' good Lord. Yep, by jiminy, ye best be listen', ye had!"

"What do you want of me?" Marty's voice was low and uncertain, and his still-boyish face wore the exact expression on his childish features as when Uncle Joe and Young Wil (a junior deacon) had led him and True into the river to be baptized, wanting to swim but fearful of water.

"Patience, lad, patience," O'Higgin admonished. His voice was rough, but True had the feeling that he was stalling—not for words but to assess the situation, study Marty's reaction, and calculate the outcome of the proposal yet to come. After all, wasn't Marty released to the older man's custody when he foolishly allowed himself to be led into an act of rebellion against the railroads, that of a minor part in the train robbery? Authorities had demanded someone outside the immediate family.

True felt her husband's gaze and lifted her eyes to meet his. Young Wil's dark eyes showed a rare touch of anxiety. But they were turbulent with affection. Boldly he winked. She blushed. Gentlemen did not wink at ladies. And then she laughed inwardly. When was she going to get used to the idea that she was his wife? The wink had communicated love and intimacy—and more. They were sharing a secret, she realized. No matter how serious O'Higgin's revelation of the "condition," the prankish man was enjoying his role.

The idea dispelled a bit of her apprehension. And, right or wrong, Young Wil's look of pride made her happy about something she would never voice lest others think her vain: True was glad her husband was proud of her. She paid little attention to the mirror, but for her husband she was thankful that she was, although a wee bit too slight, not of the Amazon variety, had eyes larger than a garden pea, and a laugh that nobody had ever said would wake the dead. Of course, nobody had said she was kittenish (like Midgie) either. She was too independent; but for Wil she could be anything he wanted her to be and everything the Lord found pleasing as a proper wife. Already she found herself fidgeting, wanting this meeting to be over, eager to establish a home here...

With an effort True brought herself back to the now of things. Finally Irish O'Higgin was coming to the point. Forgotten were her ambitions. Forgotten, too, her appearance, although the sun sent red-gold waves shimmering through the natural gold of her hair and filled with sunbeams the pools of her violet eyes where myriads of tiny stars made daytime homes. The shock of O'Higgin's words were far too great for ambition, vanity, or frivolity.

Somebody had asked if Uncle Art had died. O'Higgin's answer had been to blow his nose, apologize, then say that his uncle had been a cross, crotchety old man and that there was no need to mourn the passing of a very old man. Still, he could have been kinder to his benefactor...and now that his carousing brother had sat in a drunken stupor while a slow train ran over him (at which Midgie gasped with horror and Marty, to True's surprise, placed an awkward arm around her narrow shoulders)—well, things looked different. Lots of regrets, but life must go on.

"So!" O'Higgin withdrew a crumpled paper from his pocket with all the black-crepe severity of a lawyer preparing to read a will in a tone that sent premonitory thrills down the spines of the hearers. " 'Lastly, th' property, real an' personal—includin' homestead grazin' land 'n stock thereon—I bequeath t'me—my—nephew—on condition. One Irish O'Higgin's t'occupy—or have occupied by another of 'is choice and a suitable wife, one versed in th' Word an' abides by it—populating the earth—which means bearin' of one heir within th' year o'their required occupancy an' provin' up on th' claim as well as provin' their worth, which is that Irish, or 'is chosen, will show before suitable witnesses, also designated and sent together with said heir, that he be—is—capable o'managin' rangeland an' further—re-peatin'—wife of same bear—' "

A white-faced Midgie gasped. "I won't—won't—" she choked.

O'Higgin's eyes lingered on the girl, weighing, testing. "Then ye be willin' t'rob th' man ye vowed t'stand by of 'is chance? An'," his voice dropped back to its original tone of defeat. " 'Low th' roof t'be taken from me'n me Mollie? Be ye so cruel?"

A fountain of sparks ignited in Marty's eyes. "Leave her alone—I refuse the conditions, too." Then, with every drop of color drained from his face, he met O'Higgin's eyes squarely. "I can't refuse, can I? You've got me cornered and you know it." His voice spilled over with bitterness, and the rebellion True had seen in the child now reappeared in the man. "You are right—that uncle of yours knew how to mess things up all right!"

"Or straighten 'em out. Give a wee bit o'thought t'that!"

Midgie's eyes brimmed with tears and a small blue vein throbbed on her forehead. "You married the wrong wife—I—I tried tellin' you. What am I? Not able to live up to your family's classy standards—and not able to face life in a wilderness—"

"You're an okay wife, Midgie. Nobody had any right to involve you in this mess. I can't ask you to make such a sacrifice—"

"No sacrifice, laddie—if th' lass loves you. What 'bout it, gal, be ye thinkin' love's important?" O'Higgin boomed.

"You don't have to answer that!" Marty's voice had grown stronger and more protective than True had heard it heretofore. Now, if only he would not drop his head sheepishly. But he did.

It was Midgie, surprisingly, who took up the matter again. "I will go with you, Marty. Remember I promised to forsake all others—wasn't that what we said? They've always forsaken me, so I'm thinkin' it's my turn." The laugh she attempted was unsuccessful. It came out pitifully.

Young Wil let out a breath that sounded as if he had held it a long time. "I commend you, Midgie. Let's find out were 'said property' is. Who knows but what this will turn out to be quite an adventure?"

O'Higgin looked alive again. "Oh, shure 'n I got me map—land lies over th' range—very private-like, no neighbors, 'ceptin' coyotes—how about it, Marty, be ye man 'nuf t'swing all th' terms?"

"Will I have a helping hand?"

"Best helpin' hand's th' one on th' end o'yore arm! But—" and he cast a scheming glance at Young Wil and then at True, "yes, terms included witnesses—an' I got me witnesses picked."

True had wondered where they fitted in. And now she knew! *Oh, no, Lord...*

6

Understanding— and Explaining

"What will your Daddy Wil and Aunt Chrissy say?" Midgie ventured, her face whiter than her blouse.

"They are *your* family, too, Midgie—call them whatever you choose," True said gently as she touched the frightened girl's hand.

The two of them had suggested that they occupy the back seat of the buggy in order that their husbands might try to make some sense of the strange news. Too, True had hoped to bring solace to Midgie, who was finding marriage too much in such a short time—and yet had come through in Marty's time of need like a real trouper.

"As to what our family says," True continued, choosing her words carefully, "I think their reaction will depend largely on how we present the situation. We must sort out our feelings, darling—and may I say here and now that I was proud of you back there? Marty needed that. We must all take this a step at a time." She swallowed, then continued, "Please believe me when I say that I am shaken too. But—but—if we all stand together, we can build for ourselves a marriage like Daddy Wil and Aunt Chrissy's. It is more than fair-weather vows—"

36

"Oh, I will do my part. I don't want to be embarrassin' in high society—"

"Oh, my dear, we are not 'high society,'" True assured her. "We—"

But Midge was not listening. Instead, with lifted chin, she averted her eyes and half-whispered, "Me—I'd walk over burnin' plowshares in my bare feet before I'd hurt any of you—and—and if I could make Marty love me," she gulped.

True felt a tightness in her chest. "Oh, Midgie, you don't have to make a burning sacrifice, darling. We love you just as you are—and, as for Marty, surely you are sure of his love. What bothers you?"

"Young Wil was so nice to me—gave me a job in his office when other people thought I was dumb—and then he introduced me to Marty—" Midgie's childish voice shook and her breath came in little gasps. "I—I—think Wil may've thought I would be—uh—good for him. And, me, I up and fell in love. I'll make him love me, True—I promise I will!"

What was there to say? True made a weak protest, then paused. There might be a measure of truth in what Midgie was saying—not on Wil's part but on Marty's. Had he taken the vows seriously? "Please—*please*, Midgie, try to be happy. Smooth going does not necessarily result in happiness. In fact," she said, realizing that the idea was new to her, "it may very well be the other way around. And you will have us with you—"

"Honest to gosh—I mean, honest to goodness, True? You're sure enough *going*?"

True bit down on her lower lip, feeling a sharp pain shoot around her heart. What business had she to make such a commitment? Why, she didn't even want to go on this wild-goose chase that some mischief-making old man may have dreamed up in wild delirium. And, most important of all, she would never, *never* make a decision without listening to her husband. Leaving here meant surrendering all their plans...his practicing medicine with his Uncle Wil, the only father he knew ... serving the needs of the valley folk he loved so dearly ... and it meant putting an end to her aunt's dream of her teaching as Chris Beth had done before her ... and, small as the matter sounded, she and Young Wil had wanted to live in the little cabin that was just whistling distance across the creek ...

"Some fathers would never consent to their daughters going to a wild, new country—Ooooo, those coyotes— but I guess my father wouldn't care where I went as long as I was out of his way. He put me in an orphanage, you know, and said he would come for me. I waited and I waited—" Midgie's chin quivered and her eyes glistened with unshed tears, as if she had waited all these years to weep her heart out.

"There must have been a good reason," True soothed. "It would be difficult for a man to care for a baby alone. Mr. Callison *did* come for you, and he looked so proud—"

"Proud because I'd made a good marriage—"

"You have been hurt, Midgie, but try to be fair to your father. He showered you with gifts—"

"Which never quite make up for love," she retorted, then added bitterly, "like I told Marty. "But—I promised." Then quickly she went back to her previous comment. "What will *your* father say? Will he try to stop your going?"

"Daddy Wil would never stand in my way of happiness, no matter what. He loves me too much to hold on too hard, and yet he refuses to allow me to cling. And," she smiled in effort to lift the other girl's spirits, "our fathers have no right to make our decisions now, Midgie. Our husbands have that responsibility. Our place is with them—"

"I know—I said I'd go and I will, takin' whatever crumbs I'm offered. Whatever will we do for money?"

"We will work for it, Midgie. Yes, it will take hard work, and a whole lot of faith. Has it occurred to you that

God may have had a hand in this—that there is a job out there He had in mind that even—"

"Old Nick didn't know about?"

"*Uncle Artie.*" Midgie laughed. Then True sobered as she said, "Midgie, trust yourself. Remember, darling, that sometimes detours offer more thrills and adventures than beaten trails." True wished she were sure of her words.

The Big House was ablaze with lights as the two couples reined in before the front gate. A lump that True found hard to dissolve rose to her throat. No matter what the hour, there would always shine a light in the window when one or more of its inhabitants had not reached the protection of its loving wooden arms. How could she leave them again—something she had vowed in her heart never to do when she returned from Atlanta? But life never revealed its pattern.

In minutes the twins, with a pack of dogs (including Tonsil and Lung), surrounded the four of them. There were embraces without questions—just an invitation for all to wash up for dinner, which, True knew, was over an hour later than they usually ate. Bless them!

Prayers said, Aunt Chrissy, refusing help, brought in a hearty stew and cornmeal muffins. She had been out calling on some new neighbors and Daddy Wil had delivered two new babies. Conversation seemed so normal. True wished she could erase the happenings of the day, just settle back, and live life as she knew it and loved it. But somehow she must find a way, once she found out what Young Wil had planned, to accept it—even try to make it sound appealing to Midgie and Marty. Her double role would not be easy. But she squared her shoulders and let a warm flood of joy flood her being: She had Young Wil!

True had a chance to talk briefly with Chris Beth once an exhausted Midgie was tucked in. The men remained, in Dr. Wil's office in conference. True planned to wait for a report, but once alone with Aunt Chrissy in the upstairs bedroom that was always hers, she found herself spilling out the whole story. Her aunt listened without change of expression, nodding only on occasion.

Then with a faint smile she said dreamily, "History repeats itself."

"It *does* parallel your life story and my mother's in some ways," True said slowly, letting the revelation sink in. "What should we do?"

"Talk it out with your husband, pray together, and review your mother's diary. Whatever you two decide, we will stand by, my darling."

7

Charting
a New Trail

A million conflicting questions crossed True's mind during the week following O'Higgin's outlandish proposal. *Outlandish* was the only word she could think of to describe its strangeness. The man was a born tease, known all over the valley for his shenanigans. But this? A man as devout as Irish O'Higgin would never stoop to so cruel a hoax. Why then did the uncanny feeling persist that there was more to the story than the red-whiskered giant had revealed?

Where was this mysterious land? How would they get there? And what would they take? These practical questions must be answered, and there could be no answers until the men could provide more information. True longed inwardly for time alone with Young Wil. In fact, she found herself resenting the invasion into what should have been her honeymoon. She felt robbed of sunlit days and star-dusted nights that should have been theirs. Honeymoon indeed! Why, she hardly saw her husband. He, Marty, Daddy Wil, and O'Higgin spent hours and hours poring over maps, talking with Thomas J. Riefe (the big-jowled president of Centerville's largest bank), and a stranger who wore half-moon glasses, had pink skin which looked as if the sun had never touched it, and carried a black umbrella even when there wasn't a cloud in the sky. Isaac Barney was his name, True learned in a brief introduction. He was the lawyer who had prepared Uncle Nicholas' last will and testament.

True wished she were a child and could pout. Not a single preparation could she make until somebody gave an order!

Well, she was no child; she was simply behaving like one. Certainly she could prepare—prepare for unemotional farewells, prepare her heart by reading the Bible, which she had been neglecting, and by leafing through Mother's diary again. The hardships recorded in its pages would make her own troubles seem trivial.

So, while Aunt Chrissy spent time getting to know Midgie—answering her questions about Marty, reexplaining the complicated family relationships, and reducing some anxieties about the girl's "fitting in"— True devoted herself to the demands of the twins. "Little pitchers have big ears" (Grandma Mollie's axiom) certainly applied to those two! Somehow they knew that their three idols were going away again, and they dogged her every footstep, accusing her with great, round eyes. How could she reassure them when she had no answers herself? Trumary North, the iconoclast. She hated herself in those moments. Then, feeling like a martyr who would never be catalogued as a saint, she turned her fury on her husband. How dare he show such neglect!

But she would reckon with him later. For now she must think of the children. So, as she had always done, True devised games (that nobody else in the world knew, she whispered in conspiratorial tones). Then, noisily and gleefully, they romped up and down the stairs with the dogs yelping at their heels. "Tonsil's learned to bark!" the twins shrieked.

Chris Beth shook her head in mock despair. "True is to Jerome and Kearby what Young Wil was to her and Marty," she explained to Midgie, supposing True to be out of earshot.

"I wish I could let go that way. I never got to play—or be *me!*"

"You will, darling, you will. Just wait until you spend a year around those two!"

Two. Even Aunt Chrissy failed to count Marty in—a fact which did not escape Midgie. "Marty never did count," she said to herself wistfully.

That night True spoke to God a long time about her brother. "I guess You are using this delay to help me develop patience, Lord, and to reach a decision in my own heart about this unexpected move. I guess You know what my answer has to be. Other people must come before my own selfish desires. So, if that means sacrificing a year for Marty, I will—providing You give me some sign that it is Your will and my husband's choice. Maybe he needs a sign too."

Mary Evangeline North's diary lay on the lowboy within reach of where True knelt beside the bed, her face pressed against the sweetness of the sun-dried double-wedding-ring quilt. She reached for it and read her mother's last entry:

> God bless you one and all, my wonderful family. Know that I will remain with you always. I will blossom with the dogwood in the springtime and hum with my bees in the summer sun. I will sparkle with the snow-flakes and in the ribbons of each rainbow. I will laugh when you laugh. Cry when you cry. So long as you are together! For I leave with you my legacy of love.
>
> Your Vangie

So long as you are together. True turned the wick of the lamp on the nightstand low and extinguished the blaze with a ragged puff of breath. The words continued to burn in her heart. She squeezed her eyes shut, but they continued to glow in the dark. Then tears of acceptance came in a flood of relief. "Angel Mother" had said a sad-sweet goodbye to a heartbroken little girl—leaving behind a legacy of love.

"All right, Lord, You've had Your say. You'll have to help me—"

And there, fast asleep, her husband found her.

"Hey, sleepyhead, the bridegroom is in your chambers. Is your wick trimmed?"

True blinked. There was so much to say! Instead, she flew into his outstretched arms...

8

By Rail
and by Trail

Midgie had scarcely spoken since boarding the heaving, obsolete, inland-bound train. White-knuckled, she gripped the rough boards of the wooden bench that she and True shared. True gave up trying to draw the frightened girl into conversation. *If only Young Wil were here,* her own heart kept whispering. But orders from a shirtless man with freckled shoulders and a chest like a bear were that Wil and Marty must ride the cattle cars: "An' iffen you two got a gun, she better be loaded, less'n you plan on losin' them prize cattle yer transportin', an' (he grinned, revealing the absence of two front teeth, the remaining ones yellowed by tobacco), them purdy women—they look like prize stuff, too."

Young Wil, face whitened with restrained anger, nodded. Marty, always impetuous, doubled a fist and stepped forward before Wil could place a restraining hand on his shoulder. "I'll not have you speaking of my sister and—uh—wife in that tone. They are not cows!"

The big man spat, leaving a brown tobacco-juice trail oozing down his chin and lodging on his massive chest. "More like heifers," he leered, "not yet full-grown. Keep yer shirt on, Little Britches, else them two'll not be reachin' cowhood! Injuns in these parts

45

ain't human—too lazy t'work—'n I'm here t'tell you greenhorns they'd steal you blind, bust yer bellies, 'n leave th' insides fer th' buzzards. Dunno who begun th' rumor back in yer Injun-lovin' settlements that th' savages are *people*. Dum' animals'd ruther have a white woman's scalp than her body! Keep yer distance, Boy, from th' bloomin' redskins, from me—I ain't took myself no likin' t' th' likes uv you neither—'n from train robbers, white men—"

Marty's face blanched, all bravado gone. He slumped forward as if shot by an arrow. True understood. How far was it that the men figured they would travel by rail? O'Higgin had arranged through Isaac Barney for a so-called "foreman" (a squatter who gladly exchanged his services for "squatters' rights") to meet them. The sooner the better for Marty's sake, but how far was it that this rangeland was from the railroads? Maybe Midgie would remember. But Midgie's face was a white mask of horror, her young body stiffened against reality. And that was when she seemed to drown out reality. She appeared to be dozing now. True pulled a lightweight shawl around the girl's thin shoulders and glanced around her.

She had known all along that the two of them were the only women aboard the wheezing locomotive, so different from the modernized train she had taken in her cross-continent trip. Each time the train stopped, True had hoped that another woman would be among the rain-drenched passengers who entered. But always it was gawking men, soaked to the skin, their ragged jackets smelling like wet wool. The smell, added to the ever-thickening cloud of cigar smoke, was almost overwhelming.

Would any of these men be their neighbors? True's eyes traveled the distance of the now-crowded car as she moved an inch toward the sleeping Midgie in order to accommodate still another rider. Aunt Chrissy had told her about the long ride West by stage, where, interestingly, she had met Miss Mollie, O'Higgin, Wil North, and "Brother Joe." Certainly there were no such persons riding on either side of this narrow aisle. Across from them sat a man with a paunch in his middle, head down and lost in sleep. His left nostril twitched when he exhaled and his domino vest appeared ready to split until he sucked in another noisy breath. Beside him a man wearing bright yellow doeskin gloves kept fumbling in his pockets as if counting his change. And next to the narrow door marked "Use only when necessary" a rangy man sat soldierly-straight, a beaver hat covering his entire face except for the point of a skimpy goatee.

Gooseflesh prickled her arms. Why search here for a neighbor? She would rather die of loneliness. Only she would not be lonely! Loneliness was a state of mind. *Solitude*—that was the word. A lovely solitude that she and her husband would enjoy together. She would consider Aunt Chrissy's suggestion about taking the correspondence courses in order to further prepare herself for teaching. The two of them would study together, since Young Wil planned to pursue his medical research. Their happiness would rub off on Marty and Midgie, given time.

Forcing her eyes from the unsavory faces, True's gaze wandered to the clerestory roof of the rattling confines, examining the three brass kerosene lamps, so badly in need of polishing that they appeared to droop as they swung ceaselessly to the jerking movement of the clang and clatter of the segmented column of the centipedelike creature called a train. Up and up they crawled now without conversation, the quiet broken only by the rusty squeak of the "Necessary" door's periodic in-and-out swing. It was fitting, she thought, that nothing was visible beyond the smoke-stained window except a white sheet of driving rain. Try as she would, it was hard to maintain the lift of spirit sensed a moment before. Doubts and fears kept nipping at her heart as she reviewed the peculiar twist that her marriage had taken. All for Marty, she thought a little bitterly. Marty, who had maintained a somewhat hostile aloofness as the rest of them prepared for the journey.

At True's request, the family did not accompany the four of them to the station. O'Higgin and Grandma Mollie took them instead. True wondered how much the older woman knew, but she did not question the "why" of the journey. Instead, there was a constant homey flow of conversation centered around domestic matters. Did they bring along enough dried beans and canned fruit? Surely they remembered the blanket spread, enough quilts, and the black dinnerpot? Yes, yes, yes, True kept saying mechanically. And, yes, of course she would write often. Nothing of real significance except at the last moment.

As Mollie Malone O'Higgin hugged her for the third time, she whispered, "Now, you brung them stout boots. Jest make double-sure you keep that sweet heart as stout, my child. It was right generouslike of th' parents of this brood to make all of you feel comfortable with cash-money as a weddin' gift. Th' Good Lord's gonna be watchin' out fer you, but, well, marriage takes work 'n understandin'—just you be promisin' me one thing, that you're a-gonna remember that God gave you a husband at that altar 'stead of a brother!"

True promised fervently, although her smile felt faulty and uncertain.

They all would have to do a lot of adjusting, she knew. She had devoted a lot of time checking out the region of the Inland Empire, once she heard the name. Living there would be far different. There had been no gold rush, nothing to bring the wagon trains into the area in search of a fortune. So population would be sparse. Well, the ground was rich—or would be if there were more water. But clouds from the ocean dropped the needed moisture in the beautiful valley system first. Having dumped their burden, the thin clouds climbed the higher mountains, whose peaks squeezed them even drier. By the time they reached the eastern Oregon plateaus, the clouds were drained, weak, and tired. The land was all right for grazing; it welcomed stock, cattle, and sheep (if one could avoid range wars, dodge poachers, and chink up the cracks of his cabin against nasty winds and bitter cold). In fact, there were sections of land tilting up to the south that were receptive to wheat and gardens, especially when situated near a lake. Thank goodness, the vast acreage edged against a lake on one corner, according to the lawyer's crude sketch.

"Trees I can sacrifice for a time—maybe. But to give up fresh vegetables and bright flowers would be like giving up my life."

True spoke the words aloud without realizing she had spoken until curious eyes turned invitingly her direction. "Eh, Miss?" "Well, whadda ya know? Th' doll can talk." "Got ye'sslf a man, Woman?"

True gasped in relief when the conductor in greasy overalls ambled in to punch tickets, asking and answering questions amiably. His eyes lit up noticeably when they focused on True. "Better wake up your pretty companion, Missy," he said, punching True's ticket, "next stop bein' yours. Now, I do hope that you two ladies ain't plannin' on goin' it alone here."

The words renewed the interest of the uncouth passengers. There were suggestive remarks, a few whistles, and, in the eyes of some, unmistakable lust. True felt her blood curdle. *Oh, Wil, where are you?*

Praying for strength, she received it. "Our husbands are with us," she said in a dignified manner, her voice much louder than necessary.

For some unaccountable reason, True felt stronger. She had met one crisis. God would help her through those to come, maybe in ways she did not expect or understand. But help He would!

"Wake up, Midgie, darling," True said almost gaily. "We're there!"

"There" proved to be far removed from what was to become home, True realized as she looked at the vast grasslands with not a dwelling in sight. However, it seemed a good omen that the unusual gift of late rain had kissed the whole plateau with its special favor, then skipped away. Now the sun sifted gold dust on the stand of cottonwoods, which had appeared like an oasis in the open country. Meadows were ripe with sweet-breathed clover, bitter-scented white poppies, and wild daisies bobbing their heads as if to shake free of the rain. The train whistle startled a flock of quacking ducks, back from the warmer climes and now dining without conscience on a wide field of wheat. Alarmed by the din of human voices and complaining bellows of the cattle being unloaded, the fowl took to their wings, circled, and regrouped, finally wedging in departure. Were human sounds so foreign to them? Whatever True had expected, this was not it. This was surely another state, another country, another world.

Taking no note of the new surroundings, Midgie's anxious eyes searched the length of the train for sight of the men as the black monster puffed out a cinder-studded doughnut of smoke and prepared for departure True followed Midgie's gaze and felt her heart leap with joy and relief when she spotted Wil. With customary efficiency he was instructing a dazed Marty in the art of coaxing cattle down the gangplank. One by one they hitched the cows together by means of securing their halters with ropes. And all the while Young Wil talked to the frightened animals in low, soothing tones. How wonderful he was at everything he did! Perhaps she judged her brother a bit too harshly, expected too much. It was unfair to compare him to her husband. Still—

"Look! The dogs!" Midgie's startled exclamation broke her long silence and passed it along to True, who stood speechless. How on earth had those twins managed to smuggle Tonsil and Lung into that car? And then she realized that it was comforting to have companionship, which obviously was a scarce commodity in this strange land. Too, the fat, wet-nosed puppies would be a constant reminder of home—and, yes, she was homesick already. She smiled to cover the sadness—a smile which was cut short by a scene, innocent though it might be, which caused her heart to lurch. Maybe she should try to distract Midgie.

"Midgie—wait!" True tried to stop her sister-in-law's flight. But Midgie either failed to hear or chose to ignore her. She ran as fast as her long skirt would allow. Stumbling over the wagging puppies, she failed to see the short interlude which gave True her first hint that trouble was brewing.

The tall man with the beaver hat had approached Marty, said something which caused Marty to pale, and reentered the train. The stranger's face was still partially covered by the wide brim of the hat, so there was no recognition on True's part. All the more reason that a thrill of apprehension tightened her spine. The man had lifted a long-boned finger, resembling a talon, in salute to *her*!

There was no time to give the incident further thought. Young Wil spotted True, and in what appeared to be one long stride was at her side, his arms around her. Undaunted by the tedious ride, he grinned broadly. "Do I smell like a cow?"

"How would I know? My nostrils are too filled with smoke to do their duty. Who cares about smells anyway?" True snuggled closer. Over his shoulder she saw Midgie reaching her arms imploringly to Marty like a small child begging to be scooped up. Marty obliged with about as much emotion as if lifting a sack of grain. His face looked strained and morose, the expression which spelled out a touchy mood. Inwardly she shrugged. Marty North best read his Bible and heed the words of Paul: "Every man shall bear his own burden."

"Are you all right, sweetheart?" Young Wil's voice was filled with concern.

"Perfect!" And she was—*now*. They were a perfect team *anywhere*—

He was about to answer when a drawling voice drew them apart.

"Hi'ya, Mister North, I'm guessin'—th' bossman of Double N—gave 'er a name when we heered you wuz comin'. Welcome, Boss!"

They turned to see a withered little man with a face like a prune beneath a high-crown felt hat, some two sizes too large, with the brim turned up and secured with a nail. His legs were bowed out either by a quirk of nature or from riding horseback more than he walked. But the grin was genuine and heartwarming. True liked the little fellow at once, comical a picture as he presented.

"And you must be the foreman," Young Wil said cordially, seeming to ignore his appearance. "I am *one* of the Norths," he continued, "but neither of us is the owner of the ranch. Since his name is O'Higgin, I suppose rightfully we should call it the Double O."

"No sir—it was him that ast fer th' N--'n me, I carry out orders."

"Good for you! But I failed to catch your name?" Young Will extended his hand.

The man took it awkwardly. "Goldish—Billy Joe Goldish. But th' fellers never could say it proper—pure devilishness, I'm guessin', when they dubbed me 'Goldfish'—so, jest call me 'Beetle,' what I'm knowed as."

"Beetle it is, Mr. Goldish—and may I present my bride?"

Beetle turned twinkling eyes on True. "Oh, my my! How purdy, jest like a picture—my wife'll be liken' th' sight of you—yep—"

True favored him with a bright smile. "So you have a wife. Oh, that makes me happy! I had hoped to meet another woman—well, several—"

The little man shook his head sadly. "Ain't many, ma'am. An' sad t'say, but—but my Mariah ain't able t'speak no English—jest Spanish—"

True felt absurdly near tears with disappointment. The disappointment then focused on Billy Joe, the Beetle. The little man was regarding her with unqualified approval—and hope. Hope, True supposed, that she would be able to teach Mariah to communicate other than in her native tongue, when the only words in Spanish she knew were *Señora* and *Sí!* But why dash his hopes at this point when the cross-currented lines of his mouth increased with a broad grin? Instead, True smiled back, wondering if Young Wil had also noticed that his foreman's hat flattened his ears so that they looked as if the Almighty had fashioned them as a hat tree. The answer came when his twinkling eye caught hers.

Billy Joe scratched his right temple in concentration beneath the ill-fitting hat. "I'm plum outta idees 'bout how we're gonna get all that stuff 'crost th' trail," he said doubtfully with a nod toward the household belongings and trunks piled alongside the tracks. "So muddy sometimes th' gumbo gits right up t'th' hubs uv th' wagon wheels. Glad I brung th' burros—stubborn critters, but they come in handy."

"Thoughtful of you, Beetle—you know, I like Billy Joe better—any objections?" A look of pleasure crossed the man's face, and Young Wil continued: "Marty, how about a hand here?"

Soon the three men were loading the bundles and boxes onto the protesting wagon, leaving some of the heavier items for the slat-ribbed donkeys in order to provide seat room for the ladies.

"The rest of you are going to walk?" True said with concern. "How far is it?" Young Wil and Marty turned questioning eyes to Billy Joe.

With palms up he guessed it to be " 'bout 25 miles down-slough," then up a little rise from Slippery Elm. "Got er name from a grove uv elmwood, but, by jiminy, sure wuz a fittin' name follerin' sech a rain."

So it was decided that they would spend the night in a

sleazy little hotel in Slippery Elm. Midgie wondered about
bedbugs. Marty complained about the situation in general.
True ate cold mutton, white with tallow, and a muffin that
failed to rise, and held onto Wil's hand—with a smile.

9

Mixed Feelings

Washing down the tasteless meal with water, True suggested stepping outside for a breath of air. Only Young Wil accepted her invitation. Midgie had chosen bedbugs over Indians and Marty—well, who knew what he was thinking?

Slippery Elm was no town—never would be—although it showed signs of lost ambition. There were no boardwalks and no plan laid out—just remnants of sod slabs, half-roofed with heavy thatch or canvas. The weatherbeaten hotel, which served as an inn, post office, and telegraph center, bore a proud sign: SLIPPERY ELM. Underneath it, more visible than hoops beneath a lady's skirt, was the peeling paint of the original sign: SQUATTER SOVEREIGN. The only other building was something passing for a general store. It would pass for Aunt Chrissy's description of what Centerville's first store looked and smelled like. It was more of a barn in appearance and was filled with barrels of sugar, flour, and coffee beans. The lid was off the vinegar barrel, allowing emission of such tartness that one was forced to clutch the throat to clear the windpipe. True had taken one glance, eyes misted over by the tartness of the vinegar, and expressed that they would not be doing their shopping here.

To her embarrassment the operator, a man with a mastiff face, bald head shining like a mirror, overheard her. Lifting hands that looked like 12-pound sledges to tear off six yards of calico for a waiting male customer, the proprietor stopped short. He set her at ease, however, by favoring her with a surprisingly gentle smile. And his voice, when he spoke, was apologetic and almost sad.

"Guess they's no choice—nothin' else in these parts. 'Silver 'n gold have I none, but I will give thee such as I have'—ain't that th' way th' Good Book says it, now? Meanin' I'll carry you folks from one crop to t'other. Right glad t'meetcha. North, ain't it, now?"

"News travels fast," Young Wil had smiled. "And your store's fine."

"Ain't much, but what we git, we share."

Telegram and all, True found herself thinking as she acknowledged the introduction and stepped over a hound stretched full-length between her and the door. "Curly" Caswell lifted the hinged board which would allow True to enter the dry goods section (where bolts of material were stacked along the walls) and bade her come in. She declined politely.

Once outside, True determined to make the most of what was beginning to look like a bad situation. She held onto the wooden banister of the sagging porch and concentrated on the sunset until Young Wil joined her. The total absence of fir-clad hills imbued True with a sense of loneliness. But the grasslands were green and the twilight was a beautiful blend of crimson and gold. The air was still fragrant with freshly scrubbed earth, and a meadowlark trilled across some distant meadow. In a final goodnight, the sun sent a last afterglow that rivaled a blazing forest. Just as it died away, leaving the old buildings squatting in shadowy shapes, Young Wil's hand closed over hers.

"Are you sure you'll be all right here, darling?" His voice held a curious choking sound. Her own emotions found vent in a little cry of delight as she turned to be swept into his arms. All right? She would be all right anywhere with him. *Nothing* could defeat her!

"I will be perfect, darling—once I wash off three layers of dirt and soot, and get a decent night's rest. Two nights jostling on that wooden bench have shattered my backbone. No way to wash up or brush my hair without being invaded by one of the men in need of the 'Necessary.' My teeth need brushing, and I must smell like a stogie—"

"Better that than cows and chips!"

Together they burst into laughter. Then True sobered. "Where did you sleep?"

"Sleep? What's that? I did well to find squatting room in the straw, most of it being taken up by bellowing, four-legged critters."

"Oh, darling!" Then, in retrospect, it all seemed funny again.

When the air grew chill, they went upstairs to a barren room dominated by an ancient iron bed with a straw mattress. Young Wil looked at it and claimed to feel right at home in the straw while True wearily poured water from the granite pitcher into a cracked pottery basin and splashed her face. As she was brushing her hair, the sound of Midgie and Marty's voices came through the thin walls. Midgie was sobbing while Marty's voice was low but angry. At least, whatever the problem, he had the good sense (and through Aunt Chrissy, good breeding) to keep it between them. But honeymoon? What could he be thinking?

True told Young Wil about the little scene between Marty and the stranger in the beaver hat then. It seemed important that he know.

Wil nodded thoughtfully. "I saw that—what do you make of it?"

"I don't know—I just never did know how to help Marty, I guess, although goodness knows I have tried hard enough—"

"*Too* hard, True. We will stand by him, and keep our prayers going up for him constantly. But promise me that you will let him grow up. This is his chance. It will either make or break him."

True agreed and climbed into the bed of thistles, too tired to flinch. Anyway, she was with Wil, so... what...did...anything matter...?

She was fast asleep.

10

The Double N—
Home?

Overnight the ground appeared to have soaked up the water thirstily. Not so with the trail, hardened and rutted as it was. The heavily loaded wagon began complaining while it was still on level ground. The wheels moaned and groaned as they hit pools of water, churning up fountains of mud over the two passengers. Midgie, eyes still red-rimmed from last night's weeping, gasped in horror as the murky water splashed onto her clothing, then struck her face. And then, as if almost relieved to have some way of explaining the tears, she began to cry again. Little sobs. Sounds of despair. It was best to let her cry.

True glanced away tactfully. "Oh, dear! Look at our poor husbands!"

The exclamation drew Midgie's thoughts away from herself. "Oh, how awful—they're like mudballs—" she hiccuped once, then went into a regular spasm, causing more tears. "How—how—can—we—h-hel-p?"

As True looked at Young Wil plastered in mud (and looking for all the world like an amateurish sculpture turned out with the aid of an eggbeater), she was tempted to join Midgie in tears. But for now, action was needed.

"I'm going to help."

"You stay put, young lady!" Young Wil ordered. "I don't want to have to worry about *you!*"

"Then don't!" True said saucily as she leaped from the wagon and put her shoulder to the front wheel right alongside Wil.

Together they hitched forward, paused to inhale, and—with eyes closed against the mud—hitched forward again. The mules strained in their harness, their mouths white with froth. True lost track of time and eventually her sense of reality. They were on board an ailing ship, helpless on a high, choppy sea—unable to move forward or backward, with water washing over their heads. And yet some determined captain was bellowing, "Heave—ho! Heave—ho!"

Crazily, True realized that she had heave-hoed all she was able to. And they were sinking, sinking—to the hole in the bottom of the sea. One more heave, no more.

The tactic, whatever it was, worked. The wagon lurched forward with such a lurch that True fell forward, biting her lower lip in the fall. But they mustn't stop now! They must push as never before. She was on her feet instantly, and, hooray! they *were* moving forward as if by pull of an unseen force! True kept pushing with Billy Joe's every command, spitting mud in the process, and squinting in an effort to see.

And what she saw caused her to falter and almost fall again. Midgie, helpless little Midgie, was pushing with all her strength on the opposite side of the wagon. Something about that touched her heart. She hoped it touched Marty's, too. The girl looked so beautiful in spite of the sad condition of her clothing. Her eyes shone and her lips curved in a smile of triumph. True knew the feeling. For a moment, Midgie and Marty had conquered the world all by themselves.

Feeling invigorated and oddly refreshed, in spite of still walking in a dream, True allowed her face to be wiped free of mud by her husband's clean white handkerchief. And for once she made no reply to his scolding, for she was seeing a vision: of their new home glowing like a precious stone, blessed with Mariah's colorful touch; of a blazing fire which would dry out her matted hair; of firelight dancing from bright saddle blankets, beaded garments, and vivid landscapes captured in oil and resting in hand-carved frames to the book-lined walls, where a giant white cat, now rosy with the changing color of the burning logs, stretched lazily on the mantelpiece. How cozy... warm... alive... welcoming!

The vision was to fade suddenly, for there was an abrupt stop at the foot of a little slope. "Thar she be!" Billy Joe announced.

This? *This* was where they would live—this cabin roofed with dirt and hay? True tried to tell herself that it was a mistake. But Wil's quick intake of breath said otherwise, allowing her dream (which had grown with beanstalk rapidity) to wilt just as quickly. Not a tree. Not a shrub. Just a single-story shack over which desertion had cast an evil spell. In the bright sun two dirty windows, panes cracked, stared sadly through their sagging frames. Stained and weather-warped, the boards of the crude building appeared ready to give up the effort of standing. A creaking door, standing ajar, told its story without words. Someone had inhabited the place recently and had hurriedly boarded it up, but another person (Billy Joe, undoubtedly) had made a vain attempt to rip away the boards and make the place respectable.

While the others stood pondering what to do, True moved forward as if drawn by an invisible magnet. With her heart winging its way into her throat, she pushed the door open cautiously, giving no thought to possible danger inside. Her concern was simple: What could she create from such chaos. But the interior held no answer.

Once over the threshold, she sensed a recent presence. Could it still be occupied? In the dimness, the sparse furnishings were shapeless. When her eyes adjusted to the shadowy interior, the cracked stove, orange with rust, came into focus. Then a table with remnants of food and abuzz with flies crawling along the faded oilcloth covering. True shuddered and forced her eyes to traverse the rest of the room. Benches made from packing crates. A three-legged desk leaning against the wall for support. A dilapidated bunk. And a door leading to another room, which lay in total darkness. It was easy to imagine a man or beast lying in waiting. She was going to be sick. She must escape—now. Spinning on her heel, True hurried out.

It was good to feel the warm rays of the sun and to see the *real* faces of her family. Real, yes, but concerned. And all eyes were focused on *her*. God had given her another assignment.

Valiantly, True North squared her shoulders. "Well," she said, forcing a smile, "welcome home—to the Double N!"

"Is—is it *hor*-rible?" Midgie's teeth were chattering.

"It is that! I need some volunteers who have no fear of dirtying their hands, a barrel of soapy water, and a good disinfectant!"

Young Wil's eyes flashed appreciation as he and Marty went inside to inspect. Midgie clung to True's hand. "What—can—can we do?"

"We can be brave—like you were on the trail—and wait for our men to make some decisions, darling. And I guarantee you an adventure!"

The men came outside. Marty looked ready for burial. Young Wil, bless him, looked ready to split with laughter—something only she could understand. But he pulled the corners of his mouth up stoically and nodded with Billy Joe offered assistance with unpacking. Maybe they could just bunk, he suggested. Then, come tomorrow, he and his Mariah would be back to help clean—oh, his Mariah *could* clean! Right shamed he was now, not being able to invite them to bed down with them. But, well, they had only a tent, and what with three "young 'uns"—they did understand? But at least they'd not be starving, not with Mariah's dinnerpot chuck-full of red beans (with lots of pepper) and lip-smakin' good.

The next morning Young Wil announced some emergency steps. He and Marty would go back to Slippery Elm and pick up a few emergency supplies. As he recalled, there were stacks of lumber in the shed of the combination inn-store-and-whatever-else-you-need building.

"If you girls are game?" His voice was sober with concern.

Marty answered before they had a chance. "Midgie's going home."

"Your decision or hers?" Wil's voice demanded an answer.

"This *is* home," Midgie said, her small chin lifted in pathetic appeal.

Marty could not meet her gaze. "I guess we have no choice, have we? he said bitterly. "And you're enjoying my misery—"

"Get with it, Marty!" Young Wil said sharply. "Life always offers choices. God gave us free will and expects us to take charge of our lives. As I remember O'Higgin's terms, *you* are in charge—so, what's your pleasure?"

Put that way, True thought with a desire to laugh, Marty *didn't* have much choice! She felt a thrill of joy that Young Wil had placed the burden squarely on their brother's shoulders. They would go!

Once the men were out of waving distance, the two young women looked at each other, first in desperation, then in grim determination. And without words they understood each other.

Thank goodness Aunt Chrissy and Grandma Mollie had thought of everything—even rags for cleaning! Midgie drew a bucket of water by hand from the well (the pulley having rusted beyond repair), and the two of them shredded lye soap into a large granite pan. Then with rags, brooms, and brushes they went to work.

True's back was breaking, and her hands were bruised and bleeding, but in her heart was a song.

"Work, for the night is coming!" she sang out, and, to her surprise, Midgie joined in. Why, the girl's voice was beautiful. Something told True that she had sung before under different circumstances.

11

Renovations

The sound of hoofbeats startled Midgie, bringing her to True's side. The child had a million fears—strangers, new situations, bugs, and mice. Now she was sure that she and True would be murdered. By whom made no difference. Child? True told herself for the thousandth time that she and Midgie were the same age, with Marty but three months their senior. She *must* stop treating them like children.

"See who it is, Midgie," she said briskly, wiping her hands and laying aside her mud-stained apron.

"Halo, halo—anybody home? I brung Mariah 'n th' brood—"

"BillyJoe!" Midgie whispered in relief. "Thank goodness—"

The two young women moved to the door to welcome their first guests. Billy Joe, "foreman" of the Double N, looked as relieved as Midgie. "Never can tell who might be lurkin' inside. But thangs are a-gonna be diff'rent with me 'n yer men in charge." He exhaled as far as his flat chest would allow.

True had hardly heard. She was preparing to welcome their neighbors—"squatters," wasn't that how O'Higgin referred to them? Billy Joe dismounted the aging mule so that Mariah, who rode behind him, came into view. Heavy, braided, dark hair swung forward and the near-black eyes, fixed on "El Señor's" family, were questioning. The high cheekbones showed signs of former beauty, weary and weathered though her face was. There was a plea in the woman's face, a begging to be accepted.

The three children, all boys (who, True guessed, ranged between five and seven), rolled dark eyes from their mother to the two strangers standing in the doorway. Poor dears. They were all but hypnotized with curiosity but had obviously been instructed to "behave or else!" In that split second, True lost herself in a dream of possibilities... Young Wil would make a wonderful father... a quickly spawned fantasy which ended abruptly with a startling memory: A part of this strange bargain had been that Marty and Midgie bear a child, preferably male... how foolish could conditions of a will get? An eccentric old man trying to dictate people's lives from his very grave! Then came the realization that Midgie had reacted with a stout refusal. "I won't!" She wished the memory had lain dormant.

Billy Joe's family continued to observe True and Midgie in fascination. "Forgive me, Billy Joe," True said quickly. "Bring them in by all means!" She flashed them a warm smile and beckoned an invitational finger. Her reward was a beautiful, pearly-toothed smile from Mariah and then the wordless scramble of the three boys as they slid from the back of the other mule obediently and came to her shyly.

"*Buenos dias, Señora,*" they said in unison, then scuttled away.

"They know how to work, too!" Billy Joe said with pride, which signaled the trio back to the mules (burdened, she saw then, with crude tools). Billy Joe helped Mariah to the ground, keeping up a flow of conversation. Wonderful woman, his Mariah—sole survivor, as far as he knew, of an ambush. Indians? Billy Joe scratched his thatch of hair that looked as if he'd borrowed it from the shack's roof and said it was more like a bunch of "white trash" that attacked the lone wagonload of Mexican immigrants bound on stock-raising. Stole the livestock, of course, and some right good horseflesh excepting one stallion that galloped to the hills faster than the winds could blow. What with Archibald—yep, that was the stallion's name—and wild horses abounding, there was a great opportunity.

Of course, horses needed good grain for wintering. And wheat needed watering. For winter, that was. No problem in summer, with grass belly-deep. No problem with milk-giving critters either, excepting for poachers. Great opportunities if men had a will, and it was plain to see that at least one of the two North bosses had horse sense. Billy Joe paused to laugh at his joke, glancing at Mariah, and then, seeing that Midgie had established a friendly communication, lowered his voice confidentially.

"My Mariah warn't so lucky as th' stallion, tryin' t'run fer th' brush like she dun—" Billy Joe's voice trembled with anger. "She was captured 'n th' whole shebang taken after her—'n—there wuz a life-'n-death struggle 'fore public fornication—"

"You mean—" True was too horrified to go on.

Billy Joe's mouth twitched pitifully as he nodded. But beneath the ill-fitting hat his eyes were live coals. "They ravished my Mariah—all th' stinkin' filthy cowards. Me, I went no fu'ther—runnin' ain't no answer. It settles nothin'—'n me, I'm a-gonna square thangs one day. Lucky I found her wanderin' 'round like th' stallion—jest her 'n her *git*-tar—them purdy eyes glazed like th' dead 'n sangin' words I didn't com'prend—but I'd seen enuf t'know—I know how t'shoot—them animals 'll pay—"

True could understand his feelings, wrong though they were. What she could not understand was Midgie's reaction. Having apparently overheard some of the conversation, she had stopped scrubbing and stood as if carved in granite. True shook her own head to clear away the image that floated before her eyes of an angel chiseled in a tombstone.

Without speaking, Midgie dropped back to her knees and resumed scrubbing. A throbbing pulse on her white neck like the delicate wings of a dove beating against a cage was the only sign of the inner turmoil that True knew was there. It was as if her sister-in-law faced some uncompromising danger from which there was no escape. Even if freed, inevitably she would be caught. What was the look? One of total change. As if being Mrs. Marty North—maybe even this faraway place—had offered refuge. And now the haven was but a thin illusion. Instead, something sinister and forbidding had taken its place. Maybe life had taught the peculiar man known as Uncle Artie more than any of them realized; how quickly values change to shift like shadows in crises!

All day they worked as if driven, each buried in a private vault of thought. Even the children—Carlos, Rafael, and Eduardo (who, Billy Joe explained, insisted on being addressed as Carl, Ralph, and Eddie)—were quiet as they brought fresh water into the shack and pulled weeds from around the doors and windows outside. There was no mention of lunch.

The afternoon sun dropped behind distant hills. Inside the air was sultry, but there was the smell of freshness and livability. A tinge of rose replaced the gold of the afternoon, the changing color now visible through the windows. Almost without warning the color faded, and twilight came like the flapping of gray wings to let in the dark. Somewhere a coyote howled. Resolutely True shook off the eerie feeling that they were being watched as Billy Joe struck a match on the sole of his shoe and lighted a lamp polished by his wife's capable hands. Immediately the room was flooded with a warm, mellow glow.

Mariah said something to the children, who shyly whispered to their father. Billy Joe nodded. "Time to wash up," he beamed, "fer my Mariah's corncakes, pep-perpot, 'n coffee—puts grit in th' craw and greases th' innards, 'sides bein' lip-smackin' good!"

Mariah's cooking was all that her husband prom-ised—and more. Several times True found herself grabbing for water to put out the fire in her mouth. But the food filled up the empty spaces in her middle that all the stooping, lifting, and scrubbing had created. She was grateful to the stouthearted woman who had endured so much so bravely, yet clung to her faith—a faith evi-denced by the simple gesture of dampening a finger with her tongue and making the sign of the cross on her forehead before partaking of food. The children fol-lowed her pattern. True was uncertain what was ex-pected of her, so said a quiet "Amen." Mariah smiled at her across the table, which, thanks to her husband, now had four legs. True was eager to have the men see the change.

The lean-to kitchen would accommodate no more than two, so True walked to the front door. The men should have been home long ago. She listened for the sound that might signal their return. Nothing. Nothing except the hair-raising howl of a hungry coyote. Billy Joe was at her side in an instant, shotgun raised.

"I—thank you, Billy Joe—I dislike those creatures—"

"No need fearin' 'em, ma'am. Cowards they are—iffen a sheep wus t'turn 'n look 'em in th' eye they'd hightail—jest like some men I know—'course now, a body's gotta be watchful, make ready."

"Life in such a place is challenging, isn't it?"

Billy Joe thought the statement over, then answered with judicial like deliberation. "Ain't th' place fer them what don't cotton t' quiet. Me, I call it God's Country—ever'thang here a man could be wantin'."

True stepped out the door and stood breathlessly star-ing at the overhead canopy of shimmering stars—so close she could pluck them from the sky. The breeze was fragrant with nightbloom—and wasn't that—?

All thought of danger gone, she ran out toward the trail with a small cry, her feet flying in her haste to meet the loaded wagon that Billy Joe had lent them. "Wil, Wil—*Wil!*"

In his arms, she whispered, "Is it wise to be out—in—the—dark?"

"Wise? How can a man be wise and in love at the same time?"

12

One Step Forward—
Two Back

In the days that followed, the group was to see a lot of one another. The Goldish family spent every waking hour assisting with repair. Spreading canvas salvaged from covered wagons which had collapsed, been abandoned, or fallen prey to marauders, Billy Joe proceeded to remove sod from the roof. The little man, hopping about in the dirt, *did* bear a comical resemblence to a beetle, True thought with a smile as she handed him tools for prying away and replacing the sagging boards underneath. Later they would chink up the cracks between the logs, he said, and 'twasn't much, but—

"We'll make do, Billy Joe. Wil and I'll spend only the remainder of this year—"

The foreman stopped his work, turned his head aside to spit, and accepted a board he had asked for. "Yer meanin' that th' other 'un—th' one what don't look *at* a body, jest *through* it—*that* boy'll stay?"

"*Man*, Billy Joe, and his name is Martin, Martin North. He may stay—"

"Well, now," Billy Joe said as he scratched his chin, "Martin North's got hisself a heap t'learn—'bout ranchin', human bein's, 'n bein' a husband—"

True started to say that they would all have to help him, then paused. That was against the new rules she and Wil had agreed on.

Billy Joe took her silence as a rebuff. "Sorry iffen I offended you some, Miz True. But a man'd be stone-deaf 'n blinder'n a bat not t'take notice. Thick-skinned as a buffalo 'n sharp as a thistle with that tongue—sorta like he's a-tryin' t'duck out on life—"

Billy Joe may have talked on. True was thinking about Marty and Midgie. In fact, she thought about the four of them. A house—no matter about size and location—should be a refuge, a *home*. A home meant peace, love, and protection. How could this be so unless something was done? And indications were that her brother was unwilling to do *anything* to stem the emotional tide that was washing his direction. True had hoped it was only her instinctive desire to protect Marty that caused her concern. But an outsider's taking notice dashed that hope. This would become a house of strangers—alienated and fenced off in the private domains of their hearts unless they could talk the situation out. Up till now she and Young Wil had done all they could to make life normal and bring happiness to the other couple. But they were battling a formidable adversary. Marty's sulkiness spelled out a single-mindedness on some problem too great for him to handle. He was sick but unwilling to attempt recovery. His attitude now was one of bitter resignation. *Face it, True, an ingrate!*

Wil, on the other hand, had remained pleasant, even enthusiastic, and—unlike herself—determined not to allow their brother's problem to grind him down. But something had to give. The strain was more than Marty had a right to expect any of them to contend with, especially Midgie. She was trying so hard—*too* hard—to win the love of a downright spoiled brat! True suddenly wished that Midgie would simmer inside, warn Marty with signs of reaching a rolling boil by coloring with indignation at some of his insults, tighten her fist and voice, and then explode. Wouldn't that clear the air? Shake some sense into him?

And then it occurred to her that perhaps Midgie had no idea what this was all about. That in her naivete she felt she deserved no more—that "this is just the way the world is for people like me."

True determined then and there to have a talk with her.

For just a moment she feasted her eyes on Young Wil, so handsome in canvas-colored Levi's, sinewy arms—slightly sunburned and soaked with perspiration—hammering away at the window frames. Odd the effect he had on her. One look at him gave her a feeling of homecoming. Well, why not? They were of one flesh—one house which was God's temple—neither complete without the other. Feeling her gaze apparently, Wil paused, wiped the sweat from his bronzed forehead, and pushed at a rebellious lock of hair which crowned his smile. Oh, how God had blessed them! Even in this ridiculous situation they were happy.

On pretext of needing a cup of water from the barrel, Young Wil dropped his hammer and came to where she was picking up rusted nails. Then, pointing to a log, he led the way to it. There they sat down, his arm around her, a teasing forefinger tickling her ribs.

"Problems?" he queried, pushing a straw hat to the back of his head.

"Stop that tickling, Wil North. This is serious!"

"I know, darling—that's why I teased, he said gently.

True told him her concerns, leaving nothing out. "I'm sick with worry about poor Midgie—passive as a little lamb and just as docile, letting Marty walk over her. She tries to see life as sunshine and roses and what is her reward? He—Marty's going to destroy her, Wil."

Young Wil was silent for a time. At length he said, "Marty has been insulated from hard knocks, True. But no more. It's too bad that it has to come all at once, but that's the way he chose it—meaning that I am going to lay it on the line this time. I am tired of his childishness—one step forward then quick-stepping back two when nobody's looking!"

And she would talk with Midgie. But much was to happen before the plan materialized. There was so much to do. But, thank goodness, the cabin was hardly a shack anymore. It actually looked like a house now.

13

Strange Encounters

July came in hot and sticky. But the sky remained a constant blue, and True noted with glee that the sparrows which nested along the eaves of the cabin had hatched and were trying their soft-feathered wings. They touched her heart, striving as they were to cling to life as opposed to establishing a degree of permanency—somewhat like Slippery Elm, which was little more than a tent city and was apt to stay that way. Unless, of course, the vague plan materialized that she overheard mentioned in the lobby on the night she, Young Wil, Marty, and Midgie were guests.

The disheveled-looking town had come to mind because of plans to make a trip for wiring to patch up the corral fence at "roundup" time (Billy Joe insisted he could bring the stallion down and that the wild mares would follow), for some plants for a fall garden, and to search for a few temporary laborers to harvest the grain that Billy Joe had seeded by hand. The wandering harvesters would work for a dollar a day, he said, and it would cost a dollar thirty-five to feed them ordinarily. But his Mariah knew the shortcuts and could stretch a buck and still stretch a man's stomach. Not much profit in this year's harvest, to be sure, but a man had to look ahead, save good seed—improve 'em—

"Feed that horde, try to stay alive through a devilish winter—what kind of future is that?" It was Marty who spoke—bitterly as usual.

Midgie opened her mouth, obviously hoping to soothe his anger or cover for his rudeness, then closed it.

Billy Joe had eyed him with ill-disguised disgust. "What kinda future you got elsewheres? A man's gotta carve out his own by th' sweat o'th' brow, 'cording t'th' Good Book. Any venture's a gamble—iffen y'ladies'll be pardonin' th' expression. They's a way t'survive. Hunt, man, hunt! We kin larn a heap from our red brothers 'bout harvestin' th' fowls, deer, 'n rabbits—like hare stew?"

Marty's lip curled slightly in disdain. This man he thought crazy had touched a nerve with his mention of gambling. Any onlooker could see that Marty was not a man committed to work out a friendship with the new land. He was condemned to it.

Billy Joe Goldish made a lot of sense. True agreed with Young Wil in discovering a lot more intelligence than they had first attributed to him. Marty had dropped out of the conversation when Billy Joe referred back to the talk overheard at the inn. "Shippin's always brung problems even if a man can turn a profit, but some o'them pipe dreams 'bout extendin' th' rails could be more'n cracker-barrel talk. Folks 'round here stick to th' idee with leechlike conviction!" Billy Joe said.

"Not that we have much need for transportation," Wil laughed. "Unless," he sobered, "we *can* develop a new strain like you say—"

His voice trailed off and True recognized the look. Always interested in botany, Young Wil's fine mind was out there somewhere climbing trees for a better view of the land, sorting seeds for developing a hardier hybrid strain, and finding a method to irrigate. She saw his dark eyes light up with inspiration as he said, "Maybe we can do the same with horses, not concentrating on how many we can breed, but creating a finer breed—improving—"

"Righto! That's 'xactly whut I'm meanin'!" Billy Joe's short legs bowed out dangerously as he literally jumped up and down. "Iffen th' weather cooperates 'n we kin find them hands tomorrow, hang onto th' harvest, it's possible t'git this place in th' black ink—providin' we gotta 'nuf cash money fer winterin'—"

"We have it."

"Then, by jiminy, we'll do it—it's our bounden duty t'prove it! Ain't that th' whole purpose?"

"Well, in a sense, yes—proving up on the claim there in the western corner." He made an effort to catch Marty's eye, but failed. "And certainly it will be a challenge," he finished, flashing a jaunty smile at True.

True smiled back. If her husband needed her support, he had it. He had Billy Joe's too; seeing the entire matter as a "duty," he was a willing serf, tied to the land, and he knew all there was to know about ranching. His family was a delightful bonus.

Her thoughts traveled on in a strange comparison of the three men. Duty for Billy Joe, yes. Challenge for Wil, yes again—but more. It was a moral charge, a sacred obligation. And Marty? While the dwarfed foreman would crawl on all fours to fulfill his self-imposed responsibilities, Marty's face revealed the awful truth about his own attitude: He was being punished, condemned, scourged to do penance for some heinous sin he did not commit.

True sighed. If his older brother had talked to him, it had accomplished nothing.

On the way to Slippery Elm, Billy Joe commanded the team to the right with a loud "Gee!" where the trail forked. "Been hankerin' t'show this," he said with pride.

This proved to be a broad expanse of farmland where wheat shocks, scattered like a disorderly army, waited for orders. "Scythed it myself 'ceptin' my Mariah 'n th' boys—could'n git no help er no loan—so we jest had t'let a heap uv it be."

"Did the rain sour it?" Young Wil asked with concern.

"Nope, me now, I covered jest 'bout all with them wagon sheets. Ain't no noticeable damage done."

Billy Joe pointed to sections remaining for harvest— acres and acres. Farther north lay a narrow band of uncut grain still green with summer and stretching away to the horizon to lose itself beyond a rise in the terrain. In the clearing, nature had repaired the damages by sending squadrons of golden-yellow poppies and purple daisies to cover the stubble. The flowers stood at attention until a playful breeze set their heads to bobbing, their slender stems bending in exaggerated salute.

"Oh, True, look!" Midgie reached out her hand and pointed to where the road appeared to fork again. "That's where I'd like to build our cabin—no," she dreamed on, "make that a sprawling white farmhouse and matching picket fence...shakes for a roof...a fat chimney attached...and—what am I saying? It— ain't—isn't possible—"

"Of course it is! responded True, caught up in the dream. "Anything's possible with the Lord. It will work out, darling—it has to!"

That would have been a perfect beginning for the talk that True so wanted for them. But this was neither the time nor the place. Even the wagon seemed to know. One wheel dropped into the deeply rutted trail and took its toll. The wagon, already flirting with collapse, shuddered. The two pine boards on which True and Midgie sat bounced, almost tossing them overboard. And then the wagon stopped with a telltale splintering sound. The wobbly wheel had made good its threats. A spoke was broken, Billy Joe announced without irritation. No problem—good place for a rest. Take no more than an hour to fix it.

Whistling, he set to work. With Wil's help and some grumblings from Marty, Billy Joe made good his promise.

Slippery Elm looked even sadder to True's eyes than before—just remains of a conglomeration of thrown-together buildings with dirt floors and rusting single-pipe contrivances through which smoke could escape. The few windows with glass looked like blind eyes wearing glasses, staring hopelessly as if waiting for those who had passed through to return. Silence hung over the treeless town like a plague, except for the tinny notes of an out-of-tune piano coming from somewhere in the inn. A few men sauntered past as Billy Joe tethered the mules at a hitching post—grizzled, ragged, and unwashed men, some gaping, others smirking at True and Midgie. They seemed to be the only women around.

"What's all the ruckus, boys?" the innkeeper barked from inside.

A tall man with a hacking cough and a withered arm yelled back: "Women!"

Marty took a long stride forward, coiled and ready to strike. "Ladies!" he ground out as if something about the town or its people rekindled a fire within him.

The man fumbled at his belt with his one good arm as if in search of something. A gun?

The swinging door creaked and Curly Caswell, the proprietor, stepped out. "Plannin' on usin' that weapon, eh, Gun Slinger? I wouldn't be advisin' it—be gittin' on home!" Wiping his massive hands on an apron that was none too clean, the big man turned toward the prospective customers, recognized them with a smile that sent half-moon wrinkles up from bushy brows onto his bald head, and bade them come inside.

"Tillie!" he called loudly, "come on downstairs 'n meet th' lovely ladies I tole you 'bout!" Again, the smile of pleasure.

Tillie Caswell, hair tousled from the cleanup work upstairs, appeared wearing a cheap gingham floor-length dress, ill-fitting and washed free of its original design. Her eyes were lovely, True noted, but as blank as unstamped coins. Life must have been cruel to her. Starved as she was for the sight of another woman, she was shy and fearful of strangers.

There were introductions, and True drew her into conversation. "I'm glad you're here, Mrs. Caswell. While the men stock up on supplies, I would like to have you show me some material for curtains. Too, I wondered if you had some colorful fabric for a special dress—what are they called, these full-skirted ones with lace that Spanish ladies wear for—"

When she paused, Tillie Caswell supplied the word, "*Fiestas?* Oh, then you are one of the two Mrs. Norths." Her voice was low and musical, her diction perfect. "You must be meaning Billy Joe's wife, Mariah? Oh, she's never had anything so nice!"

True smiled. "She has more than earned it." And this time she entered when the swinging board leading to the yardage was lifted.

Mrs. Caswell suggested a soft fabric of sunny yellow with small red flowers in circular design, plus black lace for trim, and wished for some patterns but assured True that Mariah was clever enough to make her own. True agreed and felt a surge of happiness when she saw light come into the woman's eyes, an awareness of her surroundings.

In fact, she appeared downright excited as she led True to a remnant counter. "I wish I had more selection, but very few peddlers come this way. Feel free to look these over just in case something here will fit your windows—or I can order from Meier and Frank's—"

"In Portland?" Midgie asked excitedly. It was the first time she had spoken after the brief "How do you do?" The rest of the time she had wandered around restlessly, casting her eyes up the stairs frequently as if in search of something she hoped not to find.

"The same," smiled Tillie. "Your home, too? I came from there—"

She paused as if talking too much and went on to tell the story obviously dear to her heart. Aaron Meier was himself the welcome peddler once upon a time—made door-to-door house calls on foot with his bags of calico, by-the-yard elastic, paisley shawls of breathless beauty, and mysterious Eastern gadgets. Oh, how Aaron lightened the hearts of pioneer housewives—lightened their thankless burden of mending threadbare garments, too, with his gift of a darning needle.

"A darning needle?" Midgie looked puzzled. "One?"

"The same," Tillie Caswell said, biting off a thread that wrapped the soft pink-checked material that True thought would fill the bill. "And how precious it was! It was passed from one household to another, miles apart, by children—runners, they called themselves. The needle was stuck for protection in a raw potato and always threaded with red yarn. My, My! how that paid off," she smiled, remembering. "Once a boy stopped to gather some hazelnuts along the slough and was startled by a she-bear and her cub, so he dropped the spud—not that a soul blamed the child—"

"A *bear*?" The pupils of Midgie's eyes enlarged, but her curiosity overcame her fear. "And then what happened?"

"Will that be all, Mrs. North? No? Well, just make yourself at home and I'll answer the other Mrs. North's question. Oh, the whole family went hunting for the precious commodity—found it, too—do you know how?"

"The red string?" Midgie clapped her hands like an excited child. "I guess we don't have it so bad after all,

True. But," she opened her oversize purse, "maybe we'd better take a supply of needles just in case."

The three were laughing together when the men returned. As they shopped among the tools and coils of wire, True prepared to pay her bill. That was when Midgie moved close to Tillie Caswell and, her face as pale as death, whispered: "This place—uh—it isn't a place—"

True was shocked. But Tillie Caswell's voice portrayed no emotion.

"A brothel? No, my husband's a God-fearing man. Just wish there could be a church here." Two questions answered, True had intended to inquire about the church, holding little hope that one existed.

But Midgie? Why on earth would she ask such a question? And why the look of relief? Surely she didn't suspect Marty—

Quickly she put the revolting thought from her mind. It had been a strange encounter, as if both Midgie and Tillie were leaving something unsaid. Or was she imagining things?

Certainly she did not imagine the next two incidents which happened almost simultaneously.

True was unaware that a train had arrived. Probably the continuous slashing away at the keyboard by a self-styled pianist who knew only one song had drowned out the noise. The arrival of a few newcomers and the sight of a cloud of cinder-studded smoke sweeping close to the ground beyond the single front window alerted her to the activity. Peering out the window for sight of the men, she noted that the sun, trailing ribbons of crimson through the smoke, had dipped below the horizon. Twenty-five miles of travel in the darkness held little appeal.

Looking anxiously for sight of Young Wil, who surely must be loading the wagon, her eyes caught a glimpse of Marty. What she saw stopped any attempt to get his attention. He was talking earnestly with the man she could only identify as "the stranger wearing the beaver hat." Both were gesturing and in turn glancing to see if they were detected. Thank goodness Midgie was looking on a counter marked "Milady's Toilette" and asking Mrs. Caswell if she could hope to find peroxide for her "roots."

True had grown more uneasy by the moment, and now this. If she could get the mail and find the men— yes, she preferred traveling in the darkness to—what?

"Mrs. Caswell," she called, "I failed to inquire about the mail. Have you anything for True North or—"

"True North! As I live and breathe, it's you. True North," the remembered voice repeated as if tasting the word, "so she did not marry, after all—"

Michael St. John!

14

Dreaming?

The sight of Michael's tall, sandy-haired handsomeness rendered True speechless. Moments ago his very name would have meant only a near-stranger from her past, a ghost of a whirlwind "understanding" (had she really expected to marry him?) from her past. But now, hearing the low, throaty voice and looking again into the hazel eyes which in any situation seemed to twinkle with amusement, he was as real as the day they had said goodbye in Atlanta. The time between folded like an accordion.

There had to be words to cover the encounter. Michael St. John meant nothing to her. Never had—at least, not in a This-is-the-man-I-am-going-to-marry way. It was Young Wil then. It was Young Wil now. It would be Young Wil forever. Michael had been an important link between finding her roots and cutting the cords which bound her to the past. And, of course, it was he who helped her dispose of the railroad shares. She was grateful, nothing more. It was only the shock of seeing him, a poking into the ashes of a dead love...

True inhaled deeply and hated herself for glancing down. When she met his eyes again, his gaze was bold and complimentary, out of keeping with his still-boyish face. Out of keeping, too, in view of her marriage and new title of Mrs. Wilson North.

"I—I must be dreaming," she murmured, the words sounding foolish in her own ears. Obviously they sounded equally so to Michael, as revealed by the beginning of a smile below his closely cropped mustache.

"It is no dream, my dear. I am flesh and blood—see for yourself." Michael extended a hand, which she accepted and then withdrew too quickly for the gesture to be called a real handshake. "It is more like a dream come true," Michael went on. "I have always felt that we would meet again, even when you denied the possibility—unfinished business—"

He seemed to be waiting for her to say something. And there was indeed something that needed saying. But how could she say it? "I am married...I am Mrs. Wil North...there seems to be confusion on the name; I *did* marry the 'kissing cousin' you teased about, who is no cousin at all"? None of these were right—too much too soon, too defensive. Casual, she must be casual. She wanted no wrong impressions.

"What brings you here, Michael?"

Michael had removed his hat and was running restless hands through the shining thickness of his hair. "The railroad, what else—unless—"

"There is talk of extending the inland route, I understand. I should have realized that you would be involved—owning as many shares—"

Michael laughed. "How little you've changed, little True North. That was our problem, wasn't it? The railroad's being to me what your religion was to you. There's so much to catch up on. But I prefer hearing about you than talking business. What are *you* doing here and—"

The sharp warning of the train whistle cut short the conversation. "Last call, Mr. St. John!" Tillie Caswell called. "Oh, I see you've met Mrs. North—"

A look of incredulity crossed Michael's face. "True, I must see you—"

But his voice was lost in the hissing sound of steam as the train shuddered and tried its wheels. Michael St. John, hat still in hand, ran forward, his retreating figure lost in smoke—the way dreams always end.

15

"Let There Be No Misunderstandings!"

Seeing Michael was no dream, True realized as her eyes roamed the darkness of the hotel room that Tillie Caswell had assigned to her and Young Wil. "I always try to accommodate newly-marrieds with a room having a door instead of a drape," the woman had said with a smile, "and the latch works. You see, it is safer that way—not that we expect trouble. But it's best being prepared."

Fleetingly, True hoped that the hospitable Tillie had made no such statement to Midgie. Looking around for spiders was enough for her to cope with for now. True herself had been relieved when Young Will suggested staying overnight. They could get an early start and . . .

Her thoughts drifted back to the events of the afternoon. Marty, Tillie, and Midgie, and then Michael. Why did she feel a connection?

After a plunge bath, scrubbing with a cake of coarse yellow soap that left her skin feeling stretched across her body, True had braved the mattress with Young Wil. She had planned to speak of the three incidents but he dropped off to sleep. Careful not to awaken him, True lay so still that a stiffness began at her neck and spread over her entire body . . . a long accumulation of fatigue, which she chose to ignore. It would be nice to get away from this place. On the other hand, she almost wished for some time to explore it further, enduring the gibes and leers of the stragglers, to learn what puzzled her: the background of the ranch that Uncle Artie had left to O'Higgin... the real status of the railway's present and future... and, most importantly, how Marty and Michael would fit into those plans. Both were deeply involved, but in entirely different ways. She would keep her ears open and her mouth shut.

Sleep came fitfully. The stiffness had traveled down to her heels, and in turning carefully she thought there was the sound of footsteps outside their room. Was it locked? Barefoot, True padded to the door. No sound. But her motion had awakened her husband.

"Morning?" Young Wil sounded wide awake, rising on one elbow to look at the low-in-the-west moon shining palely through the loosely woven burlap serving as drapes. "Doesn't Slippery Elm bother to go to bed? I'm sure I smell coffee."

True dressed hurriedly, then lighted the stub of a candle on a stool table. By its sputtering light she took note of the pole bedstead with the tick mattress that had been about as comfortable as a sack of broken crockery. Their featherbed sounded like a luxury... as was their breakfast when they joined Marty and Midgie downstairs. Eggs 50 cents apiece! She was afraid to ask Young Wil what the coffee cost. It was strong enough to walk, so worth whatever it cost, but not bracing enough to stop Midgie's complaints about the eggs. She would get some chickens, that's what. Maybe *sell* eggs. Or exchange them for staple groceries.

"Just set a trap," Marty suggested, his mood seemingly improved. "I saw some wandering around the ranch, looking wild as quails."

"They belong there but have gone sort of native since—well, for a long time," Tillie Caswell said as she leaned across the scarred oak table to heat their mugs of coffee. "With a little grain, you'll have the birds eating right out of your hand."

"Good idea," was Midgie's reply. And the faraway look in her eyes said that she was speaking of more than chickens.

———————————

Tonsil and Lung came bounding out to meet the foursome returning to the Double N. The puppies were becoming dogs . . . a reminder of how time was slipping past. Seeming to read True's thoughts, Young Wil suggested that they get the fall cabbage and collards set out at once. Yes, the late-summer sun would do them in unless they were watered by artificial means. Marty was skeptical, saying there were no means out here in the "wilds." One needed pipes and know-how. Billy Joe, who was equipped, Young Wil said, with more than one set of ears, heard the dogs and appeared from nowhere.

"Smart young feller like'n yourself oughta know ir'gation's older'n history," he said, his voice rising a fraction with annoyance. "Read Genesis, my boy, secon' chapter: An' a river went outa Eden t'water th' garden.' 'N iffen that ain't convincin' 'nuf, flip over t'Kings—you *do* read th' Good Book, I'm a-takin' it?—sez there 'Ye shalln't see wind er rain—yet th' valley'll be full up with water that both ye 'n yer cattle 'n beast kin drink'—ain't that th' way it goes, Wil?"

"Close enough," Young Wil answered. "With three-fourths of the earth's surface covered with water, one day man will discover how to distribute it 'and the desert shall bloom.' For now, nature does a satisfactory job, what with the snow—at least, here. However, now and then nature needs a hand—"

"So we're to make a Persian wheel or Archimedes screw like I saw you reading about?" Marty's voice carried a jibe which Young Wil ignored. His attitude troubled True, however. Why must he behave like a wary foe, thrusting and retreating on the slightest pretext? Puzzling.

Young Wil and Billy Joe went on with the conversation. It would be a simple matter to plow ditches from the little lake. Walled up a bit, the lake would serve as a reservoir for capturing melted snow. Good that gravity flow was on their side. Would it work? Course 'twould, Billy Joe said smugly. "Look what them Mormons done in Utah, 'n that's desert, man, real desert."

Young Wil's dark eyes were alive with excitement. Of course, there would come a time when all the creeks and lakes would be fringed by more farms—then they would have to work out a more complicated system. But for now, "Well, let's get those cabbages planted!"

Marty scowled. "At least we have enough ground here so settlers can't inch in much, tap into our water lines. We'll see to that."

Billy Joe's small eyes became smaller. "Well, least-wise, yer thinkin'—allus a good sign. We're bound on makin' a good rancher uv you. An' one o'these days that mouth o'yorn's a-gonna open 'n let somethin' good come out!"

Marty actually grinned. And then the frown was back. "Could be we're facing a bigger problem than poachers, carpetbaggers, squatters, wild animals—and more. If those railroad thieves try cutting in—"

"Marty, please—" Midgie's voice was that of a pleading child.

"We'll worry about that when the time comes." Young Wil's answer declared the subject closed.

For the next month they all worked together, including Mariah and the three boys. Nobody complained, although True was sure that every bone felt twisted out of place every back fractured. The men plowed a sizable square of virgin soil and pulverized it with a harrow before going on to break furrows for the water to follow. Midgie helped Mariah stake even rows by using string while True and the children crawled on hands and knees to drop tiny seeds, pausing only for drinking water or driving away the troublesome canines, who between chasing rabbits used the newly seeded garden for a speedway.

When the job was finished, the timing was right for presenting Mariah with the makings of her fiesta dress, True and Midgie agreed. Something had warned them that the woman was proud and very well might mistake any gesture of kindness as unearned charity.

But they were surprised when she refused the material even after her hard work. Vigorously, she shook her raven hair in refusal. But strangely, her dark eyes were shining as her tapering fingers made a desperate try to communicate in sign language.

What could she be trying to say? First, Mariah held the precious cloth to her own face and nodded. Then she shook her head sadly and pointed to Midgie, still clinging to the fabric possessively. When she pointed her direction, True felt a flicker of understanding.

"She loves the material—probably the loveliest thing she has ever owned—" True began.

Midgie caught the message and interrupted excitedly. "But she wants to make similar dresses for us. Oh, True, could we?"

"Of course we can! What a lovely thought, Mariah." True hoped that her smile and nod would fill in for the English words.

They did. Mariah jumped over a row marked "BEANS" and, with many a *"Gracias, Señoras,"* she smiled through a mist of tears.

"The men will be going for the laborers the last week in August," True recalled aloud. "We can see if Tillie has more selection—and both of us must have letters ready to mail the family."

"The dress will be the beginning of my new wardrobe," Midgie said dreamily. "Nothing I have is right— and you are too nice to say so. It's wrong here—and there with your—our family—wrong in Portland. No wonder Marty got the wrong impression—we still have to talk—"

Her voice trailed off at the sound of Young Wil's whistling and Billy Joe's singing (which was more of a croak). One day, True had prayed over and over, their attitudes (admittedly taken from Paul's—"I have learned in whatsoever state I am, therewith to be content") would rub off on Marty, allowing him to be happy.

"Yes, we must talk. We all need to be open and honest—"

Although the back door was opening, Midgie tugged at the folds of True's long dirndl skirt. "*Can* we be—and still love each other—I—I mean—*really* be truthful?" she whispered.

"It's the *only* way," True whispered back with a reassuring smile.

But Midgie needed proof. "Then tell me I am right—that my clothes *are* wrong—*look* at me, True!" Her voice was desperate.

True looked. Midgie was wearing a gimp two sizes too small, making her look 12, its colors screaming for attention. Inhaling deeply, True said kindly, "Yes, darling, the dress is wrong—but believe me, there is nothing wrong elsewhere. You are growing—truly you are—and your spirit has outgrown that dress!"

It was true. There was a change in Midgie's face. Her eyes were still searching, sometimes filled with fear and confusion. But she no longer looked lost, utterly defenseless. There was a look of discovery, as if she had looked deep inside herself and found a certain strength. And now she was ready to look *outside* herself.

"It's true, isn't it? I am stronger—I can face the truth—and share it! If I can just make Marty see—he just has to love me. Losing him would be second-worst to losing the Lord. Why, I'd be like an elephant without a trunk!"

True laughed. "You aren't going to lose either of them," she promised. "Just let there be no misunderstandings—"

"Let there be no misunderstanding about this, my beautiful brat—your man's hungry. This cow-punching whets the appetite, creates a desire for food, drink—and love!" The man with the appetite had his arms around her.

"Wil North—" she gasped and then stopped. His hug was so tight that she saw seven varieties of stars.

16

Developments
at the Double N

The furrow-canals finished, the men experimented with allowing some of the little lake's water to trickle down to the gardens and field. The men watched with pride. Midgie watched not at all, her mind devising a way to capture the roaming chickens she had caught sight of. True, while sharing Young Wil's enthusiasm, found her mind taking an unexpected detour in fantasy. The earth-tone water, picking up loose soil in its downward course, turned to silver froth winding and coiling from a laughing waterfall. The scrawny stand of timber changed complexions from sunburned green to crimson-blushed forests climbing up the timberline to where forbidding rock peaks lost themselves in the ragged edge of gold-lined clouds. *Mount Sinai!* The mountain to which Moses had climbed to receive the Ten Commandments. Now his garments in her mind's eye blended with the filmy-white of the clouds obscuring his shining upturned face while below the whole of Israel stood in awe—seeing, hearing, believing...

True blinked away the vision, but another took its place: The foothills of home, junction for the five-fingered streams created by melting snows of towering mountains to water the broad valleys below, loomed before her eyes. The bountiful gardens. The endless expanse of cultivated fields. Aunt Chrissy's undisciplined flowers, which Daddy Wil vowed were soon to reach over the rooftop of the two-story house.

Face it, True North, you are homesick. Homesick for the protection and familiarity of the Big House and its beloved occupants. Family and home. A lump rose to her throat, a lump which dissolved quickly with another startling realization: She was equally homesick for the loving fellowship of her church family. True, she and God had remained in close communion, but didn't He expect more? Something told her that, yes, she had a mission in addition to helping Mary and Midgie, but she wished the Lord would speak up, tell her...

The trend of her thoughts was interrupted by a commotion. Midgie was screaming, and with a different quality from when she spotted a mouse or expected to be scalped. She was laughing victoriously. And Marty was laughing with her—*Marty?*—while the dogs went crazy.

A loud squawk told the story even before Midgie yelled, "I got him—I got him—cock-of-the-walk—only rooster in the crowd...and the ladies'll follow. I—I—done—did it by myself—and now I can sell those golden eggs—"

True looked up and burst into laughter with the others. Midgie had tolled the feisty rooster to her by using up most of the precious cornseed. But the results were obviously worth the price. When the cock had paused to scratch coaxingly to his harem, Midgie had leaped from a furrow and grabbed him, managing somehow to avoid his deadly spurs. What she *hadn't* avoided was the rush of water released from the lake. She was an absolute mud ball, her hair an inverted mop.

It was a riot. And it was—*Oh, thank You, Lord!*—the very first time the four of them had laughed, genuinely laughed, together...

True inhaled deeply of the air, now gloriously asparkle with bubbles of life. It was all going to work out. One day there would be a rambling structure with an inviting sign reading WELCOME TO THE ABODE OF MR. AND MRS. MARTIN NORTH! And, as if to guarantee that welcome, True, dreaming again, foresaw well-graded roads approaching the ranchhouse . . . corrals . . . barns . . . bunkhouses . . . towering silos. All spick-and-span with whitewash. To the east, looking down on fenced-off hayfields and meadows dotted with thoroughbred stock and cattle grazing in a varicolored mosaic, there would be—

Raising her eyes to the top of the tallest hill of which the terrain boasted, she finished the dream with a dread reality: There at the top was a natural gap through which pioneers had passed. There was now a man-made one, newly scarred, familiar to those who knew the method as a sort of divine-right move employed by the railroad to declare a right-of-way. Unfortunately, the law was on the side of the shareholders. And True's experiences in Atlanta had taught her that ruthless men encountering any resistance with landowners were not against use of force at gunpoint. Unfortunately, too, there were landowners who believed in fighting fire with fire. That had been the youthful Martin North's downfall. Easily led, he had fallen in with bad company. While her adopted brother in his emerging selfhood saw an opportunity to protect the senior Wilson North's rights, leaders of the gang were mercenaries, and knew a scapegoat when they saw one. It was easy to convince him that their Robin Hood tactics were acts of heroism.

What had Marty learned, if anything? Which side was he on now? If only he were less aloof, more approachable! She was tired, tired, *tired*.

That night, after a sponge bath (most of the available water reserved for the disheveled but happy Midgie) and a hearty meal, True snuggled close to Young Wil in the confines of their bandanna-sized bedroom, their only place of privacy. She tried to tell him everything, whispering for privacy which the thin walls failed to provide. The gap ...the feeling about Tillie Caswell and Midgie...Marty's meeting with the "beaver hat" stranger...and, finally, the surprise appearance of Michael St. John.

"Not sorry you came?" he whispered. But True was fast asleep.

17

❖

Discoveries
in Slippery Elm

The late-August trip to town was destined to be hot and sultry. But the sunrise was beautiful. Having left before the pink of dawn, True, Young Wil, Midgie, Marty, and Billy Joe (looking very much like "the Beetle" astride a skimpy-tailed mule) viewed the sunrise in awe from the sun's lavender warning flares until its sleepy golden rays spread over the luxuriant green of native meadows to the even greener glow of scattered grain-fields, now taking on a harvest glow. The wagon wheels were surprisingly quiet, as if listening while staggering along the aged pack-trail—so quiet that a lone rabbit ventured out curiously, wriggled his nose in greeting, then scurried back to cover. True wanted to laugh, but Young Wil's hand squeezed her hand to warn silence as the team came to an abrupt halt.

Nobody spoke and, strangely, Midgie did not let out a single whimper. Instead, all eyes followed Wil's pointing finger. Billy Joe had dismounted and crept stealthily alongside the wagon, obviously struggling with a *"Yip-pee-yea!"*

And small wonder. There beneath the protection of a mushroom-shaped rock stood the most beautiful animal True had ever seen. An enormous shiny-backed bull, a perfect specimen looking carved in the rock, stood motionless, ruminative eyes upon the group. True did not recognize the breed, but she knew the look. The satin-coated beast reminded her of women that Michael St. John's aunt introduced her to at society functions in Atlanta: in doubt as to her social status; arrogant and superior; and all the while fearful and on guard of invaders.

"Great-blooded Shorthorn," Billy whispered in near-reverence. "Prob'ly a runaway uv some Eastern immigrants—gone wild now—'n—"

Seeming to hear the sounds almost inaudible to human ear, the great animal snorted and pawed the earth, sending showers of debris between himself and his audience. When the dust settled, he was gone.

"I tole you—I tole you," Billy Joe, hoarse with excitement, said over and over. "I'm a-gonna ketch that sucker—I'll find me a way—an' we're boun' on havin' ourselves th' finest herd this side uv th' Ole Miss River. Now as t'how—"

"Ride him in," Young Wil teased, his eyes alive with excitement.

"Or let Midgie here capture him!" Marty grinned.

Oh, how good to hear him speak lightly! Better yet, to note his enthusiasm. There was no opportunity to point out the change to Young Wil. The men were too busy devising schemes to corner the magnificent animal before he was slaughtered for beefsteak or lassoed by some poacher who knew thoroughbred cattle. "Now that you seen queen's evidence, you willin' t' believe me—'n take my word that my plan's boun' on workin'?"

Billy Joe posed the question just as they entered the outskirts of a bruised and battered Slippery Elm, where a bar fight had obviously taken place the night before. True shuddered and slipped her hand into her husband's. The place gave her the creeps—or, as O'Higgin was fond of saying—made possums crawl over her grave! All thoughts of asking the excited foreman of the Double N about his plan were gone. She and Midgie would do their shopping quickly and hope that the men would do likewise. To get out of this so-called town *immediately* was not soon enough! How long did it take to find harvest hands?

Was last night's brawl too much for Tillie Caswell? She glanced at True and Midgie when they entered the store, her eyes vacant.

"Remember us? We're the Norths." It was Midgie who spoke first, reaching out with a small gesture of friendliness to touch the older woman's hand. Tillie's expression remained as blank as that of some store window's mannequin.

True wondered if Mrs. Caswell was reliving some chapter in her past. She wore an outdated cheap satin dress and her tassel-trimmed boots, once so stylish, were run over at the heels. But the pathetic part of her attempt at prettiness was the faded clump of velvet rosebuds tucked into her heavy hair.

Tillie's husband stepped in front of her unceremoniously. "May I be of assistance, ladies? My wife here's poorly today. We run a respectable place, but—" Curley Caswell paused to scratch his shining head where the hair used to grow, "well, I'm guessin' you fine folks have gathered some ain't so legitimate—oughta be burnt t'th' ground 'n them alley cats be scorched all th' way back t'St. Jo. Th' roughhousin' ain't good fer my Tillie—ain't good a'tall. She's been through a heap 'n it left her bundle o' nerves. Any excitement can trigger it—even when it's no relation uv what she's suffered—"

Midgie's face was white. "In Portland?"

"Thereabouts—in a flood, with lootin' 'n shootin' after, whilst she was all-time searching—"

The proprietor was unable to finish whatever he was about to say. Later True was to look back on his words and regret that. But for now she was relieved to see that Tillie was coming around, speaking in broken monosyllables, but present tense, with no reference to the past.

"I feel as weak as water," she said at last. "If I could have a cup of tea?" Quickly she unpinned the roses and dropped them to the floor. "I've a feeling you've come for more of that material. Did you run short? Too bad, but I am out completely. But," her tired eyes brightened almost feverishly, "guess what! We received a shipment of the loveliest dry goods ever—bee balms, scarlet, pink—reminds me of a late summer meadow. Makes you almost drop to your knees and gather in the flowers, praying a bit while you're down there."

Functioning now, she stepped behind the counter and began unrolling bolts. The fabric was every bit as lovely as she described. Excitedly, the two Mrs. Norths made their choices. As Mrs. Caswell's shears snipped away and she tore across the bolt in completion, she said dreamily, "I guess you ladies are making these for the roundup? It's the biggest thing we can boast of here. My husband told me that you planned on roping in some wild horses. Maybe the men can break them that day just before the barbecue?"

True thought of the beautiful bull and hoped he would not fall prey. But, after their near-total isolation, a gathering sounded exciting. It would be like the old days at the Big House or Turn-Around Inn. Tillie, her rational self now, made small talk while assisting with the selection of notions for completing the fiesta dresses.

"*Hola, Señor!*" Tillie said in greeting to a leathery-skinned customer who had entered noiselessly in his beaded moccasins.

Flailing his arms in excitement, the wiry little man began an endless reel of Spanish. Tillie, her voice low and musical, answered in equally rapid sentences. Then she turned to True and Midgie.

"Augie hears that there's work at the Double N. He's of fine character and as loyal as they come. Without him," she smiled, "my passing might go unmourned. Do you want me to tell your men?"

The man had an honest face and clear, dark eyes that could look another person squarely in the eye. His worn clothing spoke of need. "Yes," True and Midgie said simultaneously.

"It will take Mariah's help," True said thoughtfully. "None of us speak Spanish. Which reminds me, Mrs. Caswell, Billy Joe wants her to learn English so badly—"

"I will help her," Tillie said with a note of gladness in her voice. "And I will help Augie here—"

"And we'll *all* help at the ranch!" True was surprised to here Midgie volunteer. For some reason it made her want to cry.

Young Wil entered. Tillie Caswell introduced Augie, explaining his background and desire to work, and made no effort to conceal her delight when her Mexican friend was signed on for the harvest. Augie was overcome with gratitude, murmuring, "*Gracias, Señor! Gracias, gracias—*"

True was only dimly aware that arrangements were made with the aid of Tillie's translations for Augie to sleep out-of-doors, there being no bunkhouse. Would a temporary shelter of canvas stretched over supporting poles be acceptable? And hay would be the best they had to offer by way of a bed. Young Wil's voice was apologetic, something Augie failed to hear. He was too busy adding to the sum total of his "*Gracias—gracias, gracias*" song of appreciation.

Resolutely, True tried to appear hospitable, but it was as if some irresistible magnet pulled her eyes to where Marty stood engrossed in conversation with a portly man dressed nattily from his proper black suit to his shining patent button-on shoes. His terraced chin showed lack of exercise, as did his pale skin in contrast to Marty's. For the first time she noted how tanned and fit her brother had become from his hard work and exposure to the sun.

Suddenly a woman appeared from nowhere. "May I have a glass of water, please? This dreadful place is enough to drive one to madness. I shall be happy to bid it goodbye—if my brother and I are fortunate enough to escape with our scalps!" The voice had a metallic ring.

Before accepting the water, the woman touched her elaborately coiffured yellow hair. It glittered with some sort of glaze, totally unlike the satiny sheen of True's—where, Young Wil said, the stars were entangled.

Tillie Caswell obligingly took the almost-untasted water from the other woman's jewel-frosted fingers. "It is nice to see you once more, Mrs. St. John—Mrs. North, I believe you met Mrs. St. John's husband?"

Mrs. St. John? Michael's wife? Taken by surprise, True found herself tongue-tied, quite capable of committing some dreadful social blunder. Worse, she was staring, actually staring at this obviously wealthy person, no older than herself but already showing symptoms of middle-age curves, corseted into an expensive green frock, which was no greener than her cold eyes.

True was never sure whether either of them acknowledged the introduction. The woman—had Mrs. Caswell called her Felice?—turned away. "I do wish my husband would give up this silly notion of attempting to civilize this country—railroad or not—"

Tillie Caswell colored furiously. "Come now, Mrs. St. John—"

True heard no more. Midgie, missing the encounter by stepping outside, was walking toward Marty. Marty terminated the conversation immediately and motioned her back to where Young Wil was talking with a small knot of other men. Probably recruits gathered from their previous trip to Slippery Elm, True guessed.

The guess was correct. Marty, seemingly composed, nodded approval of "Pig Iron," a giant with an engaging grin but appearing to possess more brawn than brains. Pig Iron motioned for "Tex," a lad who looked as if he belonged in grammar school but was amazingly well-versed in the ways of wheat. "Tough work, raisin' wheat—feller's gotta keep his eyes peeled on th' elements 'n bugs. My ole gran'pa use' ta say, 'Now, Junior, lis'sen t'th' Injuns. Wheat's gotta have a lake with a mouth fer waterin' it—soil with ears that'll screech when it's thirstin'—'n a windbreak uv trees that set there 'n watch, fer protection from storms 'n fer reaching up t'th' Great White Spirit.' Golly-gee, it's work, but me, now I need work 'n there's somethin' 'twixt my brain 'n them yeller heads uv ripe wheat—you ready fer threshin'?"

Young Wil looked amused. "The wheat has to be cut first."

"Yeah, 'n cured—then comes th' flailin'—beatin' 'til yore eyeballs drop outa their sockets—"

Tex's voice had risen. He lowered it as if trying to avoid the adolescent crack he had learned to anticipate. But the crack came anyway, comically and uncontrollably. His unshaven face flushed, his bravado gone, Tex looked as if he had been caught stealing sheep. Clearing his throat, the boy tried to make amends for an imagined transgression.

"Mr. North—Mr. Norths—I mean, uh, Mr's. North—I want you t'be knowin' I ain't seen a lotta years, but they've been hard 'uns an' learnt me a heap. I'll work hard 'n," he gulped, "I'm a nothin'-but-th'-truth maniac—honest. 'N that ain't all, I brung a new strain uv seed from th' east—hardier—"

"No need to keep talking, Tex," Marty said briskly. "You're on as far as I'm concerned. Wil?"

Young Wil extended his hand. "Indeed. Welcome to the Double N!"

Excitedly, as if afraid that to stop talking would cancel the handshake agreement, Tex explained that his wheat could be planted right after the first frost but before the first freeze. Red winter wheat.

"I'm glad you like your work," Wil said with a poker-faced wink at True. "Our foreman may need help with rounding up livestock—"

The boy was off like a cannon. "What a day!" Wil laughed. True nodded, knowing that their meanings were different.

18

Secrets
of the Harvest

An eventful month passed, 30 days of dawn-to-dusk labor for Wil, Marty, and the hired hands, including a "long drink of water" (as Billy Joe described him), friend of Tex's called "Slim" and, to True's dismay, the man with the withered arm that Mr. Caswell had called "Gun Slinger." Young Wil confided that he too distrusted the man but that he knew a lot about stock and cattle. Billy Joe had put him through the third degree on longhorns, shorthorns, Holsteins, Jerseys, Ayreshires, and all the in-between mixed breeds of cattle. As for horses, Gun Slinger used to ride in a rodeo, to which the withered arm was a testimonial. A wild burro had rolled over on him—

True listened and prayed that everything would work out. In fact, she suspected that she kept God busy with her constant talk as she and Midgie worked their once-soft hands to the bone cooking and delivering meals to the fields at midday, since there was no pause for lunch. She and Midgie took turns at taking the food to the men—their only chance to keep alive the fact that they had husbands. They saw the North brothers only by lamplight at breakfast and supper.

Aunt Chrissy had done a commendable job at teaching True the art of cooking, but Midgie had had no training at all. True marveled at her, cooking as she did, awkwardly at first, but—under the supervision of True and Mariah—systematically, with no wasted effort and with every detail carried out to perfection. "I could feed a regiment," she beamed with pride. True believed her.

The only breaks in the strenuous routine were the fittings of the fiesta dresses which Mariah's nimble fingers somehow managed to stitch together between the other demands on her days, plus Mrs. Caswell's weekly calls. If Mariah was to learn English, she must have regular lessons, Tillie declared, and besides, the trip got her away from the confines of Slippery Elm.

"Mariah's a fast learner," she declared. "Has a tuned-in ear. Do you know if she plays a musical instrument?"

True did not know. But she did wonder at the way Midgie's pale face went even paler at such a simple question. She welcomed Midgie's suggestion that the two of them take along a lunch for themselves when they delivered the noon meal to the men the following day. There was so much to talk about, and the few minutes' rest would do them good.

Beneath a little grove of elms, they spread the still-warm sourdough biscuits with blackberry marmalade from Grandma Mollie's pantry. The jerked beef tasted saltier than usual, as if Billy Joe had dunked it into the salt barrel for curing instead of smoking it slowly over a hickory woodfire. Midgie chewed on a piece, made a face, and spat it onto the ground. "This stuff needs soaking before cooking with dried beans," she said. Her face looked wretchedly white, as if she were going to be ill.

Small wonder. True herself felt as if during the past few weeks they had been traveling around the world—uphill all the way. She was tired, so tired, as if every step would be her last. Poor Midgie. She was less accustomed to the rural way of life, and certainly not this style. True had written cheerfully to Aunt Chrissy and Daddy Wil about their tribulations, making them sound like a game, but admitting that she would be happy for them all when the game was over. If they could see the overwhelming exhaustion on Midgie's face, they would find her accounts less amusing. For the first time, True noted that the other girl's legs were swollen above her heavy shoes, the ones she called "combat boots."

Before she could comment, Midgie lay back—head pillowed on hands laced together behind her—and moaned slightly. "It would take more than food and drink to restore me," she said in a small voice. "Physical strength just won't keep me going—"

True's heart filled with admiration and compassion. "I know, darling, and I am so proud of you. You have overtaxed your body. Only your will, heart, and purpose have sustained you."

"Keep watch, will you, True sweetie? I couldn't run if we were attacked by Indians or a pack of wolves. I feel as if life were tracking me down—watching me grow more helpless with every day—"

"You should have told me, Midgie—drink this water, close your eyes and rest."

Midgie gulped with an effort and returned the half-full glass to True. "I'll obey all except the *resting*. You watch and let me talk."

True began to gather up the crumbs. Any smell of food *could* invite a bear. Considering the possibility, she hurried—then stopped. Midgie's story was too incredible to allow for anything but listening.

"You know something's wrong between me and Marty—Marty and me. It all started before we married, and I thought if I tried hard enough I could prove myself—make him love me the way I thought he did—be-be-before he found out the truth. But I guess I killed his love—killed it dead—only I didn't know—honest, True, I'm not a bad woman like he says—"

"Marty said *that*?" True dropped the canteen from feelingless fingers and mopped at the puddle of water with her cotton petticoat.

A tear slipped from beneath Midgie's closed lids. "Oh, I wish God could take us back—let us live some of our lives over. I wish that being 'born again' really meant another chance—"

"It does, darling—it does—you have to believe that! God does not require that we do that, just ask forgiveness and *He* wipes the slate clean—"

"Then why won't Marty do that, too?"

"I think," said True slowly, "that you will have to explain the situation instead of beating yourself unnecessarily—than we can talk. And, Midgie, remember that I love you no matter what the problem is. I also trust you—and find it impossible to believe that you have committed some heinous crime. Tell me only as much as you feel like—"

"I will tell you all of it—it's not that much, really—just a terrible, terrible misunderstanding—and me being so stupid—and lonely. Now, I ain't—I'm not excusing myself. But I've got me this weakness—about playing a guitar—folks say I have talent—"

Relieved, True laughed. "That's no weakness—"

"I guess," Midgie said slowly, opening her eyes to squint sightlessly into the sky, "you better let me finish—it gets worse."

It did. Listening, True was transported to Portland's back-street business section, where men with tobacco-stained teeth and no morals catcalled to any passing woman without hesitation. After all, no "lady" was going to venture down Rum Road without knowin' man did not live by bread alone. Ignoring them, the girl hurried into the door bearing the sign WANTED: YOUNG WOMAN PLAYING STRINGS. Summoning courage, she knocked and was admitted to a room with shades drawn. At first only the woman's thick, homely lips painted a violent red stood out, then the myriads of flashing sequins, lending an air of tawdry elegance to the sweeping folds of her black taffeta dress. A rush of footsteps said that they were not alone, but there was no one in sight as the woman led her into a large room with hobnail-scarred floors. Scattered tables and tops supporting upturned chairs spoke of night trade, as did a battered piano, now idle, in the corner. Stale tobacco smoke and the sour-mash smell of a bar were enough to make one retch. But a girl couldn't be choosy if she wanted to break into the music business, could she? The opera house was hardly a starting place. She could gain some experience here and then—

"Whatcha lookin' fer, missy? Don't look dry behind th' ears."

"I—I—came about the sign. I play the guitar—"

The woman licked her lips, looked her over from head to toe, and nodded. "You'll do—had any experience?"

"No—but," eagerly, "I'm willing to learn!"

Denver Belle, her name was, rubbed fat palms together. "So much the better, missy—startin' tonight with th' strings—then, we'll see jest how well your act goes over 'fore—"

The girl heard no more above the tom-tom of her heart. Neither did her inexperienced eye recognize that the woman had a heart of pure flint, the temper of a rabid skunk, and the morals of a she-coyote.

"Now, I provide a necessary bizness, missy. Now, they's them psalm singers wearin' black hats 'n shirt collars on back'ards what'd have me horsewhipped jest fer givin' sweet young thangs like you a chance—fer gettin' on in this world. Better git them clothes stitched up tighter, uv course, 'n drop that Sunday-school drawstring neckline down over th' shoulders—git up there 'n sang, knock 'em dead."

That was the first night. And sing she did. Even the men at the bar stopped their raucous talk and listened, yelling, "More, more!"

For a week everything went well. In her ecstatic state, Midgie paid no attention to the clientele and was oblivious to the other girls who must have "boarded there," since they seemed so much a part of the place, swishing up and down the stairs the way they did.

Midgie went on with her part-time job of helping Young Wil with his paperwork, and also continued seeing Marty. Young Wil, seeing that they were becoming serious about each other, encouraged them both. And the relationship grew, drifting into a sort of "understanding." Life was beautiful, and so was Midgie. She glowed in the warmth of being in love, something she was sure in her simple heart would be doubled when her beloved discovered that she had found success—real success—that she was a celebrity bound for the stage. She held the secret close to her heart for just the right moment. Then she would reveal her talents.

But the revelation came sooner than expected, the night of the Sod-Busters' Ball. Midgie could remember little of the preparations, she said, except Denver Belle's frenzied state of preparing for the big night when patrons would expect "quality goods." The rooms went wild with colored streamers and the scent of cheap cologne, which all but asphyxiated her as she practiced intricate strumming and fretting of the guitar, saving her voice for the performance. Denver Belle's attitude began to change. She screamed, cursed, and threatened, her face as white as the pottery washbasin, her eyes glinting with ambition that amounted to downright evil. Midgie had known all along that it was a less than ideal place for her to be; but a girl with no stage experience couldn't expect to go looking down her nose, could she? But this night she felt—well, threatened somehow. Her uneasiness grew each time her employer's eyes met hers—cold, calculating, and as hard as black diamonds in a way that drew the upper and lower lids together.

And then the crowd. The terrible crowd of leering men—full-bearded prospectors, filthy buckskin-clad trappers, and some decently-dressed businessmen with uneasy glances darting back and forth to the door as if hoping not to be recognized.

"You're on!" Denver Belle hissed in Midgie's ear. "But first git some paint on that innocent face. This is your big night!"

There was no time to protest. No time either to put her blouse back onto her shoulders when the woman jerked it even lower than usual. Midgie made up her mind then and there that this would be her last night. But first she must fulfill her obligation. She must sing. Sing as she had never sung before. Who knew who would be in that crowd? Hadn't Denver Belle said this was her big night?

And then it happened. Midway of her performance, her eyes caught sight of a table in the corner where five strangers sat. Quieter than the others, they stared at her unbelievably, the one in the shadows glowering. A regular powder keg, sitting there waiting for a fuse...

He found one. A drunken patron leaped to his feet and staggered forward to mount the step to the stage, where he grabbed at her thin blouse, tearing it to bare her flesh. "Ain't she purdy, boys?" And with that Midgie screamed as his filthy face neared hers.

The shadow at the table was no shadow any longer. Taking substance, the man leaped forward, jamming a gun into her attacker's ribs. "Move and I'll blow you apart! Let go of the woman I'm going to marry!"

"Marty." True could only whisper the word.

"Marty—and with him some railroad men. Maybe some he'd been in trouble with, maybe not. I—I was no longer aware of my surroundings—except that everybody went crazy. Marty's friends came to help. Somebody shot out the lights. And me not helping just sitting there wondering how I'd ever make Marty understand how nothing like this had happened before—and—and that I wasn't one of the madam's (yes, that's what she was) 'girls' who swarmed out of the rooms, half-dressed—"

Midgie burst into uncontrollable sobs, near hysteria at the memory of the nightmare. True wished for the water spilled from the canteen as she wiped the girl's feverish brow with the still-damp petticoat, soothing her all the while. "Oh, my darling, you know Marty would never think that. All you had to do was explain—"

"He—he wouldn't believe me—" Midgie whispered brokenly. "He said he—could never trust me again—that I couldn't possibly have been so blind—and that I deceived him—"

"Perhaps in a way you did. You should have told him, Midgie, but we all make mistakes. Someday I will tell you about my trip to Atlanta—but for now—"

True paused, suddenly furious at Marty's behavior. "What right had *he* to throw the first stone?" And then, "Did you tell Young Wil?"

Midgie was calming down, but there was defeat in her young face. "Yes, and he called Marty a whippersnapper—said he would talk to him—and I guess I'll never know if—if Marty married me out of duty—or because of what Young Wil said or did—or, oh, True, do I dare keep hoping that he does love me—and is suffering from what Young Wil called wounded pride?"

"The latter, probably," True answered, wanting to add that she wondered at this point why Midgie gave a fig for his pride. "You have been a wonderful wife. You've done everything possible—"

"Even had my hair bleached because he—Marty kept saying how pretty your blonde hair was. But—but about the child I—I'm supposed to—"

"Give yourselves time, Midgie. Babies wait to be wanted sometimes."

"Wanted?" Midgie's voice was hoarse. "*Wanted?* When he—he never touches me? Just once—on our wedding night. I—I feel so unclean—unwanted. If—if I ever conceived, he—Marty'd disclaim it—oh, True!"

19

Sorting the Wheat from the Chaff

The weather behaved. The few dark clouds which bellowed threateningly withheld their rain and there were no heavy dews to sour the fallen grain. Sun-ripened into golden sheaves, the wheat was ready for threshing now. Some of the choice crop would be saved for seed and some ground into flour for home use, as staple groceries were hard to come by. The hay was sweet enough for fodder, Tex declared, fine for livestock, "providin' we save back 'nuf fer us stayers-oners t'have fer beddin' down." The youngster planned to remain? True had made an attempt to catch Young Wil's eye but failed because Tex was going nonstop with next year's plans for his new strain of wheat.

"Back home we wuz always callin' wheat th' 'worry crop,' but added onto th' veg'tables, eggs, milk, 'n stuff, uh body kin do right well, sure 'nuf—'n that ain't countin' bringin' in them horses—"

True wished that her brother were half as enthusiastic about the red winter wheat whose case Tex pleaded so hard. But Marty appeared determinedly indifferent. It was almost as if he had set a no-win goal designed to prove himself a failure—including his marriage.

The morning that threshing was to begin, True left her breakfast unfinished in order to join her husband before Marty came outside. She wanted to exchange hurried impressions of the situation. Would the year help Marty get his life put together? Get his values straight? Recognize sacrifice, opportunity, and responsibility when they stared him in the face? Or would he continue to look the other way until something bigger than all their efforts brought him to his senses?

But the moment was too precious to waste on words. Dawn was creeping slowly up in the east to transform the world into a fairyland of beauty. The air was sweet-breathed with hay and woodsmoke of the early-risers. Somewhere toward the lean-to barn Midgie's rooster announced that the last star had twinkled out. True reached out a hand to touch her husband's. The way he clutched it, lacing his workworn fingers through hers, said that he too was reliving the fairyland of pantomimes of their childhood. Only the two of them knew that wood nymphs danced among the columbines at this sacred time of day, granting wishes and endowing children with magic passwords. But whatever magic lay in the lap of this God-given morn, True held no illusion about the raw reality behind the closed door.

"Have we made a mistake?" True whispered out of context.

"*You* may have—*I* didn't!" Young Wil declared, pretending to misunderstand. "I got myself the kind of wife every man needs—one who can stand the wear and tear of daily companionship and put up with my moods without being irritable and snappy—one with the saving grace of humor—"

"Wil North! One would have to have that to put up with you! Here we are allowed 30 seconds—"

Wil sighed. "And you want to talk about Marty," he said tiredly. "So let's face it, I am getting weary with our brother's seeing us as intruders. As a doctor, I see him as a patient with a weak heart and high blood pressure! Our coming here should have been therapeutic. Just seeing what a perfect pair we are under any circumstances ought to spur him on." He pulled her gently to him and talked over her head, his eyes watching the door for Marty. "After all, any dumbbell can get himself married. It's *staying* married that proves one's mettle."

True nodded against the roughness of his denim shirt while a vision of Midgie's white face floated before her . . . the steadiness of her gaze, behind which there was always the hint of tears. She would keep her marriage promises at any cost. How reverently she had repeated her wedding vows, although her heart must have been breaking.

"I talked with Midgie—or listened—" True began.

A creak of the door said they had only a moment alone remaining. Wil grabbed at it, speaking rapidly. "Midgie has done all she knows to do to save their marriage from the scrap heap—but I do wish she would learn the persuasive value of a laugh against his sulks—and stop knuckling under to the ingrate! I am unable to get through his thick skull—well," he shifted quickly as Marty's footsteps neared, "we outgrew the wood nymphs, sweetheart, and Jesus took their place! Ask Him to walk alongside us today—today will be no playhouse."

"You know I will! You, Marty, and all the others. Is—is—I can hardly bring myself to say the name—how is Gun Slinger doing?"

Young Wil laughed as he brushed her brow with a kiss and swung astride his horse. "Relax—no need for the name anymore. I said something of the same and he confided it was a name he'd dreamed up himself—something to improve, in his mind, his self-image. Not that I blame him much for a switch. Gervinus is hard to handle—so we call the man Gerry. Slinger's his last name."

"Which doesn't weaken his aim, you'd better believe," Marty said almost to himself as he bridled his horse. "He can shoot if need be."

Young Wil's head jerked erect. "You knew him, Marty?"

"Knew *of* him. That bother you?" Marty flung over his shoulder.

Young Wil made no reply. Instead, he was looking where True's finger pointed to a lone rider silhouetted against the painted sky of the gap.

After that, True made several sightings of the man. It unnerved her to see him sitting there motionlessly, surveying the vast ranch. There was nothing to arouse suspicion except his very presence. Once she and Midgie had ridden to the gap to check out the newly gouged earth, where stakes waving red flags were driven. True recalled her concern. Then the morning sun shot up through a fleece of clouds to dye the sloping hillside with radiance and transform their cabin into a habitation of gold. Was the rider considering robbery or poaching? Could he be connected with the railroad? Or was her imagination simply working overtime? Midgie had enough on her mind, so True made no mention of the stranger's reappearance time and time again.

September brought harvest to a close. Trees, which nobody realized were there, burned with color. Midgie's hens grew too fat and lazy to forge for themselves, so content were they with her oversized helpings of wheat. The fall garden flourished, necessitating the building of a tightly woven fence to keep out deer and rabbits, who ignored Midgie's NO TRESPASSING sign. September also brought the fiesta closer. Plans were underway when unexpected company came.

True and Midgie were canning tomatoes one sultry afternoon when a horse whinnied a warning from the hastily constructed corral. A light breeze sprang up, causing dust to swirl and eddy around the approaching buggy and muffle the labored breathing of Tillie Caswell's aging mare. In spite of the dust, the kindly woman's clothing suggested a soap advertisement. Her starched petticoats rustled as she hurried up the little path that True and Midgie had bordered with zinnias, now at their peak of brilliance. Making a megaphone of her hands, Mrs. Casewell called:

"Yoo-hoo, yoo-hoo! I've brought a guest—down, Tonsil! Down, Lung—let's not drive the Reverend away!"

The dogs looked at her in tawny-eyed reproach, sniffed the Reverend gentleman's pant cuffs and ministerial black frock coat, then went back to the holes they had dug in search of cool, damp earth.

"Mercy! Those two have grown. What do they plan to be when they grow up?" Mrs Caswell laughed with more feeling than True could recall.

"Shepherds," True laughed back. "Do come in—it is nice to have callers."

Midgie hurried to set out the tea service, one of her wedding gifts, after accepting Mrs. Caswell's kiss and acknowledging an introduction to Reverend Randall. True hugged Tillie Caswell, thinking that her friend looked exceedingly fit, then turned her attention to her companion. Reverend Randall appeared to be middle-aged, although the white hair bushing from beneath the brim of his broad felt hat added to his years. He wore a broad black tie which, even after looping into a generous bow, flowed over his shoulder like a scarf. Reflection of the afternoon sun on his glasses gave him an owlish look, an effect which would have tickled the ribs of a stoic. But his handshake was warm and firm, his manners impeccable, and his speech carefully correct.

"Randy—" Tillie Caswell's face reddened at the slip of her tongue, a slip she corrected quickly, "Reverend Randall and I once knew one another in Portland. He still brings me news when he comes this way to conduct a revival. He's one of the last of the circuit riders."

True took his hat while he mentioned his denomination—a matter to which she paid little attention. A minister of any faith was a joy to have in her household. She told him so with heartfelt warmth.

"Oh, yes, I feel a need to make the rounds—conducting memorial services for those who have passed on, performing marriages, and making an effort to mend together the broken relationships. It tears at my heart, you know, seeing couples marry only to unmarry without regard to the tragic consequences to their children—and society—"

In the small kitchen a cup clattered to the floor and there followed the unmistakable sound of splintering glass. Above the swish of the broom, True was sure she heard a muffled sob. She longed to rush into the kitchen, put her arms around Midgie, tell her everything would be all right—that the cup could be replaced. But, even as she covered the moment by chatting with the guests, True wondered if the softhearted Midgie would accept a replacement for the original. She probably was as shattered as the cup, seeing the breakage as the beginning of the end, imagining herself to be one of the "unmarrieds" soon, her heart chafing at their caller's mention of the city where it all began...

"So," Mr. Randall was saying, "I envisioned the Double N as a possible dude ranch—"

"Oh, far from it," True managed to smile. "We hope to turn the fertile acreage into a real ranch one of these days—you know, good grain, thoroughbred cattle and stock—"

Mrs. Caswell took over from there. What fine folks the Norths were! How they had enriched her life and the lives of others they had chanced to meet already! Then followed a lengthy discussion of Mariah's progress with the English language. Blessings, all of them. Much to accomplish here if they all worked together. Randy did understand? The minister was nodding. Yes, Yes—time to sort the wheat from the chaff, so to speak. And, yes, yes, he'd love to attend the roundup...

Midgie was quiet over tea and thick slices of apple-prune cake. And her smile was far away when Reverend Randall broke the news that he was acquainted with the senior Norths in Centerville and had brought a package of books they ordered: all kinds—medical encyclope-dias, educational textbooks, new Bibles—yes, yes, all kinds.

"Don't cry inside, Midgie," True wanted to whisper. And then she saw that Midgie's eyes were fastened on the gap. This time the horseman galloped down the hill a piece, stopped with a suddenness that threw the animal on its haunches, then turned and galloped away. Uncanny indeed!

20

The Roundup

"Now that the grain's finished, I suppose you'll be letting the hands go?" Marty asked of Wil the day the wind-rowed hay was tossed into mows and covered against approaching winter. He looked as if the question were important to him—as if he too wanted to leave.

Young Wil, busily saddling the roan, turned to catch his brother-in-law's eye. "Isn't it time you made the decisions, Marty? The Double N was supposed to be your project—yours and Midgie's. I suggest that you look around, see what's to be done, and do it before letting the men go, regardless of the shortage of funds."

True, washing dishes, placed them noiselessly in the drainer in order to hear Marty's answer. She was sorry to hear Billy Joe's input. Welcome as his wisdom was, his suggestions were often ill-timed.

"Let 'em go, man? You gotta be loco—what with them horses we got corralled up yonder ready t'brang down fer th' breakin' 'n matin'—"

True's heart missed a beat. So some of the animals were penned, gradually getting to know the human race before being herded into civilization. This was news—with more to come, she supposed. Not that Young Wil intended leaving her out; time simply ran out.

"Not t'mention th' cows 'n that bawlin' bull. Th' critters is gettin' a little less spooked if them trespassers 'ud keep their distance. Marty, my lad, they's gonna be a iron horse passin' this way 'n th' likes o'you ain't a-gonna stop it. Now, now, none o'that sass!" Billy Joe wagged a warning finger in Marty's angry red face. "I dunno what y'got agin' th' rails—long as they don' go cuttin' our fences 'n lettin' them valuable herds stampede—you got somebody on th' lookout? Don' answer that—guess I'm a-knowin'—an' you got th' unmitigated gall t'ast iffen we let th' few men we got go? Shucks! You gotta be plum sick—"

"I'm not listening! You're like the rest of them—think I'm a nothing! You and your whole pack can go straight—" Marty's voice had risen angrily.

Billy Joe jerked erect. "Keep a civil tongue in yore mouth, I'm a-warnin' you, son. I'm only tryin' t'help. After all, yore th' bossman, 'cording t'Mr. Wil. So, straighten up 'n *be* one. Shore, shore, y'can fire me—fire th' whole crew, but y' better be knowin' it's a sick world out there. Iffen I wuz a young man with half yore opportunity 'n brawn—well," he sighed, "never mind, what cain't be changed, cain't. But afore y'let us go, best be considerin' th' vast majority figger it's uh whole heap easier t'rob, steal, murder—whatever it takes—than do sweatin' labor. One uv th' coyotes'll knife you 'n take that herd well as yore wife less'n you larn t'lower that voice 'n raise yore sight!"

Young Wil's comment was an understatement of what he must be feeling. "Think about it, Marty. He's right, you know. I understand the railroad's hiring on men, so the powers must be sure the contract is in the making—maybe signed. Better hold off letting our men go. Pig Iron's loyalty is without question, and he can do the work of ten. Tex is as well-versed in the ways of wheat as he claimed. Slim and Slinger—well, there's no reason to question their morals, and as far as handling horses goes, they've proven their skill—Augie's a marvel—"

" 'N me, now, I vowed t'brang down that bellowin' bull, 'n by jiminy, I'm a-gonna—yep, yep, yep, so hurry them dogs along fer herdin'. Time they paid fer their board 'n keep. As fer th' heifers, they're boun' on fol-lerin'—one o'them oddities uv nature, ain't it now, how purdy womenfolk knows us strong leaders? Th' Lord knowed what He wuz doin' when He created Adam powerful 'nuf t'go losin' uh rib without lettin' it cripple 'im up! Soooo, Mr. Marty, sir, what 'bout it—gonna keep me on?"

Marty made no direct response. Instead, he swung expertly astride the sleek chestnut mare and said, "Let's go."

"He *has* made a decision," True whispered, turning a thankful face heavenward. Then, wiping her hands—reddened from oversoaking in the lye-soap lather—she turned and all but bumped into Midgie. How much had she overheard? Enough, her white face said, so her words came as no surprise:

"Poor Marty. What a dreadful way to start such a beautiful morning! We—we had a fight—"

"Good!"

"Good?"

True nodded. "You've tried all else. Maybe standing up to him will do him good, Midgie."

Midgie's face said otherwise. "He said some ugly things—about me—that I—I had lost my pride—didn't care how I looked—but he was right—"

"Midgie, stop putting yourself down! Marty had no right—"

But the white-faced girl was not listening. "It's true that my hair's awful—half black, half-yellow from the peroxide—and it's true that I've gained some weight. I let all the tight dresses out—the ones he hated me in—but now they're tight again—"

True remembered the swollen legs. "Midgie," she suggested, "have Wil check you over. He *is* a doctor, you know."

Later True wondered how Midgie would have answered had Mariah not arrived, her face aglow with ill-concealed pride. And with good cause! Behind her, where the three boys used to ride before becoming "cowboys," were the three fiesta dresses, more spectacularly beautiful than True had imagined—and the first new garments that any of the women had owned in what seemed like forever.

October first—the day of the fiesta so looked forward to by so many, most of whom, True realized with a jolt, were strangers to the hosts. Undoubtedly that was the cause for the weak feeling in her middle, the sort of gnawing dread. It was understandable—the few inhabitants being so widely separated in this vast area which for the most part was unclaimed—that they would have met so few of them. What she failed to understand was the seeming lack of interest in neighborliness, their suspicious attitudes, and their lack of desire for improving the situation when there was a need for roads, schools, and churches. Her mind bolted ahead on an investigative journey as to why no church.

Thought of a church was like rubbing the magic ring. From around the bend of the narrow trail the Reverend Randall appeared like the Arabian Nights Tale genie. If possible, he looked even more likely to challenge the risibilities of other human beings: same black Stetson, same oversized frock. But, oh, it was too much—his wearing rubber hip boots (revealed by the lifted folds of the black material) in order to avoid the dust! "Dry land fishing," it must be called here, True thought, stifling a giggle. Then, remembering her manners, she ran out to offer assistance, for the good man was as heavily laden as a back-peddler. His Bible, a large basket, and—what was this? Fish! Real fish, beautiful rainbow trout, the first she had seen since leaving home. So he *had* been fishing!

"Come—let me help you!" True urged with starry-eyed excitement as she grabbed the string of trout which would pass inspection even back in Centerville, where they were so plentiful.

"More in the basket," Reverend Randall panted, "lots more. May be needing loaves and fishes, according to all reports—already on their way. I passed some resting in the groves—travel for miles, you know, this being the once-a-year custom, as I guess Tillie and Mariah explained." Guests, she supposed he meant, not fish!

"Where on earth did you find these—and how in these parts?" True asked in admiration. "I would hardly have expected a fish to know how to swim around here, even if there were water—"

The travel-weary man dropped to the ground, removed his hat, and wiped his sweating brow. "I always come— only this year it was lonely, camping out beneath the stars without my friend Artemis. We always spent a week just sitting on the bank of the stream that few know about—yonder about, oh, say, 30 miles or so— sometimes talking, sometimes speculating on the Next World, and," he chuckled, "sort of hoping the fish wouldn't interrupt us by biting. But," he dreamed on, "they always did—God's way of reminding us that we're not Up There yet. Ever wonder what it's going to be like?"

"I guess we all do sometimes," True admitted. "But I've decided it makes no great difference as long as I and my household are there together, sitting at the Lord's table."

"You are wise, very wise for your age. But," his eyes roamed the illimitable spaces overhead, "with Artemis gone on, I find myself wondering what he knows that I don't—sort of looking forward to following to see if flowers have the same fragrance and birds sing the same songs. They should have learned *something* on this earth. Sitting out there all alone this past week, I kept thinking of all the Creator has given us down here, all the beauties that too many fail to see, and I got to wondering if they would see them Up There either. Maybe the blind will stay blind, refusing to see the light in both places. But I think it's going to be twice as nice when this spirit's no longer hampered by a body—that is, when my work's all done. Which reminds me, it's my job to fry the fish."

True laughed delightedly. "I'm sure you will have no competition, although the men have the barbecue pits dug and the beef has been giving out mouth-watering smells throughout the night." She pointed to a mound where a thin spiral of smoke rose, source of the tantalizing aroma of hickory-smoked beef below the bed of coals.

The minister sat up with an effort, massaged his legs, helped himself to a shovelful of coals, and kindled his own fire. "Folks gather early. They like to watch the sunset, and," he wiped his watering eyes that smoke had filled when a frolicsome whirlwind whipped at his fire, "they like inhaling the special ozone that only the wide-open spaces have to offer. I always take care of the Lord's work while the food cooks; soaks in better than on a full stomach—"

"You mean," True found herself reaching for words, "there's to be a prayer meeting, a sermon—or?"

"All of those—maybe some baptizing up in the slough. It happens sometimes. Some want their babies dedicated. Some want to be married. And would you believe there are those who want their animals blessed? Right or wrong, I draw the line there."

True grew increasingly excited. What fun to entertain and have absolutely no idea of what to expect at her own house! Hers? It occurred to her then that Midgie had failed to make an appearance. She must check. But Mariah and her excited brood arrived on pack mules, the only draft animals strong enough to bear the burden of her pots and pans, tons of paper streamers, extra lanterns, and mysterious boxes.

"*Buenos dias, Señora,*" Mariah called out with brown eyes dancing. "*Mis*—my—*flores*—roses bloom brighter seence you come—yes?" She held out a lovely bouquet which, judging by her gestures, were intended for the ladies' hair—scarlet, yellow-gold, baby-pink, and pure white. "*Señora* will pardon pleese—I speek so leetle *ingles*—English—"

"The roses are beautiful, Mariah, and you manage English far better than I manage Spanish." Nevertheless, True was relieved to see Tillie Caswell's buggy rounding the bend.

Mrs. Caswell looked fresh out of a mail-order catalog, and her wealth of dark hair wound becomingly around her head, giving the lady-proprietor a regal look. The blank look once dominating her face was erased by a wholesome smile. What had happened to change her?

There was no time to think on it further, as the practical Tillie had taken over, talking first in Spanish to Mariah, then remembering to address her in English. The pair worked with feverish enthusiasm which was highly contagious. True found herself looking forward more and more to the event while feeling, strangely, that it was out of her hands. The gnawing sense of near-dread lodged around her heart and refused to dissolve. How could one be excited and afraid at the same time? she wondered as her feet took her back and forth to the kitchen storing the Mexican chili beans (which must have been prepared in a washpot, judging by the amount), greasing the potatoes for baking whole in the coals, and scrubbing the tin plates left behind by previous occupants of the shack.

Once she knocked on the door leading to the bedroom that Midgie and Marty occupied. There was no answer, but the sound of tearing cloth was reassuring. Midgie was putting her hair up on rags, something she never dared do when Marty was around. The men, of course, had been working at rounding up the horses and cows in preparation for the big drive (carefully timed, Tillie told her, for an hour before sunset). There was plenty of time, yet Tillie and Mariah seemed to rush, as if they too felt a sense of urgency. True wanted to help Midgie dress, and there was need for a dishpan of garden greens for salad.

Stepping out the back door, she inhaled the deeply wood-smoked fragrance of the Indian-summer air. October had suddenly awakened to soften the sun's rays and bring the bees humming back as if it were spring. The sun was still warm enough to bake sweetness from the stubble, the sky swept clean by a light breeze. Against its interminable blue, three black-enameled birds circled as if looking for a landing field. Crows? No, they were too large. Not hawks either. The color was wrong and their wingspread too wide. Lower and lower they circled, swooping down at a point just below the gap. There, caught in bright sunlight, their heads revealed their identity. Buzzards! How could the vultures hope to find anything nonliving on such a day? Had some wild beast killed a domestic animal—or—?

Poachers! The word came from the nowhere of True's mind, causing a shudder that rivaled a physical pain to run the gamut of her being. Hurriedly she finished picking the fresh vegetables from the fall selection, then joined Tillie and Mariah. There she stopped, awe-stricken. The transformation was amazing. The entire yard, and on beyond in all directions, had taken on the air of a carnival. Lanterns, strung on wires overhead and winding through the fences, created a million rainbows, and far to the right, toward the gap, men were nailing together rough boards which would serve as bleachers.

"My Curly closed up early," Tillie said with pride, "and took charge over there, bringing with him two neighbors and," she laughed, "all the guests at the inn— lots of railroad men, including the noted Mr. and Mrs. St. John—"

"Michael." The name came out flat and unbidden.

Tillie Caswell's eyes bored into hers. "So you two *had* met—I just had the feeling." A faint smile twisted her mouth. "Forgive me, True dear. It's a fault of mine—getting 'feelings,' one of them being," she lowered her voice, "one that concerns me gravely—a certain sense that your brother's suffering from an inner seething, a kind of protest. But against what? There I go—" Tillie spread her fingers out as if for counting. "But I suspect that you have the ability of looking inside the hearts of others too. You sensed that I had known Randy—the Reverend Randall—and you are right. Someday I will tell you about it, what a help he was to me before I met my Curly—back when the floods came and—" Tillie's face turned blank again momentarily, then sparkled alive, "I promised a *someday* talk, not today. Let's look forward to this glorious togetherness. What a grand night it's going to be! Do you realized the moon will be full?"

The crowd closed in. Later True supposed that there were far fewer than it seemed. To her, "thousands" would be a conservative estimate, so long had they been isolated. There was not a familiar face among them, and she probably would never recall their names, she thought with a spring of laughter bubbling up inside her. Maybe it made no difference. When, if ever, would she see them again?

And then she spotted Michael's wife. She stood, lips compressed tightly, straight as a ramrod. Her new fall outfit with a silver trim of fur looked out of place amid the ginghams and calicoes and out of season in the autumn-bright sunshine. True wickedly hoped the snobbish woman was uncomfortably warm, then felt a little ashamed.

"If you'll excuse me," she murmured, "I will help my sister-in-law dress," and hurried inside.

A few minutes later the two of them emerged—not unobtrusively as planned, but greeted by a round of applause. A hostess should remain in the background, according to Aunt Chrissy. It was her undisputed duty to see that guests were comfortable, their needs met. And here were two of the North wives dominating the scene. True's flush came from embarrassment at the sudden reversal of roles; but Midgie's, she felt, came from excitement. Well, proper or not, it was good to see a near-forgotten sparkle of happiness about her. And truly she looked lovely. The turquoise complemented her pale skin, camouflaging the pallor, and the white-lace trim circling the scooped-out neckline, the huge puffed sleeves, and the hemline of the skirt's four-yard sweep added to the China-doll resemblance. True had done Midgie's hair, carefully disguising the darkening roots by heaping curls on top and pinning the white roses above her ears where the "kiss curls" bounced playfully.

Mariah and Tillie had joined the two of them for a stolen moment—Mariah to hand each of them folding lace fans, and Tillie to tuck Spanish tortoise-shell back-combs in their hair. "All the rage in Paris, according to the peddlers," she confided, "although I must say that the two of you look more angelic than Spanish with those complexions."

Mariah slipped quickly into her own fiesta gown of crimson, the black lace mantilla floating over her hair, which she had impulsively unpinned and allowed to droop almost to her waist while Tillie wound a pink-dyed Spanish boa around her own neck playfully. It was a festive moment—one that True was to remember forever as a beginning and an end...

Now, more than a little flustered at the sea of admiring faces, True was relieved when Billy Joe's wife stepped forward to bow boldly in her new role, and then, leaning gracefully from side to side as if keeping time to imagined music, pirouetted in practiced ballet rhythm.

Spectators mounted the bleachers. For a moment the world seemed to hold its breath. Then, as Mariah picked up the tempo, swinging and swaying with a red rose clenched between her white teeth, the crowd went wild. Stamping. Clapping. Shouting, "Bravo! Bravo!"

True was seeing a new Mariah, a Mariah who was unknowingly urging the old Midgie to emerge further from her cocoon, she was to realize later. But for now she could see it only as a means of escape, a chance to do a quick fadeaway. Beautiful as it all was, the uneasiness within her was growing. Which was it, she tried to recall, that came first—appearance of the animals trailing down from the gap or Reverend Randall's sermon? The cattle drive, no doubt, as the air of expectation was growing. The man would have difficulty holding their attention. So where were the men? Why the delay?

Afternoon was waning. Traditionally they would watch the sunset—that was it. She scanned the sky for the buzzards, wondering why. *Stop letting your imagination run wild,* she scolded herself, only to wonder if the filthy creatures of the air had landed on a carcass. Shuddering a little, True would have hurried back to her guests except that the Mystery Man had appeared like a phantom at the gap. And what was this? This time he was joined by one, two—*four* others, all of whom disappeared so fast that she wondered if she could have imagined their appearance. In her haste to escape the thoughts invading the lovely afternoon, True all but fell into the arms of a man.

"Michael!" Did her voice sound as startled to his ears? There was nothing unnatural about his presence, considering that his wife was somewhere among the spectators. On the other hand, what was either of them doing here? She made an attempt to regain her poise. But it was difficult with his eyes sweeping over her with the kind of approval that claimed a certain propriety.

For the first time she was aware of her own appearance. Dull, she supposed. Surely she paled beside Midgie and Mariah's bright costumes. The pale yellow must give her an all-of-one-color look, blending as it did with her skin, now slightly ivory from the sun, and her blonde hair, where, without her knowing, Michael's eyes had focused to watch the sun rest in her upswept curls, turning them to gold.

"You look lovely," he smiled. "Yellow roses are my favorite—may I adjust this one? It is about to escape—"

His tone was inoffensive, but True reached to re-pin the blossom herself—a gesture that seemed to amuse him. "Forgive me," he said with only a hint of his old mocking tone. "I guess I was seeing us back in Atlanta— the elixir of the air having gone to my head. I always behave badly out here—"

"You have been here—before?" Why should that surprise her, detain her return to the party?

"Oh, of course. Old Artie and I were friends—always talking land values, the railroad, petitioning Congress for help in extending aid to both. This land was his life, as you probably know?" When she failed to answer, Michael continued: "He staked a claim—rather, his father did before him, I guess—back when guns spoke louder than fenceposts and barbed wire. Always had his heart set on raising thoroughbreds, so he'd appreciate what your men are doing up there. Or," he grinned engagingly, "do you entertain the idea that the old devil's watching from some cloud up there?"

"We've had this conversation before," True said coldly. "I must get back—"

Even as she spoke she could not resist looking uneasily at the gap again. Michael saw. "One of the calves is missing."

The buzzards! But Michael's maddening patronage attributed her anxiety to another channel. "Surely you aren't reliving the days of armed bandits, masked men who robbed trains and stole cattle. That's over now, you know—"

"Which of us are you trying to convince—oh, there they come!"

Relief swept her being, followed by a thrill such as she had never experienced before. Nose-to-tail the chestnut horses, muscles rippling in the slanting rays of the sun, trailed down, nostrils flanged but otherwise making no effort to return to the wilds. It occurred to her then that Young Wil had saved this event as a surprise. The herdsmen had broken the steeds already. There would be no need for the frightening scene of roping and tying the animals, risking injury to both men and beasts. *Oh, thank You, Lord...thank You...thank You...*

"I was prepared to dislike the lucky man you said 'Yes' to, but I find it difficult when he appears to be such a decent sort of chap. Of course, I will envy him forever—because of us—"

"Michael," True said firmly, "there is no *us*. You are married—"

"A matter of convenience, family background, money—Big Brother's shares—"

"Don't make me lose respect for you completely. I refuse to engage in such conversations ever again. In fact, there is no reason for any contact between us—"

"Oh, but there is, my dear True!" True turned away angrily and ran forward to meet Wil, who was bringing up the rear, where the cows (fatter than she had pictured from feeding on the hillside pastures) were shaking their massive heads and making sportive attempts at escaping the halters of their keepers.

"Stan' back, Miz True honey, lest some o'these mavericks git too frisky," Billy Joe called out importantly. True obliged, eyes on Wil.

Wil dismounted. "Did you find the calf, darling?" True asked as he embraced her quickly, eyes still scanning the hill. "We did—dead—mutilated—in a way that told the story—the work of man, not beast—"

21

Unfinished Song

The sun had dropped behind the western hillocks, taking with it the dancing heat signals of the afternoon. But the air remained sultry except for an occasional refreshing breeze. A tinge of warm rose replaced the day's gold. And far to the southwest True spotted an innocent-looking cloudbank—innocent to those unskilled in skywatching, but she had learned to be wary. Was the hay covered? Would the livestock panic in their new environment in case of a storm? The party in progress seemed trivial by comparison. But why borrow trouble?

The men were washing up after the long drive. They must hurry or miss what remained of the sunset. Already the foothills were crimson in remembrance, and, although the purple twilight would be long, night-birds were foretelling end-of-day already. True, joining the group, realized suddenly that all activity had stopped. The men sat motionless, not one of them contaminating the air with smoke or words. Where were their thoughts as they waited almost reverently for the Reverend to take his place on an improvised stage? Some, she suspected hungered to hear the Lord's Word. Others were curious. Nobody seemed to take note of the distant grumble of thunder.

The sky flamed with secondary glory as Randy Randall, Young Wil, and Marty stepped onto the rough-board platform. There was a moment's discussion as the three obviously debated which should greet the guests. The Reverend, undoubtedly a volunteer appointed by default, won out.

Introductions were short and applause delayed because the serious-faced minister went into his message immediately. Eyes scanning the horizon frequently, he appeared to be on guard against the enemy. Intruders or the storm?

"Bless you all for welcoming these wonderful people that God has seen fit to send into our midst," he began. "Now, in view of existing circumstances, I promise to follow the rule of the effective sermon: 'Be sincere; be brief; be seated!' "

The light words conditioned his congregation for listening. The man was human, faces of the newcomers said. Maybe he *did* have word from On High instead of Down There, the way most of the wandering Bible-beaters harped on and on. His humanness would naturally outfit him with a taste for good food, and those barbecued smells were likely as not to make the "Holy Joe" into a man of his word.

Their assessment was correct. Reverend Randall went straight to the point. There had been trouble with a missing calf, he explained—trouble which delayed the roundup. Any rancher worth his salt would never abandon a little lost animal—no sirree, the good rancher, like the Good Shepherd, would search until the lost was found.

Obviously surprised by the news, the audience leaned forward to hear more, clinging raptly to each word. True, happy with the wisdom of making use of an analogy with which those present could identify, prayed that he would make use of the parable of the lost sheep. He did.

"I read to you from St. Luke, chapter 15, verses 3 through 7." Then, placing a finger between the pages to hold the reference, he further drew the congregation to him by returning to another situation with which they were familiar. "If ever any of you want to read my Book, it is yours for the asking—lots of wisdom here on how to handle animals, rotate crops, build houses—not to mention manage wives!"

Little snickers passed through the crowd as men nudged one another in the ribs and a few dared reach forward to shake the shoulders of women seated on the lower bleachers. "Most of you are familiar with the story well-known in these parts about Aaron Meier, the peddler, who furnished the one darning needle for sharing. Seems few know the rest of the story—how he came one day with a needle for every single household! Well, one day that's what I hope to do—put a Bible in each home as your almanac, your guide for days when the going's tough—and your road map to heaven!"

Randy Randall reopened the Bible and read to the openmouthed listeners:

> And he (Jesus) spake this parable unto them, saying, "What man of you, having an hundred sheep, if he lose one of them, doth not leave the ninety and nine in the wilderness and go after that which is lost, until he find it? And when he hath found it, he layeth it on his shoulders, rejoicing. And when he cometh home, he calleth together his friends and neighbors, saying unto them, 'Rejoice with me, for I have found my sheep which was lost.' I say unto you that likewise joy shall be in heaven over one sinner that repenteth more than over ninety and nine just persons which need no repentance."

"Oh, friends, Jesus loves you! Right now He is searching here among you, longing to bring you home. If you want to be found, simply raise your hand and we will pray for you—if I sound like a tyrannous, radical old Turk to you—well, it's only because Jesus and I care—"

At that moment the last remnant of color faded and there was the curious calm that precedes a storm. The fast-spreading clouds slowly rolled down a curtain of premature darkness so that buildings began to lose their outlines in the deepening gloom. But hands were visible—one, two—they became countless—waved back and forth desperately. There could be no doubt about the sincerity of their gestures.

"Then let us be merry—the lost is found! Right now the weather seems up to some mischief, and I know most of you are hungry enough to digest a mountain lion, so rejoice in your new state and join us at the Lord's table!"

There was a flurry of activity—men pumping the minister's hand, some tears, and men whistling and laughing softly among themselves as if they had heard some good news, which indeed they had. Woman bustled about with such urgency that True failed to make note of Midgie's disappearance again. Once the men had uncovered the browned-to-perfection barbecued meat and carved it, the ladies busied themselves with dishing up the remainder of the feast and set the enormous granite pot of steaming coffee back on the coals to keep warm. The men dived in hungrily, smacking their lips in appreciation, the older ones struggling to hold back beards from a bath in the bowls of rich, thick beans as— when eyes were turned safely in other directions—they lifted bowls to their mouths. An occasional dentured guffaw tattled when one of the male diners was unsuccessful. The air was charged with excitement—and electricity that none seemed to have noticed.

True cast an anxious glance at the threatening sky and slipped toward the corral unnoticed. The buildings were nothing more than a blotch of darkness, but the rustlings in the pens told her that Young Wil, Marty, and the hired hands were checking on the livestock. She caught sight of her husband as the shadows crisscrossed from the lanterns that someone had thoughtfully turned higher.

"True?" Wil was beside her in a moment. "Don't worry, sweetheart. Everything is perfect here—just keep the party going—"

Billy Joe, panting from exertion, rushed to join them. True was a lady—wife of the boss man—and therefore to be impressed. "Play 'possum, Miz True—you know, dead t'th' storm what's boun' t'pop. Thet wind's blowin' up a balloon—boun' on bustin' any minute—callin' fer help with these beauties. So see thet they're fed 'n calm—get my Mariah playin' t'soothe th' atmosphere—"

Billy Joe drifted over to where Marty was talking low and soothingly to a disturbed filly. Pleased, True took time to smile up into Wil's face. He nodded. "I had a chance to talk with him again," he whispered above the uneasy lowing of the cattle. "Things will be better if—"

Young Wil was unable to finish the sentence. There was a warning zigzag of lightning and he motioned True back to the group. There the thoughtful Mariah, accustomed to the sinister pranks of the elements, had begun strumming the strings of her guitar, gradually increasing the volume as the thunder grew closer. Mrs. Caswell had joined her. "Why not have everybody join in singing the words—or humming, whistling, even stomping their feet?"

For a time it worked. And then the unexpected happened. Her face glowing in the lantern light, Midgie slipped forward and seated herself beside Mariah. And strapped over her shoulder was her guitar!

True held her breath, remembering the terrible incident which so far had held Midgie and Marty apart. Surely Marty would appreciate his wife's overcoming her fear of crowds, her valiant efforts to help. And yet she felt sawed apart, like the illusions created by a magician, her eyes seeing one thing and her heart convinced it was untrue.

But there was no time to stop the show. In response to Mariah's smile of welcome, Midgie drew a long, tremulous breath and joined her in a mellow Mexican sonata, softly at first, and then—gaining confidence—taking the lead. Her playing was beautiful, True realized. In it there was a rare brightness, an ethereal quality to the classical music which musicians usually took too gravely, causing the average listener to turn a deaf ear to intricate numbers. Her slender fingers slid from note to note in slow motion in a way which brought a lump to True's throat. Midgie was speaking to Marty with each strum of the strings, begging, pleading—for the slow movement of the sonata gave the sense of a glorified voice.

"An angel—sure as shootin'—a real live angel," one of the men marveled in a near-frightened voice. What had that preacher done to him? "Angels *do* play on harps, don't they?"

The man beside him shrugged. "Dunno much 'bout angels—but I knowed a girl once what sung like that in Portland—an' she sure 'nuf warn't no angel!"

True's spine stiffened and she prayed that Midgie had failed to hear as she and Mariah exchanged a few whispered words. Mariah was lowering her instrument. Then Midgie was going to solo? True felt choky inside as she surveyed the eager, wistful faces turned to her sister-in-law from the now-overflowing bleachers and benches that someone had brought from the picnic tables.

And suddenly Midgie, looking like a slowly unfolding blossom, began to sing in a voice so clear and sweet that one could be charmed easily into guessing that she had dropped from the Great White Way. The men were mesmerized, their weather-browned faces resting on the girl's white throat where the music originated—or was it sent from Above? The women wore different expressions—more dreamy, reliving another time, another place, before hard work robbed them of romance. And something more, a sparkle of hope that romance, like the wild horses, could be recaptured and brought home.

Midgie sang on and on—soft, sweet melodies, then ballads. And finally rollicky folk songs. Once she would have stopped, but Mariah leaned forward to whisper, "Pleese, Señora, a leetle more—*usted* fine ladee—sing on, so they be good, never bad—or have hunger eeven wheen bellies have no *mucho* food. They fill bellies with fine music—yes?"

Midgie looked into the pleading face where the black eyes, appearing too large for her thin face, glowed with spirit—a spirit seemed to overwhelm her and tranfuse lifeblood to those around her.

"I will close the musicale," Midgie said boldly, as if addressing an audience in a fine concert hall, "with a composition of my own. Listen to the words, then join me."

> Day is done and night has come
> As stars turn on one by one,
> Lighting lanterns in the sky,
> Giving light to travel by,
> Till we join God in the sky . . .

The exquisite, languorous notes floated over the countryside as she paused to repeat the words. Then, strumming a few chords, Midgie nodded. The men moved forward toward the stage and took up the song. The women followed and knelt as if seeing once more the tender picture of mother, brothers, and sisters—now gone—and perhaps a small village church where they had surrendered their lives to God. They were watching their men do so now. For this angelic little singer had taken over where the Reverend Brother left off.

Playfully, then—almost coquettishly, Midgie, sang out: "Good night, ladies, good night, ladies—" drowning out the nearing thunder. As she reached the final line, "I'm going to leave you now!" there was a jolt of thunder, so loud it was as if some resident giant of earth suffered a passionate rage and prepared to jerk the rocky crowns from the mountains, clashing them together to destroy the broad valley.

Which indeed was what happened—except that Martin North was the giant and little Midgie was his victim. Glowering, he rushed at her, ignoring her touchingly uncertain smile of welcome. For a split second his half-crazed eyes rested on her hair, which the first wind-driven raindrops had whipped into little-girl tendrils of silvered bronze. Then, with shaking hands, he grabbed the guitar, jerked it none too gently from her neck, and dashed it to the ground. It splintered.

22

Gone!

As if tired of being ignored, the storm struck with all its fury. The wind inhaled, seeming to suck up everything movable, including the benches and chairs, then exhaled with such gusto that it shook the window frames and doors of the small house in much the same manner that an angered chaparral cock would shake a rattler. The lanterns flickered, steadied momentarily, then sputtered out. The world lay in total darkness, void and without form, except for otherworldly tongues of fire that bruised the sky.

There was bedlam as the crowd sought cover. They huddled beneath a straggling cluster of trees until Reverend Randy screamed against the snarling wind, "Don't tempt nature's forces by behaving like cattle! Get from beneath those trees—lie flat if need be—and pray while crawling on your bellies—"

Men fumbled in the darkness for a tarpaulin, waterproofed with tar for protecting the hay. If only they could erect it on the poles which held the now-unlighted lanterns—but the wind snatched it heartlessly away just as the rain came down in sheets, rattling and crashing against the distant hills. The frightened crowd pushed toward the cabin, some crawling beneath the wagons, as the wind gave one final gnash of its teeth—and stopped. In the final flash of lightning, True saw to her horror that the remains of Midgie's guitar had been picked up, twirled in midair, and carried away—broken and bruised like its owner's heart.

Where *was* Midgie? She should look after her chickens. The downpour could drown them unless they were cooped. True called her name softly, then more loudly, knowing in her heart that it was useless. Her voice would never carry above the roar of the storm and the frenzied sounds from the barnyard and corral. Knowing, too, that Midgie was crouched somewhere in the purgatorial darkness, shaking with fear of the storm, and weeping her eyes out with hurt and humiliation.

The men had managed to light a lantern in the barn, and through the cracks between the imperfectly matched boards True saw shifting shafts of light, enough for her to crawl on hands and knees toward the cabin as fast as her wildly thumping heart would allow—the kind of thump that a well-regulated organ gives when its owner is frightened for others but brave enough to act, knowing the risks. She must find Midgie, check on the safety of Young Wil and the others, try to bring Marty back to beg forgiveness—

The wind changed to a high-pitched nasal moan. Or *was* it the wind? The question had no more than occurred when the answer came. For in her path lay a human form—injured, judging from the sound of pain. A shift of the light from the barn allowed one quick peek at the face. "Mrs. Caswell—oh, Tillie—you're hurt!" The light shifted, but True could feel the hot stickiness that said blood. She felt for the wound and found it—a wide gash on Tillie's right arm. Without hesitation True ripped the bottom ruffle from her new dress and went to work. "There—that should stop the bleeding—now, to move you—"

However, the flesh wound was less serious than Tillie Caswell's emotional state. There was no budging her body, stiffened with fear as it was. The voice was thick and gutteral—beyond recognition.

"The flood—the flood," she gasped hysterically. "They'll all be drowned—and the baby is overdue. What did you say—they're dead? Dead—all dead—all three— Oh, I don't want to live—" she sobbed senselessly. "Let me die with them—they're all I have—bury me—"

And then, miraculously, the full moon peered from between the scudding clouds—its face innocent, seeking out and finding the disoriented victims below. Somewhere a shot pierced the sudden silence. But True's nerves were too taut for her to take notice of the reverberating echo. Somebody would be on guard. And surely the crack of the rifle would be less disturbing than the thunder drums to the livestock.

That the firing of a gun signified trouble far greater than what they had all experienced did not occur to her at that time...

The storm was over. It was time to assess the damages, correct what could be corrected, and get on with living. There were conflicting reports from the hands. One of the choice heifers, probably the best for breeding the fine herd, was a spirited critter, Tex said, his schoolboy face lighted with challenge. He could cut her off at the pass and bring her home before Papa Bull knew that a member of his harem was missing. Fortunately, he knew every square foot of the wide valley, having fished the streams in order to exist between harvests before landing what he referred to as a "steady job." Billy Joe, obviously a little jealous, said the boy had miscounted— better be getting his bearings and checking on the horses, which were still somewhat crazed from the storm—flare of a match could undo them. Thanks to Pig Iron's locomotive strength, corral fences were under repair, and Slinger, unhampered by his withered arm, dragged poles to him as fast as the stronger man could nail them in place. Slim was running the fences. Hands cut and bleeding from the barbs, he snipped, cut, and nailed, aided by Augie's holding a lantern high above his head to aid the moon. Loyal group...but True must check on those closer to her.

Tillie Caswell had regained control of her emotions—uncannily, almost as if nothing had happened to trigger the memory of her bitter secret. While other guests prepared to depart—*no, no, they had no dread of the long journey, just needed to be home by daybreak*—Tillie and Mariah busied themselves collecting the soggy remains of drenched food and shelter. Tillie talked all the while.

"It was a wonderful thing you folks did here, True. Life here becomes intolerable compared to what women knew in Portland and Seattle. Some never had much human tolerance. Most of them see all this as ugly, a land of punishment, hobbling them and shrinking their hearts. Bad weather, no trifles that color their lives—and the men are no help—here's your fan, Mariah, want to try drying it out? Husbands are too exhausted to see that the girls they once loved enough to court and buy trinkets for are becoming prisoners. Or they blame the women—have to have somebody to take out their frustration on, I guess—"

"But they aren't all like that," True protested, while letting her glance travel to every lighted spot in search of Midgie. "Your men are caring and loving—and Reverend Randall is so understanding—"

Mariah, pushing heavy hair, around which she had wrapped a heavy towel, smiled broadly. "*Si, Señora*—'tis true—"

"But the exception," Tillie Caswell persisted as she shook the tarp, attempting to dodge the unexpected downspout of water and succeeding in showering them all. "Oh, mercy! A thousand pardons!" When True and Mariah laughed, she went on: "I guess our men are different partly because *we* are! We have our problems, but we've learned to trust the Lord. Everybody with one iota of sense can see the all-too-evident conditions around here. So why waste words? A low opinion of a place—or persons—grants no license to harp on it. But when one loses respect for self and faith in God and others—well, it takes somebody like you folks to bring a special sparkle back. And that's what you did tonight— storm and all—True, I'm worried about Midgie—"

"I must check on her," True replied. She thanked the two other women and went to the barn, almost throwing herself in the arms of her husband. "Oh, Wil—darling, I'm so sorry—is everything going to be all right?"

"Of course," he said, but there was less certainty in his voice than usual. "I hope we can save the hay, keep it from souring. Billy Joe is spreading the hay on the canvas to prevent sprouting. And," glancing around uneasily, "Marty's supposed to be with him—what took place just before the storm? Nobody seems to know for sure, except that Marty behaved like a madman. Is he with Midgie?"

"That's what I came to find out," True said. "He hurt her—hurt her terribly, darling. Then she gave him a quick account of the ugly scene. Young Wil made a snort of disgust. "Oh, there he is with Billy Joe, working off his fury, I guess. But what about Midgie?"

The chicken coop? No, she was not there, and the chickens were her life—Henny-Penny, Chicken Little, Half-Chick—all of them.

"Midgie!" she called in the kitchen as she lighted the closest candle to send sinister shadows scurrying about the small room. There was no answer. A quick search failed to reveal anything—but wait! What was this propped on the dresser of the room that True and Young Wil occupied? Yes, an envelope! Midgie's childish scrawl said: TRUE.

Dear, dear True:
Don't be too mad at me—please don't. And don't worry. I will be all right. It's just that I can't go on like this—and I know you under- stand. A woman needs love. I never was a right

wife. So I have no right to claim love. Just let Marty know that he is free of me—that I'll no longer be an embarrassment. Don't let him look for me. He ain't (the word was smeared by an eraser and corrected) isn't obli—how do you spell it—obliged to be burdened. Maybe someday me and you'll meet again. I'll try to learn how to be a real lady by then. Thank you for never making me feel ashamed—and pray for me. Oh, and one thing more, look after my chickens. They *do* need me and will miss me when I'm gone . . .

I love you,

Midgie

23

Awakening?

The Norths had had no sleep. Surely the men must be famished, True mused as she kindled a fire in the monstrous black kitchen stove and busied her hands with breakfast. Her mind was harder to control. Poor Midgie—where could she be? How and with whom had she escaped what to her must have been one of the prisons that Tillie Caswell described? It had been hard deciding how to break the news to Marty. She dreaded his scowling and sniping. Left alone, maybe he'd come to his senses. Why not let Midgie's note speak for itself? So thinking, she had propped it on his pillow, where to her surprise was another envelope, different only in that it bore no name.

Now the coffee boiled in the planished pot while bacon sizzled in the heavy iron skillet. The sourdough biscuits were rising, and she wished one of the hands would find a new hen nest in the hay. Midgie's little flock was faithful, but would the three dozen eggs she had hoarded for swapping to Tillie for "something nice" for Marty's birthday be enough to feed the overworked men? They could fill in the cavities with biscuits. The butter was still sweet and the honey had not sugared. Should she add fried potatoes? Probably—

147

That done, True glanced out the small kitchen window, hoping to catch sight of Young Wil. She did, and laughed at herself for the silly flip-flop of her heart. Just seeing her husband was like seeing the morning sun, which was now rising from a downy bed of tufted clouds to scatter gold coins into the placid pools left by last night's storm. For a moment it seemed to rest comfortably between the low hills, only to spread glory over the rainwashed sky. She felt so close to God . . .

"Umm-m-m, do I smell coffee? And is that my bride of long ago? Admittedly, these old eyes are fading—"

"Oh, Wil," True laughed, "sit yourself down and— *Wil*, the other men will see you—"

"Kiss my wife? Through *that* window? Not much of a view—"

When he released her, True poured coffee for them. "All's under control for now. But the storm served to show how much there is to mend." He paused. "Including a broken marriage. I've seen mulish people, but compared to Marty, they're as flexible as grass in a summer breeze."

True swallowed coffee which was so hot that it burned her throat. "He's a stiff-neck all right—and I don't know what more we can do—"

Young Wil extended his cup for a refill. His hand was shaking. From fatigue or emotion? Both, True suspected. "We're not going to do *anything*. It will be hard, sweetheart, but—well, this will either finish him off or bring him to his senses."

True poured his coffee. "But Midgie? What about Midgie?"

" 'What God has joined together, let no man put asunder.' Helping could be interpreted as meddling, doing more harm than good. Maybe she was too patient, too clingy, too whatever. Apart, she may gain new insight, see things from a new perspective. Right or wrong if they can bring their thinking together—and it *must* be theirs—what I am trying to say is that O'Higgin (secretly I've always thought of him as the Fourth Wise Man!) had their marriage in view as well as their success here." Wil lowered his voice, "Here's Marty," he said.

Marty's face was whiter than a flour sack when, minutes later, he emerged from his bedroom. In the breast pocket of his soiled blue chambray workshirt was the envelop bearing no name. He tossed it on the table and poured himself a cup of coffee. Making no mention of it, what he said was "Smart move you made letting Billy Joe, the Beetle, remain as foreman, Wil. Straight as a barbed-wire fence, and a good judge of character. If I doubted *your* judgment, I changed my mind last night—" Marty paused to take a swallow of the scalding coffee, winced, and helped himself to scrambled eggs.

Young Wil waited for him to go on. When he did not, Wil said slowly, "I thought we, you and I, agreed on it. Decisions around here are to be agreed upon until the time you take over completely—"

"Minor ones maybe, but domestic—or shall I say," a shade of sarcasm sliced through his voice, "affairs of the heart?"

"That too," Wil said shortly. "That is, if you refer to Midgie—"

"Ha! Who else?" Marty laid down his fork, having tumbled the eggs around without tasting them. "Take a look." He fumbled with the flap of the envelope. "If my beloved's note to you—none to me, mind you—didn't make that clear, this *will*!"

He withdrew a tiny circle of gold. Midgie's wedding ring! So she really meant that their marriage was finished? True's heart bled for her brother even though she could understand Midgie's pain.

"End of a perfect marriage," he said. "So what shall I do—go into Slippery Elm and get drunker than a hoot owl?"

"If you want to lose the respect of all the hands, yes, go ahead and drown yourself. But don't expect me to defend you when O'Higgin asks for an accounting."

"You make it sound like Judgment Day!" Marty pushed his chair from the table with a loud scrape.

"That'll do, Marty!" Young Wil's voice left no room for argument. "You know better than speaking in those terms, no matter how angry or hurt you are. There will be no more lecturing, no more coddling, no more protecting from me. And from you I hope I can expect a change of behavior. We are sick of the 'poor little me' attitude. If you wish to let the loss of your parents wreck your life, go ahead!"

True had never seen Young Wil so angry. It frightened her, but she kept still, breathing a silent prayer. God and her husband were smarter than she. Together they would figure this out.

"Easy for you to say—" Marty began, then stopped. "But I guess that's hitting below the belt, since we all lost out where parents are concerned."

"Then spend some time thanking the Lord for Aunt Chrissy and Uncle Wil—and while you're at it, say a prayer for Midgie. Praying is much better than some of these childish tantrums. You know what the Bible has to say about prayer."

" 'The prayer of a righteous man availeth much.' But me, *righteous*?"

"That's another decision you have to make."

Marty sat down and, to True's amazement, took a mouthful of the cold eggs. By now they had to taste like cardboard. But it was his way of knuckling under—a first experience!

"How long do you suppose," he said meekly, "it will take to get last night's damages repaired?" Marty flinched at his own words. The question led right back to his marital problems.

Young Wil tactfully took it as Marty had meant it. In control now, he was brisk and businesslike. "That's about like asking how long we're going to live. It all depends on how we pull together—and then we'll have to get to the source of the slaughter of the heifer, as well as some of the other suspicious activities. Are you with me?"

Marty was. He made no further criticism of his wife. Had he awakened?

24

Planting, Planning, Plotting

An early frost allowed the men to get the planting done in mid-November. It also blackened the above-ground vegetables. Thank goodness the potatoes were bedded down in the haymow with dry onions and winter squash, True mused as she checked on the kraut. Lifting the heavy stone from a plate which weighted down the shredded cabbage (to keep it below the brine solution), she pronounced it perfect. The test, according to Grandma Mollie, was in the throat's reaction. If it constricted from the sour aroma, causing the tastebuds to lock the jaw, 'twas just right. True tried to smile, but the effort was less than successful. She was homesick for them all in a way that doubled the discomfort of the aching throat. Homesick—if one could use the word to describe her emotions—for Midgie, whose little hands had grated cabbage until her knuckles were red and raw, refusing to stop even as the handfuls of salt ground into the open wounds. Trying so hard to please...

Tex, coming into the woodshed for a shovel, interrupted her wandering thoughts. "Pardon, Miz True, but it ain't only th' implement I'm needin'; smellin' th' sauerkraut made my mouth set t'waterin' like a thirstin' horse. I'd swap jest 'bout anythang fer a handful right outta th' crock—"

True laughed. "You have earned it already. Do you think your red wheat will grow here?"

The boy reached into the crock, grabbed a giant-size handful, and crammed his mouth so full that it resembled a suitcase packed so tightly for a trip that the lid could not be fastened. The sight made her throat tighten again, giving her an excuse for turning her head aside to hide a threatening burst of laughter.

Then she sobered. The boy was hungry—not only for kraut, but just plain hungry. How could she have been so blind?

"We're going to have to do some arranging here, Tex, if you're still considering staying on—although there is no proper housing—"

"Oh, I hafta stay," he choked, face red, and strings of the fermenting cabbage forming a green-white goatee down his chin. "Ain't no choice—I've invested all I got in this world, my wheat seed—an' I'm much obliged fer th' boss men a-lettin' me use th' ground." He swallowed so fast that True wondered if the mass wouldn't be brought back up in a cud to be chewed a second time like some ruminating animal. Then, covering his mouth to avoid the belch that threatened to erupt, Tex rushed on: "I— me 'n th' other boys ain't astin' much—"

"You mean—you mean they *all* want to stay?" True sat down.

"Oh, yessum! 'N we'll be no trouble—fact is, we kin hep avoid what's boun' on happenin'—th' rustlin' 'n th' like. Ain't safe out here without numbers—'specially fer th' ladies. We dun foun' a place—" he reached for more kraut, changed his mind, and continued, "saplin's are fine—'n I'm experienced. Why, onct I built me a shack in a week with my bare hands—got me a roof over my head in seven days, same time as it took th' Good Lord t' build th' earth. 'Course now I'm guessin' He didn' break His back like I did. But y'all know what? He up 'n helped me, knowin' it'd get my goat, but we made it, me 'n Him, 'n that's how I got them precious seeds. I plowed roun' boulders 'cause I had me no kegs uv black powder 'n couldn' budge 'em. That's 'fore I met Pig Iron—now, he's valuable, too—he could do it. We kin 'n will do anythang fer y'all—anythang a'tall."

His pleading humbled her. "Oh, Tex," she said, tears gathering in her eyes, "you needn't try to justify your being here. It's *your* welfare that concerns me."

In her mind she was seeing Atlanta again—seeing the "haves and have-nots" of the St. John-Kincaid family of which (had God not intervened—of that she was sure!) she might have foolishly become a part. Their wealth and "fine old family background" had made them into hopeless snobs, looking with disdain upon those whose skins were black. Even now, the remembrance of their superior attitude caused her back to stiffen and her eyes to turn purple with rage at the injustice of their narrow world which they called "Christendom."

"I will never understand you people—never in a million years," she had said in a voice that she hoped was low and controlled. "You speak of the poorly educated and culturally deprived people as if they were less than your horses! How can they be other than they are when they're so ill-used—kept living in a world of unrelieved grimness?"

Brave words. Yet here, like a ghost of the past rising up to meet her, was a case not too far different. The boy, Tex—could he be more than 17?—was willing to make any sacrifice in order to follow his dream in a world of injustice which cared more about its headache than his demise. "Poor white trash," Michael St. John's Cousin Emily had called salt-of-the-earth people like Tex and the other faithful hands on the emerging Double N Ranch.

"Jesus would have loved these people," True had said—a statement which had served only to raise aristocratic eyebrows. She had stuck with her conviction. How then had she allowed personal problems to blind her to the needs of others here? She was as selfish as Marty, petty and small.

"I'm proud of you, Tex," True said warmly now. "You have stood fast in your faith—"

The boy nodded shyly. "My grandma took care uv that. When I lost her, I lost ever'thang—'ceptin' my faith—"

"Faith opens the door to all good things. I will talk with my husband and our brother, and somehow we'll manage," True promised, wiping away a sudden tear.

"Now, don' y'all go cryin', Miz True. I—I'll feel so bad— 'n Mr. Wil 'n Mr. Marty's got 'nuf t'settle. What we're facin's gonna take blood 'n sweat—then Mr. Marty's got hisself a pack uv other problems. He's battlin' with th' future 'n th' past—meanin' th' railroad which jest maybe ain't past after all. Then he's all tore up inside—losin' Miz Midgie 'n all. I tell y'all, Miz True, iffen th' Good Lord ever sees fit t'send me a woman so lovin', I'll be handlin' her like a prairie flower." Tex scratched a tuft of hair which stood at attention on top of his head. "Sad part bein' he's crazy in love, too—"

The boy mumbled some more, but True did not hear. *I should have stopped the conversation when it became personal,* she thought. But the boy meant well, bless his simple heart. And besides, his last sentence—in fact the entire conversation—had given a new brightness to the November sky...

———

True to his word, once he had the go-ahead from the North Brothers, Tex enlisted, without pressure, the services of the other ranch hands. The bunkhouse, such as it was, was ready for roofing by the end of the month. "Jest poles, Miz True Ma'm," Pig Iron said modestly, "but it'll keep th' wind an' wolves out. Even made ourse'ves some bunks, puttin' hay on 'em 'n kin cover ourse'ves with saddle blankets—right, men?"

"Right!" they all sang out in pride while Augie nodded his weathered brown face and kept smiling to reveal more teeth than True knew he possessed.

Marty was nodding too, although it was plain to see that his mind was elsewhere. It was he who had granted permission for the men to help themselves to the root crops. It was Marty, too, who suggested taking the leftover grain to town for milling.

"We'll share what we have—pool it, which will take honesty—"

True's heart sang to hear him take that much leadership. But there was little time to dwell on the change.

"That include th'—uh, beef, Mr. Marty?" Slim asked uneasily.

Beef? True's eyes questioned Young Wil.

"Slim found another heifer—calf, really—slaughtered," he said grimly. "Down in the hollow—still breathing but mortally wounded by gunshot, so—"

"It had to be destroyed?" True whispered, heart pounding against her ribs. She swallowed hard and steadied herself. "Was there a brand on it?"

"Ours," he replied. "Steady, sweetie—are you all right?"

"Perfectly," she said, stretching a point but feeling a curious touch of courage. "Then if you fellows will build a fire and put the beef to smoking—I—I'll watch while you search. I guess you'll have to?"

There was silence. Then all talked at once. They had searched high and low. No sign of human life except for hoof tracks. And, well, gunfire. No real casualties except for the one shot that whizzed past Augie's ear—and one thing more.

What? True had asked woodenly. But even before the answer she knew what it would be. Well, could be only a phantom, they said. Man's imagination had a way of tricking him—something call hal-halu—

Hallucinating, Young Wil supplied. No, it was no delusion. There was a man on horseback on top of the ridge—

"Who simply disappeared," True nodded without inflection.

"Up where the railroad has strung out red flags," Marty said, his voice as flat as her own. "Hadn't we better get the fire going?"

Leaving the other field hands to grub out stumps, mend harness, and—most important of all—keep an eye on the livestock, Young Wil and Billy Joe prepared the wheat for milling and the shelled corn for grinding. Enough, Billy Joe predicted, to last all winter.

"Mind if I go along?" True asked. "I need to do a bit of shopping."

Her husband answered question with question. "Think I'd go without you?"

How blest she was? She and Young Wil had each other, and even though circumstances had compelled them to plunge from wedding to marriage without the preparation period of a rightful honeymoon, life itself had prepared them. She often laughed at the memory of Young Wil's phrasing. "Such an advantage, knowing each other forever. This lifelong courtship's going to save a lot of red tape." *Bossy*, True had called him, while knowing he was right. This kind of love that grew slowly and steadily, recognizing no barriers, had every advantage. Their dearly familiar association had led them naturally and unhesitantly into two hearts beating as one. All this she wanted to tell him, but Marty had entered the door to say that he would be riding ahead for "some business."

Slipping into a tailored gray Sicilian skirt, side-pleated to allow for stepping high into the service wagon, she noted that the garment was showing its age, as was the box jacket that completed the suit. It was out-of-date, too, but warm. The day held promise of fair weather, but here one could put little trust in nature's promises, she had found.

For warmth, the three of them sat in the front seat. Young Wil tucked the lap robe over their legs, teasingly giving her knee a possessive squeeze just before taking the reins. The little gesture served to remind her again of her good fortune, and to wonder about Marty and Midgie. Marty had behaved much more calmly than she would have expected, but underneath the calm, conflicting thoughts and emotions regarding their problem undoubtedly boiled about. On the surface nothing resembling a solution had presented itself, but she had adhered strictly to the hands-off agreement that she and Young Wil made. They *cared*, but wordlessly.

So busy was True with the thoughts she had tucked away during the whirlwind days at the ranch that, if there were a warning above the drone of the men's voices discussing business, she failed to hear it. It was as if, on sudden impulse, the four corners of the earth simply folded together like a man's handkerchief, leaving the three in the wagon in the middle to soak up the drenching downpour. True would never look back on that wild ride without renewed thanksgiving that the prayer in her heart reached heaven—that God heard her plea and answered, giving Young Wil superhuman instinct as he bent over the buckboard and negotiated the twisting turns in what (fortunately) was a short distance, although harrowing. Overhead the sky sizzled with glistening tongues of fire to send thunder, like Thor avenging, rumbling through the passes. The swift transition from blinding light to black-ink darkness blinded her. Yet somehow between flashes she managed to find the great canvas umbrella she had learned to tuck in for emergencies. She raised it, a move which seemed to aggravate the wind. It was an inexplicable miracle that the wagon did not capsize when it struck a deep rut. Oddly, she felt no fear—then. That was to come later. For now she could feel only relief that rounding the next corner would bring them to Slippery Elm—or would have had a monster far greater than the one with which they were wrestling not reared its head. Immediately in front of them it was as if a thousand furies had been released, bound on destroying the earth. And, through the blinding sheets of rain, one evil eye—

The train! True realized then that Young Wil, in his rush to get them to safety, had taken the shortcut which crossed the railroad!

"Wave, wave somethin'—anythang!" Billy Joe screeched.

True yanked at her sodden petticoat, gave it a yank, and began waving the wide-sweeping garment as a white flag. She could hear nothing, see nothing. Would the engineer see, stop? *Could* he? Strange how she could be so objective, go on waving frantically, while facing the deadly monster that was so close now that she could see it. Long. Black. Sinuous. Sinister. Writhing like some earth-swallowing black snake shining with rain, its one eye blind.

"We're stuck—jump, darling, jump—you amazing girl!" Wil shouted.

There was no time to jump. A frenzied warning from the train whistle. A groaning and grinding of brakes and wet wheels sliding to a shuddering stop. And then bedlam. People laughing, crying, praying. While True, exhausted and dazed, and bedraggled in appearance, could think only: *I hope I do not encounter Mrs. St. John. She would love my backwoodsy appearance.*

She did—but not before she met someone who shocked her even more!

"Th' saints be preservin' us! What have we here but pea-brains, th' whole trio—what be ye tryin' to do, me lad, me lass, and me crazy ole leprechaun who, be th' legends true that roll o'er th' Scottish highlands, live forever and ought t'be versed in takin' proper care—"

"O'Higgin!" Recognition of the Irish burr, softened by a velvet heart, identified the speaker to True, who—taking no time to ponder the circumstances of his presence—was in his brawny arms even as she spoke the name.

"For the luvva Mike—if it ain't me True—and Young Wil in th' flesh. I was to be meetin' with Marty—"

"I'm Billy Joe, the foreman—remember me?" Billy Joe ran between them.

"The Beetle!" O'Higgin boomed. There was backslapping and a rumble of talk as True allowed herself to be led inside the Inn by an anxious Tilly. "We have to get you dried off, child—"

True nodded numbly. The shock was wearing off and her vision, like the sky, was clearing—only to cloud over again by a second shock wave, and then a third.

Stepping gingerly off the train was none other than Felice St. John. Her haughty eyes surveyed True with amusement and something else—what was the look, *triumph*? Looking like she had stepped into the latest in fashion worn by a Meier and Frank window mannequin, the woman had taken advantage of True's sad plight. Soaked to the skin by drenching rain, hair freed from barrettes by the wind and clinging damply across her face (then dripping down her back), she must look like a blonde witch. True felt herself coloring to the roots of her hair when Michael stepped from the coach to be greeted by his wife's crooning voice: "Oh, darling, did you see your former friend, Mrs. North?"

"True!" Michael's voice held concern. "Are you all right? And, to set the record straight, Felice, we are not *former* friends—"

True mumbled something and stumbled away as she heard the hiss of scathing words from Felice St. John. Michael was answering angrily. Well, what they said to each other was no concern of hers. But what she saw simultaneously was. For to the right side of the front door, in the shadow of the overhang, stood Marty engaged in earnest conversation with the man wearing the beaver hat. Instinctively she knew something was wrong. She also knew that it was wise to get inside without being observed—a feat she was unable to accomplish. A strand of wet hair blew across her face, blinding her and causing her to stumble against a chair. The small motion escaped her brother's attention but attracted the other man's. His head jerked up warily and for the first time True saw his face. All eyes. Gray as concrete and just as hard. Immovable and focused on *her*. Tillie followed his glance and nodded in recognition. A million questions rose to her mind. What were they plotting?

Only then did her heart begin to pound.

25

Talk and More Talk

Dressed in one of Mrs. Caswell's robes big enough to wrap around herself and Young Wil both, True allowed herself to be coddled as her hostess busied herself boiling water and setting out cups. True let her mind fly on wings of the wind—straight to Centerville, where last she had received such attention. How wonderful it would be to sit down with Aunt Chrissy and Grandma Mollie again just to talk and talk and talk...

The flight was shortened by Tillie's voice. "Would you believe you're the first woman I've entertained—you know, in a neighborly sort of way—in years!" she announced a little breathlessly. Hastily she cleared off an end of a table in her own small quarters, and, pushing a cup toward True, poured fragrant, amber tea with trembling hands. Her eyes, True noticed, glowed and her cheeks flushed.

"Are you lonely?" True asked, watching the thick cream spiral downward to color her tea. "There are so many people around, and you seem to know so many more than I realized."

"Lonely?" Tillie did not meet her eyes as she busied herself shrugging out of the Mother Hubbard apron and spooning sugar into her own cup. "Oh, not lonely as one ordinarily thinks of lonely. There are people in and out, but I get lonely for things as I once knew them. And I guess," she sampled her tea cautiously, "you and Midgie brought back Portland to me—except for the part I want to forget."

Forget, Tillie? The gold in the woman's eyes predominated, put there by some mysterious circumstance which was too painful to remember but too wonderful to forget. Except in part. And it was that part which puzzled. From somewhere deep down inside True had a growing conviction that at some point in the past the lines of their lives intersected. It took courage to follow a man into a wilderness like this, a land so vast and unpeopled that one could get lost just looking at the vast spaces about her. The thought startled her. She had never thought of herself as being courageous. Right now she was so filled with the home she had left—just as had Tillie Caswell.

True brought herself back to the present, realizing that her hostess was answering the second part of the question she had posed.

"Yes, there are people around—but in and out, not neighborly. And in my position I have come to know them all. Some, of course, I knew before coming. Randy and I are lifelong friends. In fact—well, what's past is past, but my life might have been different except for family responsibilities—then emptiness."

The gold had left her eyes, and so had all expression. True felt that she must do something—*anything*—to bring her back to reality.

"Tillie, did you know Irish O'Higgin—did he visit with his kin here?"

Mrs. Caswell seemed to concentrate. "I—think now—only after the property came to him—or maybe I saw him in Portland—"

No information there which was helpful to either of them. "And the man with the beaver hat—do you know who he is?"

For some reason the question amused Tillie. "That description could fit anyone, including women. According to *Godey's*, ladies will wear beaver hats this winter— winter is almost here, isn't it? Are you going home for the holiday?"

Would she? Wild horses could not keep her away if she had her druthers. But there were so many factors to consider that planning was impossible; it was inviting heartbreak. She must put the hope aside. And besides, she wanted to steer Tillie back onto the trail. The men would be in soon, and there was so much she wanted to discuss with O'Higgin. But first, back to her line of questioning.

"I have given no thought to Christmas—yet. But," True laid down her spoon and leaned forward, "do you know who the man is, the one," she smiled, "wearing the beaver hat?"

"Yes!" The answer came so quickly that it caught True unprepared. "But I am unable to reveal his identity. Please do not ask me to."

True's lips quivered betrayingly in spite of her effort to hide deep disappointment. Tillie saw. "I'm sorry, my dear." Her eyes lighted then, "But I can tell you a little about the mysterious man we saw in the gap the night Midgie left—forgive me—the night of the fiesta. At least, what I *don't* know, I should have said. Seemed he just dipped down out of the sky—let's see, about the time we were discussing the railroad shares and the rights of the government—"

We? Tillie must have seen the question in her eyes. "I own some," she said almost reluctantly, "as did Artie, as I'm sure you know now, since they came with the Double N, giving them to O'Higgin and then to you Norths—"

Railroad shares? True heard no more. Her mind was awhirl with conflicting thoughts and questions. Did Wil know? And what would this do to Marty, with his hatred for the railroad? And then: *So here we are again, Michael St. John and me—enmeshed in something between us. I should have known.* Would he stop at nothing in order to gain power?

Mrs. Caswell was still talking, apparently about the Mystery Man.

"He never asks for mail—never speaks, in fact, the few times he has ventured down. Whatever it is he does, he's dedicated to it. Strange thing about the man—he seems to drop out of the sky and go up in smoke with nary a word. Some say he's a being from another planet, and truly he plays a harmonica—the only human sound anybody has heard him make—like it was an angel's harp. If you can imagine grand opera notes made by inhaling and exhaling on a mouth organ! Asked to describe him, I couldn't. And yet I seem to know when he's around—sometimes feeling he is here even when I don't see him. Sometimes a Mystery Man, sometimes an Invisible One. Sort of spooky, but I'll wager he knows every train schedule."

An idea took shape in True's mind. "Then," she said slowly, "he may have been listening to the music that Midgie made? If so," she mused slowly, "that would eliminate him from suspects—I'm speaking about the slaughtering of the heifer. There was so much commotion—"

"And Midgie's going. Not meaning to pry, but I care about her more than you could understand, and," Tillie swallowed, "I'm wondering if you feel you could confide in me as to her whereabouts."

"I care too, Tillie. I care so much it hurts me to remember—but I can tell you nothing, including who took her away—"

Tillie jerked erect. "You don't suspect foul play!"

True's heart have a lurch and leveled off in painful beats. "I never thought of that—oh, Tillie, Tillie, keep her in your prayers."

O'Higgin's *haw-haw* laugh rang through the Inn. Mrs. Caswell picked up the tea things and True rushed upstairs to dress. Dinner was simple but sustaining—a

rich potato soup with loaves of fresh-from-the oven
black-crust bread. The latter Billy Joe dunked in his soup
unself-consciously, sucking on one end as one sucks
through a straw. The sound was less than pleasant,
causing Mr. Caswell to cast him a shriveling scowl. Billy
Joe took note and cast his host a superior glance. After
all, the foreman of the Double N could take his food as he
pleased.

"Where's your sense of humor, my good man?" Billy
Joe jibed. "Remember, eatin' ain't quite th' same onct a
body's teeth is falsified."

"Down, boys!" O'Higgin ordered as if addressing Tonsil and Lung. "Ye both be causin' me ears t'ring like
bells." He rose and felt inside the pockets of his mack-
inaw tossed carelessly on the pier table alongside the
high-domed clock beside the front door. What he found
was cotton, which he promptly stuffed into his ears.
"Protects me from th' bloomin' noise o'th' train," he
bellowed, unable to hear his own volume. And then he
grinned widely. "Glad His Majesty and Lady St. John ain't
amongst us—too rich fer our blood they be—dinin' in
th' special car o'th' Iron Horse. Big laugh, thinkin' he
owns th' monster while us commoners hold th' purse
strings."

True saw Marty's eyes widen. What he heard was
news. So the man in the beaver hat had nothing to do
with the railroads—or did he? Perhaps he felt as strongly
against their coming through the rich farmlands as her
brother. She tried to read Young Wil's face but found no
expression there—just an admiring smile.

When at length he and she were alone with O'Higgin,
they fired questions at him so rapidly that he threatened
to stuff the cotton balls back into his ears. Yes, all was
well at home. And, no, he was not here to check on the
ranch—wasn't the agreement for a year? All seemed to
be going well from her letters, he told True. Too bad the
family couldn't have Thanksgiving together, but better
that way—the weaning away, you know? They'd have

one glorious celebration when the "trial period" was over (no mention of Christmas, no mention of Midgie). The twins? Oh, pimple-faced and giggling over "the facts of life."

O'Higgin checked his gold watch. "Oh, I'll be leavin' 'fore th' mists is off th' heather come morn—th' rest o' th' night is Martin's!"

26

Winter's Lock

"Mark my words, sumpin's brewin'.". Billy Joe's voice
had the ring of a bad-weather forecast. "What's th'
world comin' to when Caswell, peaceful man as he is,
goes totin' a pistol holstered t'his hip—sez murderin'
renegades are gittin' thicker'n puddin'—strangers, too,
added t'them unsavory-lookin', impoverished prospectors who know full well ain't no gold hereabouts but stay
on. Cain't tell who's who—meainin' both sides uv th'
coin looks th' same—like thet satchel-carryin' St. John."
His eyes scanned the rising terrain on either side of the
return trail. "Then *him* up yonder in th' gap—I tell
ye'both somebody's gonna git his skull separated from
his body, er worse—"

"Worse?" True found it hard to keep a straight face
even though his words made her shudder.

Young Wil seemed unaware of the conversation. His
eyes, too, were on guard. "Did you pick up anything new
concerning the railroads, Billy Joe?"

"Oh, they're boun' on railroadin' their way through,
some kind uv merger's in th' wind—already recruitin'
hands." Billy Joe's voice was nervous and hurried. "Even
as't me 'bout our fiel' hands—'n since you wuz tied up in
conferrin' with O'Higgin—good t'see that ole wheeze!—

I up 'n took charge, sayin' we'd all look after ourse'ves. Oh, 'n sumpin' else peculiar-like. I ain't never knowed Tillie, who's so tight-lipped, askin' s'many questions—mostly 'bout Marty. Wonder why."

"I have no idea." Wil's dark eyes were resolutely on the road, but there was tension in his body wedged so closely to True, as if some inner magnet were tugging at his eyeballs elsewhere. True wished, as she did so many times, that they were alone, that she could reach up and stroke the furrows from his forehead, reassuring him of she knew not what. Life simply seemed unfair sometimes. *Stop it!* She told herself; *it's only for a year.* Until then she must think of others beside herself. She was relieved when Marty's horse overtook and passed them.

"Did Mrs. Caswell—or anyone else—ask about Midgie?" She aimed the question at Billy Joe, but it was Wil who answered.

"I did not hear her name mentioned. I wonder how Marty handled that part in the long talk with O'Higgin. By the way, this is a small matter, but did you notice that O'Higgin addressed him as Martin? We've never used the name—"

"How'd he come by that handle—uh, name?" Billy Joe parried.

"Family name—I explained about his parents' drowning to Mariah—oh, there she is!" True replied. Mariah's feet took wing, the boys running a close second.

It was a joyous homecoming for them—and suddenly for them all: Tex, Pig Iron, Slinger, Slim, and Augie, who was trying to greet them in bilingual tongue (Tillie called it "Spanglish") above the shrill barks of the two dogs as they bounced, ran circles, and set the hens to cackling. Yes, this was a part of her family now. Yet she had shared physical food with them but neglected the Bread of Life. *This I will correct, Lord,* her heart promised, *beginning now!*

"We are all going to have Thanksgiving at our quarters. And that's an order!"

Great smiles carved their faces into jack-o'-lanterns of joy.

Their reaction gave her the needed courage: "We have so much to praise God for—"

"And I have more than anybody!" Young Wil whispered in her ear.

The next three days were spent in preparing for the feast. Using Grandma Malone's recipe, True set cracked-wheat loaves to rising. The bread promised success by filling every cranny of the house with a tantalizing smell of yeast. Aunt Chrissy's walnut-prune cake looked so good that True hid it behind the lard can from which she dipped in making pastry for the sweet potato custards. From the garden came carrots and collards. But meat? The men were tired of venison and bacon.

"I'm so hungered fer chicken 'n dressin' with thickenin' gravy," Tex said on one of his excessive visits to the kitchen, "I kin smell it—it's like my granny wuz back agin—say! I've got uh idee, we could use one uv them hens. They're lookin fat 'n ready fer th' pot—"

Marty had been busy nailing a storm window into its frame. Suddenly he slammed into the house like the storm he prepared for. "Get back on the job!" His voice was an angry order. "And no! You are not to lay a hand on Midgie's chickens—*not ever*—is that understood?"

Mumbling a "Yessir," the boy stumbled out hastily.

True gasped, but before she could make sense of the scene, Billy Joe rushed in like a spring squall. "S'matter with Junior?" he asked in his usual let's-get-to-the-bottom-of-this manner. "Come outta here with his tail between his legs, eyes as watery as uh fresh-opened can uv oysters. Been cryin'—huh?"

There was an awkward pause—a pause which True broke with the truth. "Tex was wishing for family, I guess—asking for a dish his grandmother used to prepare—"

Marty did not allow her to finish. "Wanted to kill one of Midgie's hens. Over my dead body!" he spat out.

Billy Joe's eyes narrowed to slits, which he fixed on Marty while fingering his grease-spotted hat. "When'er y'goin' after her—yer wife, I mean, not th' chicken?"

"She left of her own accord—" Marty began angrily, then stopped. His fury had bounced from Tex to Billy Joe, veered off to Midgie, and now returned to the foreman. "Did anybody ever tell you what a meddlesome busybody you are? If I had my way—"

"I'd be gone, I reckon, but iffen that'd solve yer problem, it's uh sac'erfice I'd make. 'N thet's th' gospel truth." Billy Joe shook his head sorrowfully, "Y'young' uns ain't never been tolt, I'm guessin', thet gittin' hitched is easy. It's *stayin'* thataway what counts—wisht I could come up with sumpin' surefire fer salvaging th' pieces fer'ye."

"Who said I wanted my marriage salvaged?"

"Hit dawg allus hollers—" Billy Joe commenced. He stopped as Young Wil entered the back door.

"May I have a moment with Marty—alone?"

Billy Joe, unabashed, strutted out the front door. True, her heart in turmoil, turned toward the bedroom door. Young Wil motioned her back. Marty was about to let go with a barrage of words—words he withheld when his older brother lifted a hand for silence. When Wil motioned to a chair, he took it, more from respect than meekness, judging from the hostility in his eyes. True slid into a chair beside him, knowing that the air must be cleared if there was to be a proper Thanksgiving.

"Marty," Young Wil's voice sounded weary, "I realize we were not going to interfere. True and I pledge to keep that promise. However, I have a question for you—just one. Agreed?"

Do you love her? True prepared to hear him say.

She was wrong. "Did Midgie tell you she was pregnant?"

"Pregnant!" Who asked the question—herself or Marty? Probably both.

Marty's eyes clouded with shock. His face blanched and the little blue vein along his left temple which always revealed extreme emotion ballooned. Shock turned to a radiance that rivaled the sun. His moment of Creation. His Day of Revelation. There was a sacred silence. Then Marty became human again. He grinned, appearing to True's startled eyes to rise up in the east and come down in the west, and threw his hat at the ceiling.

"Oh, Midgie, Midgie, Midgie!" Turning to his brother, now a respected doctor, he asked, "When?"

"You figure that one. When *could* it be?"

Marty's face turned scarlet. "It could happen like *that*? I mean—it would happened—uh—"

"In June—on your wedding night, to be exact," Wil said professionally.

"June, July—this is November—a little March hare!"

Marty was giddily happy in a way that set True and Wil laughing, neither of them having been privileged to see this side of him before. And then a new side—one of concern for another person. He would never be the same again.

"She ought to be taking care—not overdoing—"

"Midgie's sensible, she's not glass. I doubt that she's breaking a horse. Anybody can deliver a baby—"

"Not this one! She'll stay on her feet until her hands won't touch in front! Babies need fathers even before they're born—and mothers need specialists like you. Nobody discovered this but you. So don't count on me for Thanksgiving. I'm going to find my family. Whoopee!"

———————

Thanksgiving Day dawned as bright as the good news. The Goldish family arrived in sheepskin jackets and fur caps of ancient vintage, bundled against the cold that Billy Joe predicted to arrive by noon. He was right. Wind poked at the chimney places by the time the roasted wild mallard ducks and dressing (with "thickened gravy" for Tex) were ready. Sage rivaled the sweet scent of nutmeg and cloves in the pies, and yeasty loaves of bread that Grandma Mollie would have envied—crusty-brown outside, feather-light inside—crowned the feast.

Crowded into the wee kitchen on benches of rough boards laid across sawhorses the diners waited, visibly salivating. How long had it been since the men had a home-cooked meal? And the expression on Mariah's face said this was her first Thanksgiving. Her sons, hair slicked with pomade or lard holding the middle parts intact, had controlled their manners as well. But their eyes were full moons.

As planned, Young Wil read a few brief praise passages from the Psalms, careful not to overexpose those for whom this might be their first encounter with the Bible. "Would each of you want to name something you're grateful for?" he asked upon closing the Bible. "Only if you wish."

"I dunno 'bout praying'—" Slinger's voice trembled.

"Just saying what you appreciate can be a prayer," Wil said gently.

"Later it's important knowin' thangs—know how old Methuselah wuz?"

The look cast the foreman's direction told the questioning Billy Joe that he might not reach what's-his-name's age. But Slinger answered best: "Which birthday?"

Snickers from the group broke the ice. Tex said with innocent pride, "Me, I'm thankful I'm uh good shot! Brung down four wheat-stealin' ducks. Yep! I'm glad th' Lord gimme a good aim like Slinger's, even iffen he don' feel up t'braggin' 'bout it."

A home, they said ... good neighbors ... this dandy meal ... and (from Augie and Mariah in fragmented English) *Gracias, gracias!* True longed to shout out the secret of her joy, saying instead, "Lord, thank You for love."

Billy Joe would be praying yet had the coffeepot not boiled over. The grateful men ate in silence, tossing down food with the same skill used to toss hay in the mow. Mariah brought out her guitar. They sang familiar songs of the range, then old hymns. The wind's brassy bass joined the singing to blow in the snow—winter's lock for the seeded wheat. *Praise the Lord!* "And please," True prayed in the secret closet of her heart, "let Your Word be locked inside these men's souls."

27

A Letter from Home

There was no word from Marty. There was, however, a long letter from Aunt Chrissy tucked into a bulky Christmas package marked OPEN EARLY. It was a struggle for True to wait until she, Young Wil, and Billy Joe could get back to the Double N before opening the box. It could hold a message concerning Marty or Midgie's whereabouts—better yet, both of them. But traveling home was long and tedious.

Snow had thawed, leaving the main road slippery and a bridge washed out—a gulch having turned into a short-lived river, trying the patience of men and mules. The animals were compelled to wade belly-deep and decided, with the poorly developed logic of mules, to stop in midstream. Billy Joe ranted and threatened, but to no avail.

"Git outta here, y'dum critters, lickety-split! Iffen we don' git there y'git no fodder fer uh week 'n no apple fer Christmas! Sech dum-dums," he said to True. " 'Er maybe they're smart, knowin' they git my goat worryin' me into thankin' I won' be able t'buy th' yard goods fer my Mariah t'make them fiesta dresses fer yore mama 'n gran'mama fer gifts. Wil, I'm bettin' they don' budge!"

Young Wil laughed. "I'm no betting man, Billy Joe. But if I were, I'd put no more than a dime on such stakes. Mules, like people, like an occasional *please.*"

"You joshin'?"

"Test my theory."

"*Please*, good brothers," Billy Joe said, falling for the gag.

To the surprise of all three riders, the beasts obliged. But valuable time was lost. Tillie suggested a new route home over higher ground to the south—took longer but had better drainage.

Shopping finished hurriedly, Young Wil bribed the mules with a sack of oats and loaded the wagon while Tillie asked permission to make twin Indians for the twins: a maid with braided hair and a brave wearing the paint of his tribe and carrying a fishing spear. "And, oh, True," she said happily, "Randy'll be back for Christmas week."

With some misgiving the three of them took the narrow trail overrun with brush and dill weed. Billy Joe was strangely silent as the mules strained up the gently rising hill, coming at length to the summit, crowned by a few wind-warped pines. A small creek led downward on the other side, emptying into what must be the McKenzie River, although True hadn't realized it was that nearby. The creek meandered at approximately the speed of the mules, narrowed, disappeared, then reappeared to pause where the ground rose again.

Billy Joe hawk-eyed the surroundings, obviously onto something. He was. "So thet's hit! I heered 'twas so— that th' Good Lord had emptied His pockets 'bout there, bringin' in more prospectors. Could'a landed any-wheres, I guess—me, I ain't interested in chemicals, but I smell gold. 'N," he scratched his chin, "I'm wonderin' what it's agonna add t'our problems—farmin', rail-roadin', more feudin'!"

True now recalled the clump of men talking in low tones as they stood apart on the platform where the railroad terminated onto a spur. Then the orders for a pick, shovel, and five-cent pie tins.

Her thoughts were interrupted by a faint sound—familiar, almost music, or was it the wind playing in the struggling pines? There! Again the sad-sweet notes floating through the gathering darkness. Had the men heard? Both were silent, but wasn't Young Wil urging the mules forward an indication? True looked past him and was surprised to see a sheer cliff that seemed to plunge downward and end in midair. Below were darker splotches of darkness. Tents? Overhead the stars came out one by one to crown the heavens. And by their dim light she was able to make out the rocky gap. A green-rocket falling star sped across the sky, causing her to jump. It was only a falling star, but it illuminated the Mystery Man! And then she knew the source of the music: his harmonica.

She was glad to get home. Deciding to make no mention of the incident, True steadied her nerves by cutting the ropes of the enormous package while the men unloaded the wagon.

And there, as she had hoped, was the letter!

Dear Family:
    Winters being harsher in the eastern part of the state, Miss Mollie and I decided to make extra quilts, hoping that their memories will keep you warm. You will find little patches of the past scattered at random—some of which I shed a few tears parting with: little scraps from your baby garments...Angel Mother's wedding gown for True...Marty's first rompers...Young Wil's first-day-of-school shirt (How he loved them both, the shirt and school!). I will leave the rest unexplained—although I suspect that all of you will recognize some of the colorful pieces Grandma Mollie stitched in so lovingly for your "something blue" to sleep beneath the first night. I

think all of you were a little embarrassed taking along a quilt in June—and now it is I who
sits here crying because all of you are gone,
but together! Precious moments that bind us
all into the loving family that we are...

True laid the letter aside, eyes misty with tears...
partly from sweet sentiment, and partly because it was
clear that Aunt Chrissy did not know that the four of
them were no longer together.

Later she would read what Jerome and Kirby wrote—
mostly school, how they were soloing in the cantata
"Christmas Covers the World." O'Higgin was helping
with the *grievshock (hot embers)* pantomime. *Come
home!*

But first True felt an irrepressible urge to locate Angel
Mother's diary, read it, and remember achingly what she
could of the beautiful Vangie. It spoke as if written for
True: "I will laugh when you laugh...cry when you
cry...so long as you are together..."

28

Christmas Wish Granted

Tillie Caswell delivered the colorful Indian dolls for the twins' rooms the same day Mariah brought the fiesta dresses. As they helped True wrap the package for sending home, the two women each revealed staggering pieces of news.

"I found out who assisted Midgie—I suppose one could call it befriending—in her, uh, leaving. Michael St. John! I guess we should have known."

Yes, we should have known, True's heart echoed. *He would have no qualms.* But wait! Should she be so hard on him? After all, he knew nothing of the circumstances; he only saw a girl in need—a need with which he could help. In addition, he had the lovely living quarters on the train which was leaving the next day. And, she realized for the first time, he knew Midgie's conductor-father very well.

Mariah's news had to do with another matter. Excitedly she reverted to her native tongue. Tillie listened with eyebrows raised, then explained to True, shaking her head in disbelief as she spoke.

"The boys reported seeing a woman—pretty rare, you know. Seems she was down below the cliff by the gap." She tilted her head southward. "You know children—

down there faster than jackrabbits and talking to her, no less! Can you believe she was selling barbed wire? A *woman*! Had rolls and rolls of the deadly stuff in her peddler's wagon. Mr. Caswell—Curly—is afraid to stock the stuff himself."

True looked at the women in dazed incredulity for a moment, then laughed. "If I understand correctly, you are saying that this woman is braver than—"

Billy Joe stormed in the front door, eyes flashing a warning at Mariah. "Not braver—more foolish! I tole you, wife uv my heart, that you warn't t'mention—"

"Now, now, Beetle," Tillie Caswell challenged. "Well! So Mariah spoke to me—as well she should have. You needn't stand there like a mountain lion ready to spring. What's the difference who sells the wire when it comes right down to it? Women have the same right—"

"Nobody has the right as the law stands, Tillie." Young Wil had entered soundlessly. "This is cattle country—open range. Livestock would cut themselves to pieces in case of a stampede."

"Then who would buy it?" True asked, not understanding. "I thought the commotion was over a woman's taking over a man's job."

"In a way it is. Only a cowardly man would allow that—and only a desperate, defiant, or ignorant woman would agree. It spells danger."

For reasons only he understood, Wil pulled True to him. Protectively. Almost savagely. "This spells more trouble."

Frightened, True pulled away as far as space in the tiny livingroom allowed. "Will somebody please tell me what this is all about?" Fear shaped into a frightening vision enlarging within her heart. *Supposing Midgie—in her desperation for money—or to get even—*

"About?" Billy Joe cut in bruskly, "It's about woollies! Sheep 'n cattle mix 'bout as good as water 'n oil. An' t'thank thet was sheep country we gazed 'p'on crost th' gap—"

"But why a woman?" True persisted.

"Women don' get hung—punished rightful er maybe not so rightful—but not hung by th' neck 'til dead!"

———————

Marty rode in on Christmas Eve at the speed of the rising wind, its cutting edge predicting a blizzard. He had borrowed a one-eyed horse from a lean-to that Curly called a livery stable. The animal, sniffing its more royal cousins, whinnied, and, turning its one good eye to their protective shelter, stumbled forward. At the sight of the comical pair, True burst into uncontrollable laughter to keep from dissolving into a puddle of sentiment. *Oh, Marty…Marty…what a Christmas present!*

"The prodigal's home!" Marty called, obviously glad, although his eyes showed fatigue and disappointment. True knew even before he told them that he had failed in his mission. Midgie was among the missing.

"Not a sign," he said. "She seems to have vanished. And anybody knowing anything kept it under wraps." Marty shook his head in despair.

Questions with inclusive answers. Did Marty check with Midgie's father? Conductor Callison was on a run. Did he go home? Out of the question, Marty explained, letting True take his wraps as he rubbed blue-cold hands over the luxurious warmth of the little potbellied stove. O'Higgin had hung a rider onto their previous policies when he was here: no visits home until the year ended. There was to be total breakaway.

"Guess he thought it would be easier to swallow later."

Easier for us all, True thought sadly, glad she hadn't known.

"Wil," Marty said slowly—uncomfortable in his new role of asking favors—"can we keep the fact that I left here between us, you think?"

"I see no point in making mention," Wil said quietly. "Anyway, a man would be foolish allowing any agreement to stand between him and love."

Marty's face went white. "I've been a fool; God set me straight. But I can't stay on the straight and narrow without help—His and yours. Know what I want for Christmas?" he blurted with a gulp. "You both with me—I—I know where to find her—but I need you." His face was that of a pleading child.

Young Wil looked inquiringly at True. Stunned, she nodded.

"Wish granted," Wil replied. "Are you absolutely sure she's not *here*?"

Had he thought of the barbed-wire lady too?

29

Reunion

The landscape was beginning to freeze over on Christmas Day, scalloping ruts of the isolated road with silvered ice, thereby dictating caution—a caution that Billy Joe ignored as he urged the team ahead of the approaching storm. He asked no questions, content to be a part of the drama. The boss men need pay no never-mind to anything. Wasn't he in charge? Too bad they were unable to partake of the sugar-cured ham that Mr. Marty brought home. But his Mariah would fix it up fancy-like. And, yes indeedy, they'd have the hands at their table for the feast. Prayers? Oh, my, yes! The men would know what Christmas was all about before partaking of such victuals as the loving Lord, whose Birthday they were celebrating, had provided.

While True packed a few necessities for traveling, Young Wil called the men into the cabin and told them simply that the Norths must be away for the holiday. "Your Christmas gift," he said simply, "is an invitation to share this place while we're gone. It's too cold out there, fellows. Just be careful with fires—and keep an eye out for—well, any trouble. No, there's nothing special to do, except for yourselves. There is plenty of firewood—also plenty of split rails for living quarters of sorts. Why not nail together a kind of bunk for yourselves? I will try and find you a stove, giving you warmer quarters—"

He stopped when there were tears in the eyes of the men. Billy Joe snorted with disdain, then blew his nose and faked a cough.

The train was on time and they were able to board quickly. As True waved a handkerchief of farewell to a tearful Tillie, she was surprised to feel a lump in her own throat. Six months ago she would have seen this trip as an escape. Now she felt—well, how *did* she feel?

On the way, Marty disclosed his plan. Well, maybe it would work. Just maybe. It seemed to be a last resort, actually. The ghost of Midgie hung over them all like Marley's ghost over Scrooge in Dickens' *Christmas Carol*. It would continue to do so until the matter was resolved. True refused to think of the unspeakable possibility that something could have happened to her—some tragedy—although this *was* a very real possibility. She concentrated on the beauty around her instead. Nature had been so extravagant with her paintbrush here—and it was *home*. A growing sense of excitement welled up inside her as the familiar green cathedral of the forest closed in...

The old hotel was in the exact ramshackle condition it had been when the four of them had spent their honeymoon here. Even the help in the largest diningroom in Portland remained. Seated at the long "family-style" table—deserted except for the three of them—True watched a rotund waiter (part Indian, she guessed by the black hair spilling down over his shoulders, shining like polished niello), her mouth suddenly dry. There was something about him—not sinister, more secretive— which said the diningroom had been cleared because of their presence, although he went on polishing and repolishing the silverware with the corner of his apron.

Face immobile, he applied a torch to the low-swinging chandeliers, turned them low, and marched toward the kitchen, straight-shouldered as if he were keeping step to a war drum. Did she imagine it, or was there a tilt of his shining head in their direction as a signal to some unseen figure?

She did not imagine it. The familiar face of the manager appeared at the swing-door. There was a flicker of recognition in his swarthy face. But before she could nod or smile, he disappeared.

For the first time she wondered how Marty came to decide on the hotel's being where he would find Midgie. It seemed most unlikely. The dryness in her throat worsened as she ruminated the impending confrontation if his plan for a meeting worked. For confrontation it would be—if Marty reverted to his usual pattern, letting relief give way to rage. Would he go at her tooth and claw? And Midgie—how would she behave? Let him bully her? Or would her emotional floodgates give way? She couldn't for a moment imagine that the insecure, frightened Midgie could take a meeting in stride. Probably she would catch sight of them and flee again.

Marty was obviously in a state of nerves. It was unlike him to talk so much. He veered from one subject to another with such speed that Young Wil was having trouble keeping up with him. About barley. About the scenery. About some person or persons who had been helpful, but failing to say who or about what. Then back to barley.

True forced her eyes to look out the window as the dove of twilight alighted on a tall fir which stretched to reach heaven, its needled peaks probing the blue as the light gave way. Shadows blended. Darkness settled comfortably over the land.

"Now?" a woman's voice broke into the sudden silence.

"Now," a male voice responded. And a large woman with a smiling face, bursting with obvious curiosity, set steaming bowls of soup before them.

Then she could bear it no longer. Casting a furtive look over her shoulder, making sure her employer did not see, she lowered her voice conspiratorially. "Th' missus is 'bout t'dine. Want I should tell 'er? Shock, y'know—her bein' in a family way 'n all. 'Course now it's no bizness uv mine—"

"You're right, it isn't!" Marty snapped. "The manager knew this was to be a surprise—unrehearsed—forgive me, but do go about your business. This is something I—we—must handle alone—"

The woman fled, almost colliding with Midgie. *Midgie!* Wearing a blossom-pink maternity dress, Midgie looked like a ripe peach. But it was the way she lifted her rounded chin, the simple dignity with which she carried herself, that tore at True's heart. Her smile may have been a bit fixed, but her eyes were lighted with a million stars. True held her breath as she watched Marty. No admonishing frown. No harsh words. After all, his face said, the score was even. Midgie had left of her own accord, but he had come searching in like manner.

Crushing his napkin into a ball, he flung it without aim. It landed in the soup, causing both of them to laugh. Make that four! All were bursting with mirth as Marty and Midgie ran to each other, arms outstretched.

Marty crushed her to him covetously. And nothing was going to come between them—not even their child! "Darling," he murmured.

There were a dozen "I love you's—unselfconscious, all of them.

"I'm sorry—never again—" Marty's voice broke as Midgie put a *shushing* finger to his lips. "Never again is right—no more mention of our being apart. *Ever!*"

Midgie turned to True and Young Wil, eyes shining. "No, don't go! We're never going to be apart again. I'm starved—for the first time in months! For food... news...and love!"

30

Homecoming

A shrill whistle pierced the midnight air as if vibration of the rails were not enough to alert Slippery Elm of the coming train. The short trips between the community and Portland, although irregular in schedule, occurred more and more frequently now (hopefully building "good blood" between landholders and the railroad company). But the arrivals remained an oddity—an iron monster from other worlds bringing good news and bad. And there were always new faces, those belonging to a new segment of the railroad crew. Tonight there were more spectators than usual. The usual open-mouthed gawkers appeared to be waiting for somebody who never came. The few heavily coated, bearded favorite sons leaned importantly against the sagging buildings, either to stall off trouble or start it. There were also a few stragglers, and tonight the Caswells. To welcome home the Norths?

The air was frigid, but Curly had no time for donning a hat. He had news that wouldn't keep—of that True was sure as she caught sight of his shining head, which tried to outshine the moon it reflected. As Marty helped Midgie to her feet and Young Wil pulled their travel cases from the overhead rack, True watched Mr. Caswell's keen eyes travel the length of the train as if one car were a treasure chest! He must have found it, for his face, so tense when he rushed onto the rickety platform, now suffused with color as he pushed forward.

Spotting the Norths, Curly addressed them all simultaneously:

"Th' newly appointed division superintendent uv th' railroad—yer jest in time, meetin' scheduled fer tonight or tomorrow, dependin' on which side o'midnight yer railroad time declares. Trouble a'plenty—'n—oh, I'm a-gettin' more 'n more narrow 'twixt th' horns, plum forgettin' interductions." Curly was winded but rushed on. "Wil 'n Martin, an' yore purdy wives, say 'Hello' t'Mr. Em'ry Keelin'. Th' Norths, sir; they got special in'erest all over th' valley—not shareholders 'xactly, maybe more say-so 'cause y'gotta 'ave right o' way—shake hands. Me, uh man's gotta come up fer air *sometime*, I reckon."

"I was beginning to wonder," Mr. Keeling said congenially, favoring True and Midgie with a smile. "Ladies," he acknowledged, and then turned to shake hands with the other men.

His warm, friendly manner compensated for his lack of physical charm. His small eyes, above a skimpy mustache with a moth-eaten effect, and a decidedly bulbous nose painted red with tiny veins, looked out of place above the perfect tailoring of his suit. He kept shrugging as if the blue serge coat and pants were a new mode of dressing, a uniform of distinction.

A lot seemed to have happened in the short time they were away—happenings True wanted desperately to hear about. But Tillie Caswell had rushed to her and Midgie with outstretched arms in tearful welcome, her words drowning out the men's conversation. "Oh my darlings, my darlings—let me look at you—so *that's* the secret—a baby," she marveled. "Oh Midgie, little Midgie," Tillie was weeping openly now. "You can't possibly know what this means to me—but someday—"

Why had she paused? It was not the first time True had wondered about Tillie's unfinished sentences and about her past. But now was not the time to pursue the subject even in her own mind.

"Coffee, coffee!" The Caswells were ushering the party inside excitedly. True tried desperately to marshal order from the chaos of the two conversations. It would have been impossible even without the train's endless backing and starting, punctuated by the metallic grind of brakes.

"What's going on out there?" Young Wil asked (trying, True felt, to mask his concern).

"Some new track laid—" the division superintendent began.

"More's comin', too, 'n fast—never saw men work s'fast—like they wuz tryin' t'outwit some uv us—"

True's mind went back to Curly Caswell's breathless greeting. Just in time he had told Emory Keeling... right-of-way... "trouble a'plenty..." There was more, but her mind bolted back to the present.

"Cut *our* fences—let the prize Longhorns escape to the hills!" Marty dropped his cup with a clatter. "We have to go—*now!* Can you put the ladies up for the night, Tillie—what's left of it?"

"No! Absolutely not!" Midgie jumped from her chair, fatigue erased from her face. "I'm going with you—at least, to the Double N. That way I—we, True?—will be closer."

"You can't take the chance. There's apt to be violence—"

"There's always a chance of violence. We live in a violent world. You needn't stand guard. I won't run away again. An encore would lack the punch of a first-time performance."

Even though the situation at the ranch demanded immediate attention, True and Young Wil sought each other's eyes and locked. This was Marty and Midgie? Their first expression was one of amused incredulity.

The sense of amusement turned to one of admiration and respect born of conviction. The couple had become Mr. and Mrs. Martin North, husband and wife determined to protect each other, come what may.

The drama was unfolding rapidly. Young Wil, like herself, appeared unwilling to interrupt. Not that the other couple needed help!

"I won't have you taking chances—the baby's too important—"

"To be born without a father!" Midgie finished. "Want to come with me to the—*ahem!*—powder room, True?"

Tillie followed them. The men, speechless, followed with their eyes. "We'll need horses, Curly," Young Wil said quietly, "for four."

Once alone, the women made no reference to the conversation. Neither did Tillie make mention of the crisis at hand. Other matters took priority where Mrs. Caswell was concerned. True was torn between the two. Ultimately, in those few short minutes together, she chose to concentrate on questions she knew Tillie would ask—questions which she herself had had no opportunity to pose. It was a ticklish situation—one of great sensitivity, requiring the choosing of words with utmost delicacy. And Tillie sensed as much along with True. She behaved as if about to unpack extraordinarily fragile crystal.

Neither needed have worried, for the new Midgie made it easy. "I am sure," she said, reaching skyward to relax her weary body, "you both want a quick account of my activities—and, no, you aren't prying. I am only too happy to give account. I had to get away—you both know that—find out where I stood with my husband—and look my own self in the eye. I never knew who I was. Even in my prayers I could never properly identify myself to God. There's still a lot we have to learn. But we'll learn together—and we have God with us, and all of you!"

"Did you—uh—learn anything about—yourself?" The question seemed important to Tillie.

"I learned I'm not dumb. I took classes in grammar, manners, and birthing. A baby needs a lady for a mother. Then I enrolled in a correspondence course to work on here—something new, called psychology. I learned how to listen to Marty, like we have to listen for the answer when we pray. And, oh, I made no contacts except with my father so he wouldn't worry. He paid my board without questions. Let's go!"

31

Night of Horror

"Is anything harder to bear than waiting?" Midgie pondered.

"Bad news," True answered, wondering if she believed it.

Midgie had been pitifully happy to get home, running her fingers over every inch of the spick-and-span cabin. The place looked as if the ranch hands had cleaned every corner minutes ago, but the cold stove said they had been gone for hours. Now the minutes crawled even though a fire chuckled cheerfully in the wood range and there was a lot of talking to catch up on. Midgie put the kettle on and made a batch of cinnamon rolls. True set the coffee on to boil and mixed batter for sourdough buckwheat cakes. The men would be hungry, they told each other, once the cattle were rounded up. And it was natural for daylight to drag its heels in midwinter. Well, wasn't it? They guessed so, neither of them daring to check the creeping hands of the clock.

"We should look our best," Midgie suggested. She fluffed her hair on the sides becomingly and applied a bit of petroleum jelly to her eyelids and eyebrows. "I can't do much about this figure, thank goodness!" she giggled nervously. "Oh, let me cut you a fringe of side bangs like young women are wearing in Portland!" She snipped, held up a mirror.

True saw herself through Young Wil's eyes and decided she looked more than a little acceptable. Surely he would be here soon.

The coffeepot boiled over, causing both of them to jump.

They could read the Bible. Yes, they could. They tried but were unable to concentrate. They tried praying, too, with the same results. The problem, of course, True admitted to herself, was that they were not listening for the Lord's voice, but for some sound that would reassure them that He was riding with their husbands. "The hands are studying the Bible," True began.

"My chickens?" Midgie interrupted, indicating inattention.

"They're fine."

Midgie's nerves were growing more taut. She must see them—now! True humored her. Bundling up and bracing against the wailing wind, they checked the cozily covered coops. The rooster's reassuring voice to his startled feathered hens fell on deaf ears. And the building (taking on the shape of a bunkhouse that busy hands were erecting) blind eyes looked at but did not see. Eyes and ears were fine-tuned to see and hear any clue that would tell them their men were safe.

There was sudden silence. Uncanny, coming as it did. Was the wind for or against them? Either way, it played a role. Without it, True heard the snap of a twig. It could have been anything. But some inner sense told her that it warned of a human presence. She stood passive for a moment, hoping that Midgie had not heard. If she could manage to get the other girl to safety—

The thought died before its birth was complete. A tug at her arm said Midgie had heard and was stifling a cry. Moments ago True had felt the place was terrifyingly empty of anything human—just broad open spaces leading up into the night-blue sweep of the hills beyond.

That's where the danger lay. And now it was here. Enemies squatted behind every bush. Menace lurked behind each building. Courage was dissipating like a vapor touched by sunshine. Yet mingled with fear was a morbid curiosity—or was it a form of courage for Midgie's sake?—that hypnotized her.

True would have been unable to explain why she stood perfectly still, a reassuring hand placed over Midgie's. She only knew that later it seemed wise. Rooted where they were, the two were able to hear the hair-raising combination of banshee yells and gunfire high above them.

Gunfire! Her mind did a double-take. Think. She must think. But her mind was stampeding—*stampeding*, that was it! The word alerted her to the awful possibility of a stampede of horses and cattle...animals reverting to their wild nature...fleeing they knew not what, only to trample one another to death... charging any barrier senselessly, impervious to injury of themselves or others. And the men—*oh, dear God, our men—help them! How does one cope with a stampede?*

Stop them—she must stop them. But how? She could only imagine the buildings giving way beneath the onslaught of hooves. Automatically she shielded her face from the mass of dirt and gravel which would come with such force that she and Midgie would be buried alive...

And then the incredible happened. Bounding up from nowhere, a shapeless form appeared in the shadows, and with the speed of a panther began closing and barricading gates leading into the corral. Would the fragile fence restrain the terrified herds? There were barrels of rock, she remembered, to be used in construction of more concrete irrigation troughs. With superhuman strength she bolted forward just as the bent-over form took the shape of a man, clearly visible in the light of the descending moon. Never mind his identity; he was an answer to prayer. "The barrels—I will help—" and suddenly they were pushing with more power than they knew they possessed. All three of them!

Three? "Midgie, get inside—no, *run!*" True's orders fell on deaf ears. Midgie was pushing alongside them. And the sound of hooves came closer . . . closer . . . closer. Until two strange things happened simultaneously.

Later True would discover that it was only a small stone which slipped from the barrel they were managing to shove inch by inch. But for now it might well have been a boulder rolling beneath her, causing her to lose her footing. She fell face down and lay dazed, forgetting the vital mission at hand, visualizing only the terrain along the ridge of the gap and the valley trough below it on the other side. The clump of dead trees standing spectral and black like evil spirits, almost unobserved at the time, flashed before her eyes. Fire, Billy Joe had said— fire set by arsonists, intended no doubt to warn somebody of something: Indians in order to protect their burial places—or were there any Indians here? Sheepherders warning cattlemen against barbed-wire fencing in open-range country? The other way around? Or something to do with the railroad building?

In that brief moment in the netherworld, True fancied seeing a horse half-concealed behind a dead carcass of a tree, and on it the Mystery Man—not moving, but unharmed, as wild horses and long-horned cattle neighed and bellowed past, only to fall moaning and dying beneath the sharp hooves of other animals. For somewhere up there stretched a strip of wasteland, pockmarked with gopher holes, tumbleweeds rolling, and heaping themselves like skulls of skeletons in search of their bodies. It was into those gopher holes that the irrational animals would fall, as would the horses ridden by Young Wil, Marty, and the ranch hands—and the enemies in wild pursuit. The illusion had zig-zagged across her mind with the speed of lightning streaking the sky. And then it was as if a gentle but powerful voice spoke from the ramparts of heaven:

"Why seek ye the living among the dead?" That meant *life* . . .

In response, True raised herself on one elbow, only to grow rigid with terror again. Hot breath was fanning her cheeks, salivating tongues licking her cheeks. Wildcats? Wolves?

And then there was a warning whimper, followed by a bark of concern. *The dogs!* How had they escaped the world of madness, and what were they doing here?

Tonsil and Lung had gone opposite directions and now stood like statues at either end of the corral, noses pointed up the hill—waiting, knowing exactly what to do. True shook her head to clear it, some far corner of her mind realizing that they—like Marty—though late bloomers, had metamorphosed from anaphase to maturity according to God's plan . . .

Midgie, too, had fallen. "The baby, the baby!" she was crying out. The stranger was helping her to her feet with a deep-throated order.

"In the house, both of you—*now*! We're as prepared as we can be. Get beneath the bed—*now*—they're coming this way. These buildings will go down like cardboard—unless—you know how to pray, don't you?"

True, every muscle threatening to snap, dragged a protesting Midgie inside and rolled her beneath the bed, covering both their faces with great down pillows. In the process she felt a hot, sticky substance bathe her hands. *Blood!* Midgie was injured. *Oh, dear God, not the baby* . . .

And then came the thunder of hooves mingled with voices which attempted to command and soothe at the same time. The pillows drowned out direction, but two other sounds penetrated the feathers: The dogs were barking like commanders—first here, then there. And above it all the sound of harmonica music. Soft, sad, sweet, pleading, and—above all—comforting. Of course! She should have known—the Mystery Man! He would be killed!

But what was this? Silence. Silence which came to life with voices—some familiar, others not. "We—did it—" Midgie gasped through a mouthful of feathers, the ticking having split beneath her tight grip. Hysterical laughter rose to True's throat as wildly they stumbled out the back door. Oblivious to the heavy breathing of exhausted animals, the happy yelps of dogs in need of praise, and the disappearance of the Mystery Man, they were pleading with God for sight of their husbands.

32

Aftermath

"How many hours has it been since you had any sleep, you amazing girl?" Young Wil's voice was filled with concern, but never once did his hands stop working as, together, he and True leaned over a wounded stallion. The stampede seemed like a page torn from an ancient history book.

"I'll bite. How many?" she asked flippantly. She ran a finger against the scratch on her face, her only casualty, and attempted a laugh. The laugh—after all the excitement (and goodness alone knew how many revolutions the hands of the clock had made)—was a winner of its kind. "Should I check on Marty and Midgie, or continue helping here?"

His capable fingers secured a bandage on the quivering animal's near-severed leg. "Stay with me, I think, True. I need disinfectant, and please hand me scissors from the black bag. The bull needs attention."

True obliged. "Think I should be studying for nursing instead of teaching—that is, if ever we get back to our books?"

"You've been wonderful. Without your talking with Midgie while I worked, do you realize that she could have lost the baby? And poor Marty—we'd have lost *him* as well if that happened! Poor guy—one broken arm and the other sprained—the iodine, honey. Wow! this is a spirited critter. Think you can hold this hobbler on his forefeet while I get a halter?"

Of course she could. She could do anything, even hold the world on her shoulders, until young Doctor North replaced it on its axis. Angel Mother was right: "So long as you are together."

"Speaking from the grave," Grandma Mollie had said. True called it speaking from heaven. How far-reaching a mother's love was . . . and that's how it would be with her own offspring, hers and Young Wil's . . . their love so great that it needed to find expression in creating and nurturing . . .

It must be the same with other forms of life. For it was at that exact moment that Wil gasped, "Can you believe this—a young heifer deciding to give birth instead of waiting for spring? Steady, girl, steady—" he soothed the cow as he had soothed Midgie in their struggle to protect her unborn baby. "True—come, darling, can you handle this?" All the while he was grabbing for ropes and instruments, sterilized and folded neatly away in gauze. "How many animals have we worked on—more than were in the ark?"

"The clean and the unclean," True replied. "I still don't know who's who and what's what about this whole mess. Who went where?"

He tried to catch her up as they struggled with the frightened mother-to-be. His phrases were fragmented, and True had to guess the rest. But a picture formed in her mind as Young Wil gently lifted the beautiful bright-eyed calf and placed it on a saddle blanket beside the new mother's face. "Wake up, lady—wake up and see what you've got here. She'll finish the job and let him know—yes, it's a boy!—who's in charge. Then we'd better take him inside for the night and put Mama in the barn."

True nodded tiredly, admiring him and loving him more than ever before, while struggling to put together the story of this night of horror and triumph. Their losses were fewer than could have been expected. The wounded were attended—cattle, horses, and men. Billy Joe and two of the hands were on their way to Slippery Elm...sheriff would be here tomorrow...other men were repairing fences...bullets had come close...even knocked Slim's hat off!—but they were safe. Identity?

"The whole thing was like a combination of an Old World drama with all the characters wearing masks, and just about as pagan. Like three performances in progress at once—a tragedy, a carnival, and Shakespeare's *Comedy of Errors*," Young Wil explained as they moved from one wounded animal to another, stopping often to diagnose and treat.

But the scene came alive in her mind. Make it a musical comedy, she thought, wondering if he knew of the Mystery Man's role. Yes, it had all the makings of a classical play absurdly confused with a second-rate road show. The colorful background set the stage: the starry heavens as an arched ceiling for the theater; the beautiful-at-a-distance outline of the rocky gap as a backdrop; clumps of bushes and charred trees as the wings—all softly lighted by a sinking moon as the crowning touch.

The first attacking party, according to Billy Joe and the other men (each account varying somewhat), rode up the hill with a bravado designed to thrill any audience. And, oh, yes, there was an audience—the other actors! Unfortunately, either none of them had read the play or there was no prompter in the wings, because all the actors missed their cues. A leader (as yet to be identified) made use of extras instead of seasoned actors. "Sapheads," Billy Joe called them, "not knowin' nothin' 'bout how railroads git right-aways, jest out t'make uh slick buck," but having descended on Slippery Elm to drop a few hints here and there regarding plans to destroy property. The cattlemen, farmers, and sheepherders got the word and prepared accordingly. Then the "sap-heads" made a fatal mistake: One of them attempted to recruit Slinger, the trigger-quick veteran. And so, instead of terrorizing the victims, the would-be "bad men" found themselves staring dumbly at real "bandits" (Yep, yep, yep! That's us—bandannas 'n all," Billy Joe supplied). Meantime the plot thickened. Ill-planned by all, a strange crossover began. Men joined the wrong ranks, with the railroad gang making the gravest errors of all, beginning to shoot wildly—some of the shots hitting target—

At that point the story was no longer comical—or maybe it hadn't been all along. *It was just that I am so tired, so tired,* True thought fuzzily. But now concern replaced fatigue.

"How many were injured—and was anybody—?" True was unable to finish.

Young Wil met her gaze squarely. "You know there had to be casualties, darling, But I did the best I could—"

Her breath came out in a strangled sob. "I know, darling—I know. I was so anxious—so afraid—" her lips whitened, the scratch on her cheek throbbing painfully, "I knew that with all that shooting, there would be—and oh, Wil, darling Wil (she had sobbed at that point), I know it isn't right, but I asked God to protect *you*—not thinking of how some other heart would break if—if—"

"Don't you know He would understand that?" Leaving his animal patient for a tender moment, he leaped to his feet and crushed her to him there in the barnyard, their combined tears streaking caked dirt and dried blood from their faces.

In a far corner of the lot, a cow gave a near-human moan. Duty pulled her wonderful husband away, but she followed. "Is there a way to know the number—and their names?"

"Slim found a list on one of the hired gunmen," he answered from a bent-over position. "He checked the roll, forcing them all to answer. Found several undesirables, wanted by the Federal Government. Tex also recognized several and will give testimony."

They were nearing completion, both of caring for the animals and finishing the story. But the critical questions remained.

True's voice trembled when she asked what she must know. "Were there—fatalities?" Then, remembering she had asked, "How many?"

"Four. It was inevitable. Two of the attackers shot each other, neither breathing by the time I could reach them. One rancher—and a man none of us knew." Did she imagine it, or did he pause? She could not be sure, heart fluttering like a caged bird in her throat and tears blinding her to the expression on his face. "The rancher begged for a priest. I could do nothing for him, riddled by bullets as he was, but—I—I explained that I was not a priest, not even a minister, but I could offer a prayer. Only God can repair hearts—or bodies either, for that matter. The rest of us just prescribe."

"Oh, darling—"

Young Wil tried to grin as he stood. "Don't cry, True—I can't bear any more pain. I found out the man's name and thought—"

"I could call on his wife? You know I will."

"We men can mend fences, and if we're lucky, patch up bodies—even mediate differences. But it takes a woman to give understanding and love. And by the way," Young Wil made a partially successful attempt at lightening the conversation, "you ladies were the real heroines—how on earth did you come to think up that barricade?"

She started to explain, wondering if she knew how, when the dogs came bounding out, rested, bright-eyed, and obviously demanding a medal in the form of a meaty bone. "There were a lot of main characters," True said, trying to match his mood of life-must-go-on, "Tonsil and Lung among them. There is more to say, too, but it can wait."

"Well," he said with a deep sigh of relief, "my tummy can't. Oh, one good thing came of all this unspeakable tragedy: The cattlemen, farmers, and sheep owners joined ranks. As for the railroad—who knows?"

33

The Other Side
of the Mountain

Winter closed in with tyrannical rule. The tongue of the little stream which used to trickle down the Double N's irrigation trough slowed and stopped in frozen silence. Hills surrounding the vast valley snuggled in their mantles of snow. In January they were patterned anew daily with tracks of furry animals seeking dark refuges for their long sleep. Then the pattern disappeared completely as all (including the widely scattered houses in the countryside) became a part of the white-sheeted landscape, locked in until April's key opened the door. But the plunge in temperature locked in the wheat as well. It was as snug as the Norths in their cabin and their faithful helpers, whose bunkhouse was certainly better than no shelter at all.

It was a time of togetherness, drawing them all even closer. The hired hands spent the days mending harness, whittling furniture (Tex having taught them the skill), and—with the aid of the dogs' keen noses—tracking down deer, venison being about the only fresh meat available. A cause for amusement was the young Texan's slipping (unnoticed, he thought) to the closest wheat field and trying in vain to penetrate the frozen ground with a trowel in hopes of finding a sprouting grain of his red wheat. One of the men had served as apprentice in a wagon-making shop. Together, in their spare time, the group worked on the wooden spokes and dreamed aloud of purchasing metal parts for wheels when conditions allowed for traveling to Slippery Elm. The ranch came first and foremost, of course, but just to supplement the income, mightn't it be wise someday to hang out a sign that said ON-THE-PREMISES WAGONMAKERS? Might be able to sell one for, say 25 dollars or so cash money—and look at the improvements that would make! Add profit from the wheat, maybe patenting the new strain...and the thoroughbred livestock and Midgie's chicken eggs...why, they'd all be rich someday! Life was simple and life was good. Actually, they were rich already!

And so they sang a lot, their rollicking cowboy songs a lullaby lost in the wind, except to the Norths. They too kept busy, Young Wil with his medical books, True with her educational journals, Midgie with her correspondence course, and Marty with his bookkeeping to try to figure how he could turn a profit here—and also reading everything he could get his hands on concerning the birth and care of the newborn. There were times, Young Wil whispered to True, when more of his reference books were in Marty's bedroom than his own. In fact, Marty was pushing himself. His gray eyes were too often red-laced and rimmed with lack of rest, and when exhaustion would grip him in her fist, he would drink more coffee and read on. It came as a surprise to them all when he began designing plans for a double-log house—very, very long, with wide windows looking out on a vegetable garden here and a rose garden there—a house befitting his countess and his heirs. So he planned to stay on? True prayed it could be so...

There was still time out for the young wives to make a few baby garments from the precious yardage they had on hand, and to bake with whatever their rapidly depleting supply of staples allowed. On baking day the men from the bunkhouse joined them by unspoken agreement. And there was also agreement that there would be Bible study and prayer service. Warm. Informal. "Jesus-like," Tex said of it.

True marveled at her husband's unfailing patience with the questions of the five men. Tex possessed a homespun understanding, a heartwarming legacy left by his grandmother. The boy would feel comfortable if Jesus rapped on the door, invite Him in, and bring a footstool for propping up His feet in front of the pot-bellied stove. Augie, in contrast, was possessed with the devil of superstition, having heard nothing except the dark predictions of God's unquenchable fire of wrath. Slinger, convinced that he had failed so miserably in life that no "Power up There" could forgive him, found himself more comfort in doubting One's existence than to face judgment which was already pronounced. That left Pig Iron and Slim, both wanting desperately to hear the "Jesus Story" but hampered by wrong interpretations by people with closed minds, some of them ministers. True was amazed to hear their backgrounds, once their tongues were freed enough to share without shame—colossal ignorance thrust upon them by people who ought to know better.

Augie stumblingly blurted out his fears of being struck dead if he laid money on the altar ... set on fire by the "burning bushes" ... run over by chariot wheels while the dogs licked up his blood. Midgie's mouth made a capital O of horror. "So that's what he means by 'Los perros son muy mal' and runs from Tonsil and Lung," she whispered to True. "He's afraid of those gentle crea-tures—bless his heart."

"Augie," Young Wil said simply, "those ideas are enough to scare you to death—taken from scattered sto-ries in the Old Bible and given the wrong meaning. One day we'll take them up one by one. Agreed?"

Augie was only too glad to nod affirmatively, his dark eyes aglow with new hope. Marty saw and said in the same simple manner, "Wil—if I may make a suggestion? Could we, you think, begin with the New Testament and then go back to the Old?"

"Indeed!" Young Wil agreed, causing Marty's eyes to light with pleasure.

Together, with steaming mugs of coffee and butter-and-egg cakes, they traveled through the Gospels, pausing frequently to iron out the wrinkles of misunderstanding. The men relaxed and began to enjoy themselves, actually begging for more. "It's like music in my mouth," Tex commented one evening, licking his lips as if tasting the words.

"There's so much I still can't get through my skull," Slim said, the lines in his face crisscrossed with complexity. "Sorry, Mr. Wil."

Young Wil nodded. "I know, Slim. There's a lot that none of us understand completely. Remember that God knows we lack the background of those who knew Him in the flesh—and then gave His Story to the world. But the more we read and talk, the better we understand. The Holy Spirit helps us interpret—"

Augie cringed. "Eees like—uh, *el*—thee Holy *Ghost*?" He stumbled on *ghost*.

Thank goodness, True thought, my Wil understands Augie's fears. It was evident when he replied. "Let's not worry about that now, my good friend—just remember that God loves us and His Spirit *helps* us understand. You," he placed an arm around the Mexican man's shoulders, "needn't be afraid."

"Seems like it oughta be more simple," Slinger said slowly; "sez somethin' then rubs it out. I git wantin' t'believe, 'n along comes somebody sayin' it ain't so."

"If you went duck hunting, Slinger, what would you look for?"

"Ducks—hafta know what I'm lookin' fer."

"That's right—and if somebody tried to tell you it wasn't a duck?"

208

"Hit 'im in th' snozzle with th' butt uv my gat iffen he got twixt me 'n my aim, I 'spect."

The other hands snickered. Amusement lighted Young Wil's dark eyes, but he kept his face straight, his voice respectful.

"Without violence—maybe without convincing your fellow Nimrod—you'd know it was a duck no matter what others said."

"Meanin'," Pig Iron said slowly, "some uv other folks' opinions ain't a-gonna sway us none—just gotta keep a clear head."

"I think," Marty interjected, "that God's words are clear enough when it comes to teaching about His care for mankind such as us, about sin, repenting, asking forgiveness, and *knowing* it's ours."

"That's what faith is?" Slim asked in awe. "Believe 'n heaven's ours?"

"That's salvation fer y'all!" Tex said, boyish face lighted with pride in his formative theology. "Some folks go round 'n round over little ole nibbles uv th' Bible, git theirselves all hung up like a fence-breakin' steer in baling war—wire—but," suddenly he paused as if struggling with his own understanding, "how we gonna know 'bout which doctrines is false, Mr. Wil?"

"Remember what uh duck looks like!" Slinger said smugly. "I betcha these here ladies'd know, havin' plucked as many pin feathers as they have. Right, Miz True, ma'am?"

True hesitated, her eyes appealing to Young Wil. His smile reassured her and she spoke haltingly: "I guess we have to turn to the Bible and see which messages are essential—I mean, if doctrines—beliefs—show up once, maybe twice, and no more, they're less important than what Mr. Wil has told you—those that are repeated over and over by prophets, Jesus Himself, and the Gospel writers, who told the Story which saves us."

Where did the words come from? she asked herself. Why, the Holy Spirit, of course! But the men had heard

enough. She mustn't get preachy. Already their understanding was growing. They were learning enough so
that through more reading and prayer they could live
lives pleasing in the eyes of God. *And, I Lord, am learning right along with them.*

"How about another piece of cake?" True smiled
brightly.

"Bravo, bravo!" The chorus came from several of the
men. "Shore wisht we had a *git*-tar, Miz Midgie." True
held her breath, but Tex covered beautifully. "Whatta
trip in larnin'! Feel like I'd crost t'th other side uv th'
mountain!" he said.

34

Blessed
Are the Peacemakers

A guest "from the other side of the mountain" was soon to call on the neighbors of the Double N—the very day it warmed up, March first, to be exact. The magical month of March! Midgie's month of delivery. The expectant father was jubilant with expectation. True and Young Wil had never seen Marty like this, even in his childhood years. His behavior bordered on the absurd. *His* day was coming, Marty declared to anybody within hearing range. Not *Midgie's*, and not the *baby's* but *his!* The mood was contagious. Morale, which had remained surprisingly high during the imprisoning bitter cold, soared even higher with the burst of winter-pale sunshine.

It seemed fitting that Tex should come dancing in with a handful of rich, black soil—so shiny it resembled a lump of coal. "It's sproutin'—see, whadda y'all thank I been trying t'git acrost? Give 'er a week, two at most, 'n she'll shoot sky-high—see them roots? Th' sun's a-gonna shoot th' temp'ature up, drive out th' frost, 'n pull th' grain right outta th' grave by th' armpits! Give 'er a pair uv frog-stranglin' rains, 'n we can set by yonder winder 'n watch 'er grow. This strain'll explode like a cannon, I tell y'all. Best we git sharpenin' scythes 'n hook on th' cradles—" Tex paused to grin, "th' *other* cradle, 'sides th' one we been makin' fer Junior—"

The other hands looked at him darkly. It was the wrong thing to say. Here the cradle was to be a surprise, and he up and spilled his insides. Well, what was wrong with that? Everybody knew Miz Midgie was giving birth—*the Good Lord be praised!*—but so was Mother Earth! So Tex waved his work-worn hands in an arc and raised a defensive chin. "I cain't 'spect y'all to 'preciate th' sight yore pore eyes ain't seen—a gold mine growin' topside. We'll be rich—tickle yore ears, men?"

"Mine are already tickled!" Marty declared with a look at Midgie as tender as the green shoot of wheat that Tex had found. She responded with a smile of total contentment, no more concerned with the preordained delivery awaiting her than Tex was with his own birth of nature, knowing as he did that a hailstorm could abort his dreams. A lot was at stake—turning points for both of them. Failure, for whatever reason, could change their lives. Was their faith strong enough to withstand it? True prayed that it was.

She cast a quick look at her husband, caught him off guard, and saw a flicker of concern cross his face. Well, why not? He had stood by Marty in fulfilling his pledge to O'Higgin, worn himself thin trying to point out to these men who trusted him the difference between Paul's terminology, for instance, of practices he considered "disgraceful" and "sin," the paving stones to death—and the doctrine of faith, which spelled out salvation and godly life. And now he shouldered the burden of bringing a new life into the world. Failures could weaken immature faith.

True had thought of his responsibilities and how he had met them head-on with such strength, born of his faith, so many times. And each time she had said, "Darling, you're wonderful!"

"I know," he would say smugly, knowing what to expect.

And he was right. "Wil North—" and then she would fold herself into a little fetal ball in his arms, safe and secure in his love.

Now, as her mind wandered, so had the conversation. What were they trying to do, outbrag one another? Rich? Of course, they would be. Sure, sure, the wheat would help—it *should*, this being wheat country. But don't underestimate the thoroughbred horses, the cows, and—

All within the kitchen stopped rambling conversation and vagrant thoughts at the sudden commotion in the corral. Horses were neighing wildly and the bull was pawing earth as if digging for oil. The source of their indignation was clearly visible through the sunlit window.

A crude, homemade, two-wheeled cart pulled by an enormous beast was turning in at the gate. "Hallow! Hallow! Be there anybody home?"

"Mrs. Hancock, Anna-Lee Hancock," Young Wil said in surprise.

"A-drivin' Adam's off-ox," Slim marveled too innocently to be poking fun. "Th' lady's th' widder uv thet peace-lovin' juice harp player—'n his name *was* Adam, what kept cows from millin' with that—"

"Harmonica," Slinger supplied. "You know, Miz True, th' feller what helped you 'n Miz Midgie—then started up t'lend us a hand. 'Cept some coward shot 'im in th' back!"

"Bad news, else she's been t' a fun'ral," Slim said darkly of the tiny-frame lady dressed in black from her high-laced boots beneath a cheap, somewhat skimpily gathered long skirt to the enormous bonnet which all but covered her pale face.

"I be bringin' thee a chair of which I no longer have need—'tis a high chair for the little one." Adam Hancock's widow had skillfully looped the reins around the cart's brake, stepped gingerly onto the thawing ground, and was lifting the piece of hand-hewn furniture from the back of the wooden-wheeled vehicle before any of the men could reach her and assist. Young Wil was first to take the chair. "We've met before, Mrs. Hancock. Perhaps you remember—"

"I remember," she said simply. "I be bringin' my appreciation likewise—and some good news to thee. Wilt though be calculating the subject?"

True did so mentally. The railroads, of course. But where were her manners? She stepped forward, extending her hand. Introductions were quick and business-like, and the young Mrs. Hancock, about the age of herself and Midgie, True guessed, declined an invitation to come inside.

Feeling at a disadvantage, True expressed sorrow at the death of their guest's husband. Anna-Lee's response was unemotional. "He is not dead. We Shakers believe our loved ones merely cast aside our earthly garments and change forms of existence, no more. Believe ye God be King?"

All nodded. "Then ye be peace-lovers and lovers of the land that God meted out, knowin' it be ours to guard for Him, in peace with our neighbors. We do not fight. Neither do we be backin' away. It was my husband's assignment to watch over both sides of the hill. Music was his weapon."

And it got him killed, True read in the men's eyes. Some of them looked puzzled. Others, faces blanched, stood tongue-tied. This modest-appearing little mite was a brave one; she lived up to her beliefs all right! She had walked right in here and taken over "peacefully," while they—with muscle and brawn—stood speechless. There was sure a heap they'd need be asking Mr. Wil.

True's mind had tilted the same direction. Her husband had better prepare himself to explain how the Constitution guaranteed freedom of worship, and to use this as an example of how diverse religious groups could live in harmony—providing they practiced the first two Commandments and replaced prejudice with the charity that "neighborliness" demanded.

But for now True had lost out on the conversation, catching only enough to know that her hunch was correct: The news concerned the railroads. Eight men and one woman met in Slippery Elm, Anna-Lee was reporting—no, not herself. Shaker women took no part in business. 'Twas Mrs. Tillie "who be a shareholder too." The nine-member committee outlined a plan for presenting to the borrowed judge, a Judge Grover from Portland, and his assistant, Mr. St. John. Both men listened courteously. "Nobody be goin' around in circles, just questions and answers. 'Twas not they who caused bloodshed, 'twas outlaw masqueraders who had not the fear of God in their wicked hearts." Yes, Anna-Lee's black bonnet bobbed up and down, it was put to a vote, and the news was that there be an alternate route."

"You be meanin'—" Pig Iron began, then glowered when Slim and Slinger nudged each other at his copycat language. "*I* mean, we a-gonna join them bobtails? Jest surrender our property coward-like?"

"Them ragtag renegades cain't take our property—let 'em try!" Slim scoffed.

"Maybe not—" Marty said slowly (still unsure of his position on the Double N, *and*, True often suspected, often his manhood), "but they can make it so miserable that we would have to vacate."

Faces flushed with anger. The discussion showed signs of degenerating into wrangling. Young Wil, who had said nothing, opened his mouth, then closed it. Anna-Lee Hancock had seen the men's mood change. She had the facts, and with them an ingrained sense of fairness. Let her answer.

"Both be illegal, according to your laws. That be the decision rendered by Judge Grover. We have our rights and they have theirs. We joined hands against their injustice. And now it be fittin' that we join hands for compromise. Good day!"

The gallant little lady lifted her skirts and climbed into her cart with the same agility and speed used in climbing out. Then she was gone.

"I didn't even thank her," Midgie said. She was stroking the chair.

True inhaled deeply. "And I failed to invite her again—"

"She'll return," Young Wil said, "in time of trouble."

"Maybe there will be none," Marty said. "Things seem—different."

Slinger shook his head. "Blessed be the peacemakers," he muttered, tossing his gun on the table.

35

Time and Tide

The soft, warm rains of April came, but Midgie's baby did not. The prospective parents fretted with impatience in spite of Young Wil's reassurances that babies, especially the first, often took their time. Being late was far better than being early. But True doubted if they heard.

The world around them underwent a wondrous transformation. The odds in favor of Marty's making the Double N a lasting success were good. And he, like the springtime world, had undergone a transformation. It was hard to remember his outrage at being compelled to come here, his little-boy tantrums, and his inability to see himself faintly resembling a man capable of achieving a distant goal. The change which began slowly gained momentum, becoming so big that he seemed incapable of putting a lid on his ambition. Getting the books to balance was the biggest challenge of his life—until now. Now his entire world was crammed inside these four walls. The cabin was no longer a prison. Within this castle was the sum and substance of life, his crown of achievement—the baby! His and Midgie's. God had blessed them without measure, giving them a partner in their battle here. They were the predestined victors of all odds.

Nature seemed to agree. Midgie's hens hatched out baby chicks so round and fat that they resembled buttery dumplings; and the sweet-pea seed she had planted last fall all but obscured the cabin with their twining, blossom-strewn vines. Gardens flourished. Slinger announced arrival of "th' finest colt this side uv th' Mississippi" with a whoop surely heard in Slippery Elm. But Billy Joe had to "up'n steal my thunder," he declared when the foreman elbowed his way through the admiring circle of male spectators to yell, "It's a girl—fact o' th' matter bein' it's *twins*, much alike as coupl'a peas in a pod—*yippee!*"

Tex removed his hat in awed respect. "Whadda y'all know?"

"*Niñas*—gurls—lady Norths?" Augie stumbled over the words, then threw his sombrero to the ground and propelled himself up and down on it. "*Dos*—not one God send—two!"

"Weight, 'bout 40 pounds, I'd calculate," Billy Joe said importantly. "Legs wobbly, but standin' a'ready—all 40 pounds dry weight!"

The men were stunned—all except Young Wil, who winked at True through the window. She was uncertain what the commotion was about but realized that there was a comical misunderstanding even before Slinger, already piqued, bristled. The North baby was nothing this simpleton should joke about.

"Now, man, you gotta be spoofin'—ain't humanly possible—"

Billy Joe cast a withering look of pity at his challenger. He aimed his quick tongue, always sharpened and ready, at his target and hit. "May th' Good Lord gimme patience with th' likes uv you! Now, who said 'twas *human*? It's yore bounden duty t' be knowin' which cows is about t'freshen. Purdiest thangs on this ranch, barrin' th' ladies!"

An audible sigh of relief circled the group. A few tittered then, all eyes darting between the sparring men as if attached to a single pull cord, then seemed to think better of it. "Calves," Slinger was muttering, "when you knowed you was all-time misleadin' us—betcha weighed 'em together jest t'impress us..."

"Keep it friendly, fellows," Young Wil smiled. And, knowing that this was only the men's way of friendly chitchat, he signaled True with a wave of his hand. They must make a trip for supplies.

Tillie Caswell's cheeks rivaled the color of the bouquet of wild pinks she had gathered from the east meadow and bunched into a copper kettle adorning the piano top. The reason was immediately apparent: The Reverend Randy Randall had come again. What was not apparent was his look of concern as he talked in confidential tones with—of all people—the "man with the beaver hat." True, who had all but forgotten the stranger, questioned Tillie with her eyes. And, Tillie, instead of her usual palms-up response, averted her eyes ever so slightly as she rushed forward to embrace True warmly.

"Oh, I'm so glad you came—so glad of the early thaw—glad to show you the mail!" she exclaimed breathlessly—a little *too* gladly, True thought. But Young Wil had entered, was shaking hands with Mr. Caswell, and was explaining that, yes, all was well with Midgie, but they must take care of business quickly. He doubted if Marty was up to the excitement of delivering his first-born.

Tillie Caswell went for the mail, the skirts of her becoming gray dress swishing past her Reverend friend as if to whisper a warning. Randy Randall turned almost immediately to extend his hand while brushing away the heavy white hair which, when he was hatless, tended to fall into unwanted bangs over his glasses. He was talking away as Tillie had done, running sentences together, telling her that he had seen the Senior Norths and that they were fine and sent love. His owlish eyes held True's in a way that all but dared her to turn away. When at length his gaze released hers, the man in the beaver hat was gone. So was Mrs. Caswell—after accepting a note from the stranger.

"I don't understand; I simply don't understand," True said as they returned to the Double N. "It may be nothing—only I can't dismiss the idea of the man in the beaver hat. First talking to Marty, then the minister—and now Tillie. There's a missing link, but a link for sure."

Young Wil nodded in agreement. "Somehow I get the impression it has to do with Marty, but don't ask me what. I overhead mention of the railroads. They're all rooting for him and Midgie, you know, wondering what they'll do if the wheat fails—"

"It isn't going to fail!" No answer, so she thought aloud: "They could plant orchards—and there's always a market for vegetables now that the trains run more regularly."

"This isn't the Willamette Valley, darling," he reminded her gently. "It's better suited for grain and livestock. So's Marty. I do believe he's found his niche, and I would back away from suggesting a change. He has become more like this land and the people on it than he realizes. They'd switch their wives for total strangers before changing crops."

True squeezed his hand and laughed. "Good girl!" Young Wil visibly relaxed. "I was afraid we were on the threshold of interfering again." With that he shifted subjects.

"Did Tillie make mention of Anna-Lee Hancock?" When True shook her head, he continued: "They've met now that Mrs. Hancock must do the shopping. Curly filled me in on their background. A small band called True Believers came to the Oregon Country for the sole purpose of establishing peace. A few went seaward, and a few stayed here. That separated families. Persecuted, some changed names, which meant that they were never able to reunite. So I guess they added strangers to their list of abstinences—alcohol, tobacco, meat. They scarcely venture into society except to market their wonderful cheese and hand-carved furniture—just sustain themselves without friends."

"I was honored when Anna-Lee came," True said humbly, "and I am even more honored now." *But why are you telling me this?*

The answer came flatly: "Curly said Tillie pounded her with questions—about Marty. No more questions, True. He knows no more than that—the only subject, Curly says, which is closed between them. Tillie, by the way, seems almost cured—I'm the doctor, you know—so I prescribe...*this!*" He leaned over and kissed her soundly.

"*That*—without an examination?" True gasped when she could breathe.

"I know the needs of my patients," he grinned smugly.

"Wil North—" she began, then with a giggle, "continue treatment!"

The wagon creaked on, its riders silent with their thoughts—which True suspected, were very much the same, all of them questions. Now and then one of them spoke. *The Oregonian* carried a report of the agreement made by the railroads versus the homesteaders...another "Great Compromise," the story ran. "Not that morality and decency could be legislated...up to both parties," the article concluded. But the next edition would carry news that the Government had found a peaceful solution, differing only in its verbiage, St. John had told Curly. True half-listened, her mind still on Marty. What did the letter to him from O'Higgin contain? She had only scanned the bulky one from Aunt Chrissy. No real news. And what did that enormous package from Portland addressed to *Mrs.* Martin North hold? Midgie had no Meier & Frank catalog.

Even before the din of voices, True felt a sudden urge to get home. The voices grew louder, more frantic...Billy Joe and sons...dogs...*Marty*...

Midgie gave birth with Dr. and Mrs. Wil North's aid before the foreman and the boys had unhitched the team. A perfect specimen—nine pounds ("dry weight") of manhood, a powerful-voiced welcome addition to the human race. A miracle with a red face. The apple of a weeping father's eye. The fulfillment of woman's destiny to a misty-eyed mother who felt worthy at last.

Doctor and "nurse" tiptoed out, leaving the parents alone for the sacred moment to marvel at birth, to reaffirm their love—and to pray. "The time came—babies know," Young Wil grinned with just the right shade of pride in his own wisdom. True slipped an appreciative arm about him. *"Time and tide..."* Yes, the time had come. Somewhere behind, the tide was rising...

36

Bearing of Gifts

Marty's head continued to float in the upper ozone layer. His heart lay beside Midgie (obediently in bed by his orders). His arms folded around the "March Hare" (no name yet good enough), whom he allowed nobody to touch except in "emergencies." But his feet were planted square on the ground. He was obsessed with one question: *Would he see even a small profit on the Double N?* He was beginning to doubt it.

"I question that we will break even in spite of all the hard work on the part of the hands—and the dedication of you and the rest of the family," True overheard him tell Young Wil.

"Are you forgetting living expenses?"

The two men were in the bedroom where Wil was examining the baby. In the kitchen, preparing gruel which the new mother asked for, True could feel Marty brighten. "You mean I can count that in?"

"Of course. It's a part of the profit—"

"I just take cash on hand and subtract expenses? If we break even, I'm not ready for the trash heap?"

"Oh, Marty, don't say things like that!" Midgie's voice held a note of pleading. Then it strengthened. "I simply won't have you speaking of my child's father in such terms—as if he were a loser! How could you be when—do you mind," she paused uncertainly, "if—if I go on?"

True was so touched she almost let the gruel boil over. And how good to hear her husband's deep laugh. "Set him straight, Midgie!"

"You're forgetting something, Father Martin North! You and I have fulfilled every fine line of that trifling agreement—every fine-printed line. You were to stay put—"

True sensed that Marty's head jerked up sharply in preparation for giving a reproving look if she made mention of *her* leaving. Perhaps that had been the plan. If so, Midgie shifted emphasis quickly.

"And I was to present you with a child! If Irish O'Higgin can't be happy with that, we can start somewhere else."

"You're wonderful!" Marty's voice broke. "But" (stoutly) "I don't think that will be necessary." Neither heard Wil's bag snap shut.

Dr. North found his wife wiping her eyes with her apron when ne entered the kitchen. "Hey, none of that!" he said tenderly. Grabbing her around the waist, he danced her jubilantly around the kitchen while the gruel succeeded this time in boiling all over the stove.

Breathlessly, they wiped up the spoils and fanned the smoke out the window. Then they sat down while Young Wil gave True the diagnosis which the young parents had been sure of all along. "That is undoubtedly the finest baby I have ever seen—not a flaw. No man could do better!"

"*You* could!" True burst out, then blushed.

"Oho! Well, now—I'll take that under advisement. But not before the honeymoon! Do you realize, my darling, that we have never had one? I've been thinking—"

"Dangerous!" she teased.

"You'd better believe it! The year's up in— let's see, six weeks. By then we'll have cut the hay, sold off some livestock, and settled up with Marty. I know how much you want to get home—but I want to detour by way of Portland. I'll arrange to take my preliminary exam, and you can do the same. And then, Mrs. North, we will be alone!"

Marty's duty, as he saw it for the next week, was complete care of his son. He was deaf, dumb, and blind to other responsibilities, with his mind locked around his offspring. Why not indulge him, let him take command? True suggested. All of the ranch hands agreed, but Billy Joe did not. There was a man's work to be done. Wasn't Mr. Marty in charge out there, too? 'Course he was. Busiest time of the year approaching. The Double N demanded attention of the owner (wasn't that what he was to be?). Some things he didn't understand about this ranch, and there were times when he wondered who did. But one thing he knew: Mr. Marty was strong as an ox— and sometimes about as dumb. Babies were woman's work...so...

It was Billy Joe who sent Mariah to Slippery Elm to spread the news. Just why Tillie Caswell "went nigh on crazy" was another mystery. None of his business, of course. At least (proudly) 'twas himself, "The Foreman, the Beetle, the Thinker," who found a way to get the new father back into the fields. Miz Tillie and his Mariah simply shooed Marty out of the house and took over. He'd learn in time that the baby was mortal.

Tillie Caswell arrived and dumped packages on the kitchen table, upsetting a bouquet of wild larkspur in her mad dash into the bedroom. "Let me see him!" she cried excitedly. Grabbing the baby from Midgie's arms, she pulled back a fold of the baby-blue receiving blanket and buried her face against the downy fluff of dark hair that already showed signs of a question-mark curl on top. "Oh, you darling—you adorable angel—that's right, hold onto Great-Aunt Tillie's finger!" Seating herself in the cricket chair, she began to croon softly as she rocked him back and forth. "Oh, you're just what Auntie prayed for."

Auntie? Great-Aunt Tillie? Her titles probably meant the same as Miss Mollie's calling herself Grandma. But even as she tried to convince herself, True felt a nagging sense of doubt—a doubt which she saw reflected in Midgie's questioning face . . . something in the woman's past perhaps, having nothing to do with the Norths.

There was growing evidence to the contrary in the days to come. That it had to do with the North family revealed itself with startling suddenness. Or was it sudden? Actually the signs had been there all along, True realized later—little tremors preceding a major quake, followed by a never-ending wave of aftershocks.

But for now the Double N was achieving an air of busy normalcy. The "March Hare" (Uncle Wil and Aunt True declared it disgraceful that the King of the Glass Mountain bore no name!) was a good baby from the beginning. He awoke with a lopsided smile and cooed himself to sleep counting his toes, allowing Midgie to regain her strength, while Mariah assisted True with the household tasks. The men, busy getting livestock to market and early crops harvested, ate ravenously. Midgie's other hens hatched out their broods, which ate as heartily as the men. Surely every cow in the herd brought in a new calf, which meant churning, making cottage cheese, and storing away hoop cheese to age. Gardens continued to flourish. So there were canning and drying. And the irrigation system encouraged the wild berries to grow rank and hang heavy with jelly-ready fruit. True had never worked so in her life.

Mariah took over the laundry and cleaning. It was while she cleaned Midgie and Marty's bedroom that—in the process of mopping the rough-board floor—her rag mop stuck. In trying to loosen it, she reached beneath the bed and jumped back white-faced to declare there was a body beneath the bed. "*Si, si,*—yes, yes—ees a body, *Señora!*"

True was thankful that Midgie had gone for a walk so there would be no panic. "I doubt that, Mariah, but let's see. There should be nothing there," she managed to say calmly. A little apprehensively she felt beneath the bed slats. What she found surprised her more than Mariah's wild imaginings. There it was—the package that she and Young Wil had brought home on their last trip to Slippery Elm and had given to Marty because it was addressed to Midgie. And there on top lay the bulky letter from O'Higgin—unopened. Why, when it might be of utmost importance?

Marty chose that precise moment to come to the cabin for a drink of water. "Quick! Put it back—before she gets in—*hurry!*" His voice revealed a sense of urgency. "Forgive me—I'll do it myself. It—It's a long-overdue gift. But the timing has to be right. After all," he grinned, "others came bearing gifts."

True watched as he pushed the long box back in its hiding place. Relieved and touched, she reviewed the offerings of Tillie Caswell—pound cakes, hazelnut cookies, doll-size nightshirts, and the daffodil-yellow rompers, embroidered DOUBLE N RANCH, for the baby to grow into. Mariah had made some practical, loose-fitting morning coats for Midgie until she could get her figure back into its hourglass shape. Perhaps what touched True most of all was the dainty nainsook set of matching full-skirted slip and dress (made boyish by a tiny Peter Pan collar) which all but swept the floor. Light as swansdown and white as a snowdrop, the infant's garments were handmade by none other than the thoughtful Anna-Lee Hancock, then sent over by Mariah. After all, it was not proper for her to come in person unless by invitation, once she had paid a "duty call." True sighed. She must call on Anna-Lee—

Then her mind went back to the unopened letter. The envelope was sealed, but her lips were not. She no longer walked on eggs in her brother's presence. "Marty, shouldn't you open O'Higgin's letter?" True asked outright.

He paled slightly but answered with equal candor, "Yes, I should."

"Then?"

"I'm afraid to, darling." Marty's voice was so low that True had trouble hearing. "Midgie and I have built something special here—"

"You certainly have, my darling! We are *so* proud of you!"

"Thank you," he said humbly, "without you—well, O'Higgin saw the need and saw to it that we *weren't* without you. And, you know, I think Providence had a hand in the arrangement. God knew, too."

True laughed. "Marty North, are you stalling? Of *course* both of them knew. What make you think they would let you down now?"

Marty picked up the envelope, then hesitated. "We want to stay here so badly—"

"Open it!"

He slit the flap with shaking fingers, then scanned a page with a grin spreading across his face that made him handsome. Looking at the second page, he let out a whoop of joy. "They paid off...he paid off...we—we—we...oh, read it for yourself—there's more, but I have to find Midgie—YIPPEEE!

"Marty, you'll wake the baby!"

"Of course I will! He has to know! Get up, King of our Hearts, let's find Mommie!"

He lifted his March Hare, rosy with slumber but smiling, from the cradle and hugged True all in one fluid motion. Then, taking seven-league strides, he was gone.

The letter was cause enough for elation, Young Wil and True agreed, as (by Marty's request) they studied the contents. *What* paid off? O'Higgin's railroad shares. *Who* paid off? O'Higgin—with the dividends met his loan. And, of course, *we* meant Marty and Midgie, who would be allowed to stay on, having proven up on the claim *and* in the eyes of O'Higgin, in accordance with "terms thereof." "Two things I find puzzling," Young Wil said just as Billy Joe barged in, "how did they know about the—baby?"

True was glad he caught himself before saying that it too was a "term."

"Tillie hightailed it t'meet th' train 'n sent a telegraph—*gram*, tellin' dry weight—sooo (smug in his hold on all the world's wisdom) he's a'comin'—no need readin' on—that ole talker'll tell whut 'stay on' is!"

What *did* it mean? Another gift?

37

Bewildering Revelations

True loved mornings such as this. The world lay still in those magical moments of waiting for the mid-May sunrise. Although the air was motionless, yesterday's fragrances of sun-warmed hay mingling with the sweet breath of pink clover and early-blooming petunias lingered on. There was no sound except for a few twitterings of wrens nesting in the tulip vine and the crowing of Midgie's rooster, whose wake-up call was timed so precisely that surely the young braggart had clockwork inside him. True let her eyes wander dreamily to the illimitable spaces above a mountain peak, purpled by the distance. "How beautiful, Lord, how beautiful," she whispered. "I understand Your meaning, 'Be still and know that I am God.' "

She stood very still, listening. It was almost as if God were whispering in return, reminding her somehow of His Master Plan, the intermingling of His children's lives—each a part of the other to light His world. Soon she would be going home. But this was home too in her ever-broadening way of thinking. It would be sad, leaving. But, oh, the joy of being back with family! Was that how Jesus felt when He ascended beyond that purple mountain and returned Home to prepare a place for

those who chose to follow—torn between two worlds?
What a strange thought. And yet it persisted as her mind
gathered memories into a hasty bouquet as one plucks
flowers before they can face. In spirit Aunt Chrissy and
Daddy Wil stood beside her, offering love unlimited.
Joining them was Grandma Mollie and her practi-
cality...Irish O'Higgin and his bubbling laughter cou-
pled with such hallelujah-faith that it shook the rafters
when he sang—devout and God-fearing, but always
with a twinkle...Uncle Joe, dear Uncle Joe, taken so
young from Aunt Chrissy (but not before he led the
children—herself, Young Wil, and Marty—to the Lord),
just as Angel Mother had been taken from Daddy Wil.
Mother, tender and fragile as a white violet—so fair of
face, so filled with beautiful thoughts. Oh, God was kind
to let her memory remain so faintly yet so vividly, like a
whisper of Himself. Mother...singing to her bees...
ever saying that forgotten would be the long, dark winter when spring came over the hill...then they would
look for a last venturesome snowdrop and a first daffodil
that tied together the seasons...pruning the wayward
lilac so other blossoms could see the light. Mother...
lifting the wind-tossed rose to caress each petal into
place...planting a marigold seed and teaching True the
patience the seed must learn, patience to wait for the
first warm rain. "Life," she wrote in her diary, "lies
within each clod." And in that beautiful moment alone
with God, True became a part of them all, one with her
Maker—and overwhelmed with desire to leave a part of
herself with all whose lives she had touched.

At that moment the sun topped the eastern hill to set
the world aflame. And against that blinding color there
appeared a familiar figure, easily recognizable at a distance by his usual black coat. A fish basket swung over
his shoulder, but it was hard to tell if the good man was
going fishing or returning. Either way, his long strides
told her that he was in a great hurry. "True, True!"

Randy Randall panted; "make ready for the onslaught—
they're coming, all of them!"

This time *they* translated into such a horde that True
found herself wondering if war had been declared.
There were the infantry, the foot soldiers; the cavalry on
steeds that galloped along as if delivering Paul Revere's
message; and—well, what did one label those who rode
in "chariots," namely, buggies and wagons? Had they all
camped along the roadside to arrive so early? And what
on earth were they doing *here*?

Billy Joe had linked up with the group somewhere,
looking as if he should be blowing a bugle, waving a flag,
or ordering "Charge!"

Dazed, True picked out the familiar faces: O'Higgin...Tillie Caswell...Anna-Lee Hancock (here by
whose invitation?), wearing her dark cotton and looking
a bit less pale. And was she seeing things? Could it be?
Yes, there was Midgie's father. Who had notified Conductor Callison of his new grandson? Eagerly her eyes
scanned the faces, hoping in vain to see Aunt Chrissy,
Daddy Wil, and Grandma Mollie. But they were conspic-
uously missing. Irish O'Higgin was living up to the letter
of the law all right. Even though Marty and Midgie had
met all the other requirements of the crotchety old man's
will, O'Higgin would see to it that Uncle Artie's wish was
carried out. After all, two weeks remained before the
year was up. Only then could the young Norths be
reunited with Marty's family.

It was the Reverend gentleman who collected his wits
to greet them all. And it was Young Wil, Marty, and the
hands of the Double N who returned the greeting—
thanks to Billy Joe's wild dash into the fields to summon
them. Midgie, who had been nursing the baby, came out
and looked at the crowd uncertainly. Then, with a squeal
of joy, she was in her father's arms, weeping and laughing. "Oh, Daddy, Daddy—come see him—oh, the beautiful baby—*hurry!*"

Subtract two from the group, True thought foolishly. But add two more. She had caught sight of two men laden with briefcases and books but moving with purposeful strides alongside O'Higgin. Their faces were familiar, but—

"Thomas J. Riefe," Young Wil, who had worked his way to her side, prompted in a low voice. Oh, yes, the hog-jowled president of Centerville's largest bank, holder of the mortgage on the ranch. "And the pink-skinned man wearing Ben Franklin glasses was Uncle Artemis' lawyer." True managed to nod. Oh, yes—Isaac Barney, who prepared the will.

The trio was moving toward where the two of them stood. O'Higgin was embracing her warmly, reintroducing the two men who stood as sober as undertakers, and telling Young Wil to go for Marty. They—the Norths, O'Higgin, and "associates"—must caucus while the others prepared the feast (feast?). Then Midgie's father, Mrs. Hancock, the minister, and "another" would be joining them to "shed light on the matter," after which there would be a mortgage burning and—

"Surprise! Surprise!" somebody was yelling tardily, followed by a chorus of congratulations. Then the group set to work in an orderly fashion—kindling a bonfire for barbecuing, unloading food, setting up tables. It was organized bedlam, while True felt herself being led into the cabin, wondering if she had spoken a word . . .

"So—tell me," Isaac Barney began as he peered over his half-glasses at Marty. "Has this been a banner year for wheat?" he said once they were seated.

"Yes, according to what I know of wheat's history here—" Marty began uncertainly. He shifted uneasily in his chair, looking at Midgie.

"Turn a profit?" The lawyers eyes were interrogation points of suspicion.

Marty flinched. "My husband is too modest," Midgie interrupted, adroitly walking between Marty and the owlish man. "You can examine the books for yourself. And," turning with a fond smile to O'Higgin, "I am sure you know," she said proudly, "that Tex's experiment with the red wheat was a whopping success. In fact, he developed a heartier strain—one which Marty feels he can patent. One seed company is interested—"

Billy Joe, not to be ignored, barged in. "Heered a part uv thet," he said, removing his shapeless straw hat, " 'n figgered you'd be needin' more input. Me 'n Slinger got ourse'ves th' finest herd uv Shorthorns in these here parts. Guess we all showed you city fellers a thang or two—eh, Mr. Wil? 'N Slinger's steeds claim second t'none—"

True saw the look of consternation that Mr. Barney aimed at the foreman. She also caught the tightening of Marty's lips, the look of doubt that crossed the threshold of his features. But his eyes filled with appreciation when he looked at Midgie. *We tried—even if we failed—*

"Pardon me, Mrs. North," Isaac Barney said, ignoring Billy Joe completely, "but I was examining your husband—"

"*Examinin'*, be ye?" O'Higgin's voice filled the kitchen and floated out the window. "We have a bank examiner here if there be a need—though his mission be more t'do with railroadin'. 'N there be a company detective seekin' out any hocus-pocus—so how come ye go scoldin' th' lass? Midgie here be 'is pardner—'n th' lad's one mighty lucky mon—man—'avin her likes. Many a lad's been known t'go cringin' through life, all fer th' need uv a good wife standin' by for cheerin'! Git on with th' terms 'n th' signin' over th' deed. I be satisfied!"

True's mind took a dizzy turn, then settled down to questions. So the banker's business must be the railroad shares. That figured, since they went with the original ranch, perhaps spilling over into the claim on which

Marty and Midgie had proved up according to the agreement. The railroad detective puzzled her. Was there a stranger in the crowd? Perhaps, since she was too surprised to greet each guest individually—doing well to murmur welcoming platitudes. The talk was a rehash of the terms of the will, which she knew by heart. Interesting, yet she felt her eyes drawn to the window. And there she saw Tillie Caswell engaged in conversation with none other than the man who had been the object of so many questions in True's mind as to his identity—the "man wearing the beaver hat."

There was sudden quiet, broken only by the scratching of a pen. "We'll need your signature too, Mrs. North, as witness of the fact."

What fact? True had lost out. She looked at them all apologetically—a grave source of irritation to the lawyer, judging by his condescending be-kind-to-dumb-women look. His round face wrinkled, making him look somewhat like a withered apple. His eyes were tiny green flames. Oh, dear! But the others looked elated. Elated, yes—and, in Marty's case—overwhelmed. So something wonderful had happened. Young Wil cast her a look of pride, and he irritated the squat little lawyer still further by extending O'Higgin's defense of Midgie.

"Well, since we're passing out compliments—O'Higgin having said that Marty could never have accomplished all he has here without his wife—Marty and Midgie's saying that they could not have done so without me, may I add that I could never have fought the good fight without the most wonderful wife in the world—a little brattish, but wonderful!"

"Wil North," True began, forgetting that they had an audience. Then, quickly, "The pen, please—"

" 'N th' lassie trusts us, begorry! Nice lassie she be. Observant one, too—noticin' th' mon—man—speakin' with Tillie. Might as well be callin' 'em in—her 'n th' detective. More compliments! Without Detective Dansworth there, th' one what be wearin' th' fancy hat, Tillie

Caswell never coulda regained whut be lost, includin' 'er sense uv whut was a-goin' on in God's great footstool. 'N," the great man lifted his chest high with triumph, "Martin North here woulda never known 'is background...*Come on in!*"

38

Things Always
Turn Out Right

With her breath coming hurriedly and her heart pounding, True listened to a resumé of Uncle Artie's will. In the thin spots, something told her that O'Higgin and the lawyer acted in the capacity of the Supreme Court in its interpretation of the Constitution. Certainly she had never expected that she and Young Wil would be involved in something that Isaac Barney breezily waved away in rambling paragraphs as "spirit of the law." She concentrated with an effort.

"He—the deceased—wished him who proved up on the claim, that is to say, the *new* ground, to have this," he said, beginning to wheeze a bit as he fumbled in his black bag to draw a small prayer book from among the other papers. So—?

The lawyer held out the book with a questioning look in O'Higgin's direction. The response was immediate—and shocking. "Mr. and Mrs. Wilson North, Junior," he said with a ring of power in his voice.

But—but this was not right. There had to be some mistake. True's eyes moved to catch Young Wil's, but he was accepting the book and nodding as Mr. Barney's wheeze developed into a sneeze which sent the papers askew. "Ragweed," he said wiping his eyes and ordering that certain marked passages be read aloud.

"I'm not sure I understand—" True let her voice trail off uncertainly. "*You* were the heir," she said to O'Higgin. "And—"

O'Higgin let out a whoop of amusement. "Ye be wonderin' who owns 'said property,' " he mimicked. "Sometimes methinks these lawyers be paid t'muddy th' water. Never mind, Barney, me good man. 'Tis best I tell 'em in plain English—jest be holdin' yore peace 'n *all* will read th' bloomin' paper if 'twould please ye."

The words tripped from his tongue lightly—rapidly but clearly—the flow unbroken by the arrival of Tillie, Anna-Lee, the Reverend Randy (carrying a Bible), and Daniel P. Dansworth (carrying his hat!).

Marty and Midgie were now owners of the original Double N, O'Higgin explained, while Young Wil and True owned the newly acquired property completing the vast acreage that Uncle Artie desired. The four were to "make no never mind" about him and his Miss Mollie. They would retain most of the railroad shares, as Superintendent Emory Keeling deemed proper, a few falling to the four joint owners, to whom he would turn over his proxy—all right, all right, Barney, make it "power of attorney"—as long as they could lift the burden from his shoulders. Why should a pair the age of him and his Mollie-gal have to traipse for meetings, voting, and signatures?

"None." The banker spoke for the first time revealing a mouthful of gold teeth which protruded enough to give his face a rodent-like expression. "I will take care of matters at the bank and keep you informed as to best investments, how to set up trust funds, and—"

The lawyer mopped his brow. "The reading," he reminded, obviously eager to complete the transaction and escape from Ragweed Ranch.

To everyone's surprise the Reverend Randall stepped forward. "A prayer book, I do declare—and my friend

Artemis' at that," he said in awe. "May I please see it once more? I read from its pages through the passing of the old man's spirit. It—it is a special book—the one I used for his own ceremony. Yes—Artie was married, but briefly. His beloved wife was taken early by a dread disease—but that is another story. He was hopelessly sentimental, but hid his true emotions—we were dear friends—dear, dear friends—"

"Well, *somebody* take it!" Isaac Barney said sharply, holding a finger beneath his reddening nose to forestall a sneeze.

The minister obliged by taking the book from Young Wil's hand. "Well, I'll be," he murmured, "the very words that Artemis and Miss Betsy said—and asked the congregation to repeat along with them—how about it, Irish?"

"You read 'em good feller, 'n we be repeatin'. "

Wilt thou take this loved one...to have and to hold...to live as one, according to God's holy ordinance...forsaking all others...until one shall lay the other in the arms of Jesus?

True stood transfixed for a moment, aware only that the kitchen-window curtain moved in and out as if inhaling and exhaling. The wind had changed directions which meant that the sun was moving westward as if the day had held too much already. But there was more. Much more...

Her husband laid a gentle hand over the icy fingers which must be hers. "Well," he whispered, "how do you feel, my darling?"

"Married—oh, *very* married," True breathed.

His ardent dark eyes met her violet ones. "You'd better!"

Around their private world there was sudden stirring. "Only key parties are to remain!" Isaac Barney ordered. Tillie Caswell was saying, "Things always turn out right." And outside Mariah began the soft melody of a Mexican wedding song.

39

The Residue
and Remainder

It was a case of déjà vu. True felt the same premonitory thrill race up and down her spine that she had felt—had it been only a year ago?—when the bespectacled Isaac Barney pursed his lips and read the will of O'Higgin's uncle.

"And now," he said importantly licking his lips as if to taste his words in advance, "the residue and remainder—the most important item of all." Looking over his glasses, the lawyer spaced each word, pausing between to let his full meaning soak in: "Establishing—proper—identity—of—one—individual. *Martin North, do you know who you are?*"

There was a dramatic pause.

At last Midgie lifted her great eyes, so large that they looked unreal in her childish face. But there was nothing childish in her manner. "Tell them, Marty. Whatever this man has to say cannot touch what we have—together."

Marty's hand reached out to grasp hers as if for support, but his voice was strong. "I do not know my background, if that is what you ask. But it is unimportant—"

239

Isaac Barney cleared his throat. "It is *very* important to the persons who have worked so diligently to trace it for you."

Tillie could wait no longer. "Tell him, for goodness sake!"

From that moment on the Norths became spectators of a play which was stranger than fiction. And soon to join them in the grandstand was Isaac Barney himself. After all, he was outnumbered by those with speaking parts. But they could not rob him of his rightful position. So he sat back with an air of authority that one usually associates with a prime minister or other visiting dignitary ready to challenge irregularities.

Somehow Tillie Caswell took center stage first. "This is a great moment in my life—the moment I have hoped for, prayed for, since losing track of my precious Hildred, my niece, my baby, her parents being killed in an Indian raid. I looked and I looked—all the way from Mount Lebanon, New York, to Portland. There was no sign, no trail of the little angel I had raised in my own faith but encouraged to learn of her parents' beliefs in the Shaker movement. Then," Tillie sucked in a painful breath, "she broke my heart, marrying so young as she did to a young man whose name I didn't even know. Oh, how can I ever forgive myself for—for the dreadful words I said? But for me, she might be here—and to think I objected to a Shaker husband after having her learn—"

The Reverend Randall rose from his chair to place a comforting arm around the shoulders of his friend. "Tillie, don't! Please do not torture yourself. You tried—we all did! And God *did* hear our prayers. He sent us these helpful friends who, each in his own way, led us to—him—and now you have a remnant. A fine one, I might add!"

"If thou wilt allow me to speak?" Anna-Lee Hancock lifted a slender hand, the long sleeve of her black cotton showing wear at the armpits.

All nodded. " 'Twas not thee who kept you apart. There was a time when those departing Mount Lebanon were not allowed to return. How be it then that the young woman did not bring the husband and come to thee?" Adam Hancock's widow shook her head. " 'Pride goeth before a fall,' I believe the Good Book be saying it. And the Higher Authority saith, 'Blessed be the peacemakers.' Be there bitterness left in thy heart?"

"Bitterness?" Tillie Caswell's eyes widened in surprise. "Oh, no, *no*—just remorse—no, not even that, for God has forgiven me, given me peace, happiness—restored my soul and my family!"

The other woman's eyes searched the hills as if seeking words.

" 'Twas worth the risk then of having coals of judgment heaped upon my head. If thou art at peace, thou willst be willing to restore me to the same state. So 'tis I who be seeking forgiveness for deceptions—shame I may have brought thee and thine house—"

"*You*? Not you, Anna-Lee! It would be impossible for you to offend," Tillie said reassuringly. "But," with a smile, "if it will make you feel better, what is this dreadful thing you have done?"

"I am the barbed-wire lady!"

An audible gasp circled the room. Then silence.

" 'Twas my means of gathering information for thee—and bringing peace to the valley. My people make the wire as a means of livelihood without feelings of guilt. 'Tis better that barriers separate the cattle and sheep than that men slaughter one another, offending God. But our men dare not offer the wire lest they be hanged—leaving behind families—as I have lost my husband by bullets. Punish me if it be thy wish—"

"Nobody is going to punish you, Anna-Lee. You are courageous—a fine lady. And your husband died a hero, remember that! But I guess we are all wondering why you choose to to tell us this—and at this time?"

"It *be* the time! I sought for thee information nobody else could have found among those who knew that Mrs. Caswell's niece was one of us. I be the one who could get them to speak. Others, our enemies, knew of the railroad shares, wanted the wire, and—and—forgive me, exchanged information which made my dear husband able to sign verification papers—just be saying I am forgiven my transgressions—"

"Transgressions, me foot!" O'Higgin boomed. "You were a key witness. We be praisin' th' Lord for th' likes o'you! Now, 'tis a time to be happy, not a time to weep. Tell th' good woman, Tillie!"

"I love you for what you have done," Tillie Caswell said humbly, knowing that her wonderful friend would be embarrassed by a caress. "You are sure—all of you? It—it sounds too good to be true. Oh, bless you all—I could take no more heartbreak—you are *sure*?"

"Shure 'n they be shure, me bonnie one. Reassure 'er Dansworth!"

At O'Higgin's command Daniel P. Dansworth went into action. Opening a portfolio of papers, he shuffled through them with an expert hand. "The birth certificate," he said without inflection. "It puzzles me as to why the party involved never bothered to question the attending physician." Before there was time for a response, the railroad detective held up other supporting papers tracing the Missing Person across the nation from Mount Lebanon into Oregon Country—and finally the death certificate for both her and her husband. "Cause: drowning of the latter—that would have been the Great Flood which all but wiped out the valley. The lone survivor being an infant son—no name, of course, as the former, your niece, died in childbirth, without gaining consciousness. The child was born posthumously nothing but a miracle that he survived. It took expert skill!"

"Uncle Wil has that—together with faith which sustained us all."

Young Wil's voice was the first from the audience. The performance had seemed unreal. Not one mention of a name. The miracle baby, *Marty!* True hardly dared glance at him. Would his face be blank with shock? Would he revert back to his former state of rebellion, self-pity—resentments which even he had been unable to explain?

None of these! Marty, gripping Midgie's hand, leaned forward, face aglow as if he were an architect ready to build a house that lightning would bounce off. And, in a sense, that summed it up. His faith, much like the wheat, was ripening. God had opened the windows of heaven for him and Midgie, raining down blessings. Their house would stand.

True had a strong desire to stand on tiptoe and shout. It was with an effort that she brought herself back to the occasion's solemnity.

"Then my name was Martin all along—never mind whether first or last. Daddy Wil brought me into the world and the wonderful woman—Aunt Chrissy to Young Wil and True—was then the wife of Brother Joe, who saved my life in another way. And they took me in— as their own?" Marty's question needed no answer. "Oh, I owe them so much—as I owe the rest of you. Tell me the whole story—the part each of you played in locating me, giving me a heritage to add to the already rich one. We— Midgie and I—want to be able to hand it down to our son."

Everyone started talking at once, Tillie Caswell's voice rising above them all. After all, *she* had seniority, being the nearest relative—a great-aunt to one Martin North, which made her a great-grand-aunt to that precious "nameless child" (such a pity!). But *she* had a name for herself—"Grandy" she was to be called, and—

The lawyer shifted positions. "Shall we say 'Case closed'?"

No, no, *no!* This man had a right to know the story— even asked for it. It seemed they were *all* doing some digging at the same time. Fate brought them together. *"God!"* Reverend Randall corrected, repeating what Tillie had said before. How he stood by, helped search, *prayed.* "All roads lead to Rome," somebody quoted, bringing the slate-eyed detective in touch with Midgie's father and then to the banker because of railroad connections. Yes, Mr. Callison knew there were questions—even (*ahem*) problems when his Midgie came to Portland craving more schooling. O'Higgin's homework was done for him, actually. There remained only a verification by the late Adam Hancock—with one detail missing, the family tree. Being a man of mental muscle, a party wishing to remain anonymous had studied genetics extensively and had found O'Higgin to be a "long distance" cousin to the Martins! With that announcement, Isaac Barney gave up any idea of restoring order.

40

"If Music Be the Food of the Soul..."

It had been a long day. The weary sun sought refuge behind a white city of skyscraper-clouds, pausing only long enough to light each window with red-gold light. Above the spectacle a crescent moon smiled in anticipation, while down the hill what had been a busy murmur of voices skipped several octaves, becoming an impatient ring: "Come, *come*, COME!"

In response, those in the small kitchen filed out one by one—all except Marty, who remained behind to check on his son. When Midgie would have remained with him, Marty shook his head. A look of hurt crossed her face briefly. Then she too went outside, where, the clamoring crowd reminded them all, it was time to view the sunset.

Again the overpowering sense of déjà vu. Had it *really* been a year since the four Norths came here scarcely aware of their mission? True wondered as she gripped Young Wil's hand, meditating with the others at the glory of the sunset. Truly, sunsets were beautiful here. One could see so far in the open country she had grown to love. In an odd sort of way, she would miss it. It occurred to her then for the first time that they were part-owners here. What would they do with the land?

The question went unanswered. Randy Randall was reading from Bible passages especially selected about friendship. And, bless their hearts, Tex, Slinger, Slim, and Pig Iron boomed out the heartiest *Amens* in the crowd. Augie, grinning widely, made his way to Mariah's side.

There, without aid of a musical instrument, the two of them joined in a soul-touching a cappella duet. In English! Their voices throbbed across the meadows, echoing and reechoing "What a Friend We Have in Jesus"—obviously planned in advance, as no words were spoken.

Marty politely waited until the hymn ended. Then he stepped to where they stood and said, "May I ask that my wife be allowed to join you in the next song?"

At Mariah and Augie's delighted smile, an amazed Midgie walked uncertainly to his side. Midgie's white face said plainly that she was remembering the shattering incident at the Roundup Barbecue. Marty was too— but in a far different manner, True realized, as he handed her the mysterious package she recognized immediately as the one he had kept hidden.

Fumbling at first, Midgie began tearing away the wrappings. Then, excitement growing, her fingers tore at the last scrap of paper and, with a squeal of joy, she flung open the box. As if handling a sacred instrument, she withdrew a deep-blue velvet carrying case, snapped open the hinges, and lifted a concert-size guitar made of the finest variegated rosewood. As tenderly as she handled the baby, her fingers stroked the ebony fingerboard's raised frets, three pearl position dots, and nickel-plated tailpiece. "Oh, Marty, Marty—" was all she could manage as the prolonged "Oh-h-hhhh" of onlookers rose to a chorus of "Play, Miz Midgie. Play. *Play.* PLAY!"

Misty-eyed but sure of herself, Midgie obliged, her gifted fingers strumming music from the steel strings that surely angel harps would find difficult to rival. Her touch was that of a master, delicate and commanding, as she entertained the speechless crowd with a repertoire of Schubert's serenades. Then, her eyes alight with a near-holy glow, she lifted her face to the stars. "Sing with me!" she called out gaily, and began with old familiar favorites. Hymns. Cowboy songs. And, finally, a simple Spanish song dedicated to Mariah and Augie. Spectators, unfamiliar with the language, hummed and whistled and laughed.

Midgie's already-flushed cheeks took on a deeper tinge. A breeze still warm from the sun and spiced with meadow grasses danced in to stir the curls at the nape of her neck. She was a daughter of the soil now—the vagabond impulses gone. And she was a mother! That accounted for the added shine, True thought wistfully. *Now, now, no coveting*, she scolded herself; *my time will come.*

Midgie (who, like True and Mariah, had changed hastily into the fiesta dresses) faced her cheering audience with a bright smile. Then, rising from the bench that Augie had pulled forward for her, she said resolutely, "I wish to dedicate the next number to my husband and then—"

But the soft strains of "Let Me Call You Sweetheart" drowned out the words which completed the sentence. The near-recklessness of her previous singing was gone, her voice almost pleading in its throbbing sweetness. True's heart turned over inside her, and without warning she felt her own voice join the other girl's. The others, too, joined them in a salutation of greeting and farewell, with love, affection, and kindness between. It was a love song of the heart. Midgie and Marty forgot the rest of the world.

Young Wil was making his way toward her when both of them heard the baby's wail for attention. "Uncle Willie will check on him." He managed to mouth the words to True with an apologetic grin. But the young lord-and-master of the household was already in the arms of his "Grandy" Caswell. And Young Wil was further detained by one of the men who wanted him to sample the barbecue. The crowd was starving.

In that brief moment Michael St. John stepped from the shadows to stand beside her. "Michael! You're here—I'm glad." And, oddly, she was.

He nodded, face altered by something resembling compassion in the gathering twilight. "If music be food for the soul, play on..." he said softly.

41

Anonymous Donor

Around them voices diminished to murmurous, near-inaudible conversation as people consumed unbelievable amounts of food. True felt no desire for eating; her mind was too filled with questions which could be answered only as the full story unrolled of its own momentum. A certain sad-sweet emotion swept her being, intensified somehow by Michael's unexpected appearance; or was it his Shakespearean quote, revealing a softer side to him than she had known, which undid her? He was a master of diplomacy, to be sure, but this was different.

True blinked in an effort to rid her eyes of unexplained tears. Michael mustn't see lest he misinterpret. The fragrant air was settling to the chill quiet of near-darkness. To regain composure, she looked up the incline to where the irrigation pipes began. The little ripple of water was willow-fringed now, the dark green of the leaves silver-dappled by the infant moon. A faraway coyote howled mournfully.

Michael cleared his throat, uncertain of himself for the first time. "You must wonder why I came—like," he said with an attempt at lightness, "the uninvited evil witch at Sleeping Beauty's christening. But remember," he rushed on, "that the seven good fairies were each to bear a good gift. So—will it change my image if I tell you that I have brought my token of affection?"

Caught by surprise, True could ask only, "Toward whom?"

"Everyone—but more especially you. Will you—drat it all, I hate it when I'm sentimental! So will you do the honors after I leave?"

"Of course—but what about your image? Aren't you holding something back? It would please Midgie and Marty so much and—"

"I prefer to remain an anonymous donor, True—so will you please?"

"Of course," she answered, her mind elsewhere. *Anonymous donor.* "Anonymous person." They had to be one and the same.

"You are the one," she said slowly, "who traced Marty's family, giving him and Midgie the identity they wanted. Oh, Michael, I'm so grateful—you did for them what you did for me in Atlanta—and I—I—am afraid I never thanked you properly."

"Please, no gratitude. Just a part of my job." Michael St. John ground the words out as if to recapture his stampeding composure and drag it back to safer ground. "I am a railroad executive. As such, I am compelled to trace backgrounds, locating the missing persons who hold shares. It's that simple."

"That isn't simple and you know it."

"It was in Marty's case," he replied quietly, having given up all attempts at levity. "A lot of the research was done already. I think you know that was necessary when he ended up in trouble by resorting to near-criminal means to stop the railroads from cutting through what he saw as land belonging to homesteaders. When records showed his link with the Caswell family, you can guess the rest. Martin North holds stock in addition to the Caswell shares—and that, my dear, is the gift I bear. The news, I mean—and a—a family tree for the baby—now be merciful and don't laugh—"

"I'm not laughing," True whispered unevenly. "Oh, Michael—"

Michael drew an uneven breath. At that point he could have embraced her and she would have considered it a friendly gesture. But he did not so much as touch her hand. He was, after all, a gentleman—a gentleman-scroundrel perhaps at points, but a gentleman all the same.

Voices had risen again. True turned back to the platform in time to see the long, flapping garment, the Reverend Randy Randall's differentiating trademark, pushing through the crowd. Beside him were Marty and Midgie, both looking over the heads of all others in search, she somehow knew, of herself and Wil. It was the part she dreaded: the farewells.

"I must go." Turning on her heel, True would have joined them but was delayed by Michael's urgent plea for one minute more.

"True, I wanted you to know that Felice and I are no longer together. She has gone home—to stay—along with her pompous brother—"

"I'm sorry, Michael, I truly am. A broken marriage—"

He sighed. "It was no marriage at all. Someday, if I am very, very fortunate, perhaps I will meet someone—forgive me for bringing up the past, but I met that someone once—and was fool enough to let her slip through my money-grasping fingers—"

"It wouldn't have worked, Michael," she said gently. "And, as for meeting another—surely you know that you are bound in the eyes of God to Felice. Marriage vows are sacred and binding."

"Ours were neither—either in the eyes of our Maker—or ours—not even legally binding. Felice plans an annulment—"

Shocked, True looked at him in disbelief.

"Our marriage meant nothing to either of us. Don't be embarrassed by this, but it was never consummated—"

White-faced in the glow of outside lanterns, she faced him. "Why are you telling me this?" she whispered.

"I feel a need to purge my soul," Michael said miserably. "You promised to pray for me a long time ago, and I guess it is working. I'm not a bad person at heart—just suffering from some wrong upbringing. And now guilt and disillusionment with the principles I was taught to build my cathedrals on haunt me. Thank you for all you have taught me."

"I have done nothing—nothing at all—except pray. God has done the rest. Oh, Michael, I do want you to be happy—like I am."

He laughed. "I doubt if anybody else could be *that* happy. But—who knows, as you say, what God can do? But just one last gasp before I surrender completely—let me say that if I didn't admire and genuinely like that lucky chap of yours, I'd break his kneecaps!"

True, feeling a bit giddy from lack of food and the long, exhausting day, laughed with him. "I think I've witnessed a miracle," she said—not sure whether she spoke to Michael St. John or their Lord...

———

A radiant True joined her husband at the platform, now an altar. He took her arm as she lifted the full skirt of her fiesta dress to clear the rough boards. Taking their place beside Midgie and Marty, who stood before the Bible-in-hand minister, True was surprised to have a cocoon of soft flannel thrust into her arms by "Grandy." The March Hare! At first she held him gingerly, as a maid of honor holds the bride's bouquet—ready to relinquish him on signal. Then from the cocoon there came a gentle coo as a wee, pink foot emerged. Forgetting the onlookers, True pulled back the soft blue blanket and laid her face against the warm, satiny cheek, a flood of deep emotion coloring her face. But why was Young Wil so touched? Surely he had seen a woman's face caress a baby's a million times over. But not hers, she realized ...

"Hear, hear!" True scarcely recognized Marty's voice. "As you know, Reverend Randy is here to perform weddings, comfort those who mourn—and christen our babies. Midgie and I want to dedicate this child to our Lord and Saviour—"

When his voice broke, the proud minister took over. "I christen Christian Joseph Martin North—"

Christian Joseph Martin North, sensing that unfamiliar arms cradled him, let out a lusty yell. Midgie reached for him. Making no attempt to hide her pleasure that this special child already recognized the loving hands of his mother, she leaned down to croon softly to the smartest child in the world—deaf to the rest of the ceremony.

Marty, standing straight and tall, listened intently as the minister read Hannah's promise to dedicate to the Lord's service the son she prayed for, followed by the words of Jesus: "Suffer little children to come unto me ... for of such is the kingdom of God."

That was Marty's cue. With a nod from Randy Randall, the proud father stepped forward to delineate the March Hare's name. "I have found my own lineage through the birth of our child," he said simply. "By coincidence, both my natural grandfather and my wife's father bore the given name of Christian—and there are two further reasons for our choice. His mother and I wish to rededicate our lives to Christian service—and then there is my wonderful mother, the only one I have ever known, Midgie's Aunt Chrissy—" Marty's voice faltered. Midgie reached out one hand to offer encouragement, tears sparkling in her twilight-blue eyes, and he was able to go on. "Joseph, known as 'Brother Joe,' was her first husband's name. It was he who baptized Wil, True, and me, for he—God bless him—took me in as his son." Again the catch in his voice. And then: "They gave me the name of Martin—because Martin, I have learned

through Tillie Caswell, my great aunt—that's right—"
he said above the gasp and applause, "Aunt Tillie,
'Grandy' to Christian, is family—as were the Norths,
who befriended me when 'Brother Joe' was killed—"

There was a subdued sniffle, followed by a chorus of
sniffles, with Tillie Caswell leading the Great Weep
which swept through the audience. When at last Randy
was able to break in, it was to announce the baptism of
Tex, Augie, Slim, Pig Iron, and Slinger this coming Sun-
day. Unless there were others—? It was then that
Michael St. John, the "anonymous donor," stepped out to
offer his heart openly...

42

The Leaning Tower

Night rang down its curtain. The air tingled with the arid smell of smoke, a reminder that ashes were all that remained of the mortgage on Turn-Around Inn. The only sounds, besides the operatic croak of frogs along the riverbanks in Peaceful Valley far below, were the subdued dialogues between departing guests.

Had there ever before been such a night? So happy? So sad? So filled with mysterious events? A night of revelations for sure. Just went to show you (on this they agreed) that mankind neither knew all the answers, nor would he ever. The human brain could cram itself chuck-full of knowledge, but wisdom belonged to God. Fact was, that creation time appeared to be a beginning, not an end. Why, creation was going on all around them. Pretty sobering, but the Almighty must have left the rest of the work up to His people, with so much remaining to do that He just kept on recruiting. Look at what He'd done with those "losers" hired on at the Double N. Would anybody have thought of *them* as being worth their salt? Anybody, excepting, that was, the Norths? Here those four young folks had come in acting like greenhorns and turned out to be mouthpieces for the Creator. They had downright surprised everybody—maybe even themselves.

Either way, the valley, including Slippery Elm, would never be the same. Just take a look at Miz Tillie's shining face. Look at the change.

Yes, take a *good* look—one that penetrated the heart. Tillie Caswell was darting from guest to guest making sure that every one of them had a good look at the only remaining member of her bloodline—carrying on the family name and destined to change her world, maybe the *whole* world. He had restored her sanity and her soul. Christian Joseph Martin North in a place called "Slippery Elm" was unthinkable. The foul name must be changed. Better get started on that before that big-city lawyer left...

The "big-time lawyer," his face again crinkled with worry lines (which made him look all the more like a withered russet apple), was conferring with the gold-toothed banker, who was smiling like an acre of sunflowers. Life, the two of them communicated unwittingly, was all in how one looked at it. The hog-jowled banker Riefe, having surrendered the mortgage, was already dreaming up other schemes for the new generation. Let that worrying attorney sneeze and fret a spell over the change in ownership, heirs, and railroad dividends. No, that was the mysterious Daniel P. Dansworth's lookout. Fact of the matter, he was doing so now. And sure enough, the railroad detective had joined the two men. Must be smarter than he looked. Still, he'd had the help of them all, squeezing out information the way he did as subtly as the "Ole Deluder hisself." Never could have completed his search, or course, without help from Tillie Caswell and that Mrs. Hancock. Unbelievable that the little Miz Hancock (right sweet when a body got to know her) promised to bring the entire flock of Shakers to witness the baptism...

"Jest sum it all up this away," said Billy Joe, who seemed blessed with a thousand ears, "Ole Artemis was shrewder'n we give 'im credit fer!"

True's mind was spinning even more rapidly than her guests' as she bade them goodbye. Too much had happened for her to absorb. Sometime she must piece together all the impossibles, binding them into a patch-work comforter to warm the hearts of her children, even as she must copy lines pertaining to Marty's background from Angel Mother's diary. He and Midgie would want to share these words with little Christian, and the writings would be a fine accompaniment for the family tree which Michael had prepared—

Michael! True shook her head, hoping to make her mind absorb what her heart was unable to communicate—the greatest "impossible" of all. How did Samuel's writing express it? Man looks on the outward appearance, but the Lord looks on the heart? Billy Joe, the philosopher, had said it another way in speaking of his friend, Artie: "A chestnut, that one—prickly on th' outside, but onct th' burr's busted there's a right sweet kernel uv goodness inside."

Forgive me, Lord. Michael's been "bustin' out" all along—only I failed to notice, because I had judged and imprisoned him for life...

The last hands had been shaken furiously, the last shoulder patted, and the last tear shed. Now the guests were gone. The four Norths, still dazed, remained outdoors looking at each other, too weary for speech.

A sweet-breathed breeze drifted in from lingering lilacs. Midgie's rooster crowed lustily. Soon dawn would spread pink bolts of color lavishly over the foothills, followed by the prodigality of sunrise splendor of a new day.

O'Higgin, whose knees had given out, rose and shook himself like a hibernating bear. "Well, I guess ye be knowin' I'm gloatin', lad," he boomed, reaching out to pump Marty's hand. "Allus saw th' tide o' enthusiasm in ye but feared instability might be dashin' ye 'ginst a reef—"

"You had a right to your doubts. I was argumentative to hide my *self*-doubt. I was a leaner—couldn't tread water without Wil here and True—and now—" *Marty was bustin' out.*

"You have Chris and me, darling," Midgie said stoutly as she reached for his hand.

O'Higgin scratched his red curls. "Nothing wrong with bein' a leaner. We all be leanin' on God. If th' Leanin' Tower did'n tilt, who be hearin' o' Pisa?"

43

Beyond
the Farthest Star

"I will miss the dogs," True said, meaning it but choosing this time to express affection for Tonsil and Lung in order to hold sadness at leaving in check. "But I guess they need space—"

"As do Marty and Midgie need space, darling," Young Wil said reassuringly. "They're the ones you're concerned about, aren't they?"

"I realize I'm as pale as paper, but am I *that* transparent?"

"Young ladies are supposed to be pale—"

"Who says?" True giggled. Her husband had a gift for turning phrases. Endearing—and maddening. "Name your source of information."

"*Godey's Lady's Book* by Sara Josepha Hale," he answered with a teasing air of superiority. "Mind if I ask you a question?"

"Yes, but you'll ask it anyway," True answered, playing his game.

But the game was over. "Won't it be exciting, getting back to Portland's shops, buying yourself a dress or so— doing the things a woman enjoys?"

The game ended for her, too. "I *have* been doing the things I enjoy, darling. You know I've loved it all—being with you, working together. In fact," True said slowly, "I have considered abandoning teaching and doing an internship in nursing. I have crammed three years of schooling into two—and we could be together—one long honeymoon!"

Young Wil touched her cheek with a gentle finger. "You amaze me, my darling. You truly do—and what you say has validity. As a matter of fact—" he paused to rummage through his coat pocket—"I have had no chance to tell you that I have confirmation of our test dates, and—" Young Wil paused to put a pencil hampering his search into his mouth while he located another envelope—"O'Higgin brought a note from the Portland doctor I was with—nothing to consider—but—"

True's heart missed a beat, then began to drum, drowning out the sound of vibrations along the rails which announced their approaching train. "An offer—?" she ventured.

"Something like that—sent my mind hurtling as fast as yon train. Ready, sweetheart?"

To board the train? Applaud the offer? Advise Wil to consider it? Or turn around and go back to the Double N? What she wanted to do was none of those. If only they could turn back the hands of the clock, finish their honeymoon, and return to the Big House afterward... back where Aunt Chrissy and Grandma Mollie were baking every known cake, pie, and cookie, grooming the already perfect grounds, and planning a "surprise party," while Daddy Wil rearranged the office furniture to accommodate his nephew's chairs and books and spread news to every patient that the prodigal young doctor was coming home. In bowers of flowers the twins would be planning every known prank. Even the river would sing a bit louder, practicing its welcome for their return to Paradise. All this O'Higgin had told them— and more—before boarding the train weeks ahead of them.

If only... if only... but time did not turn counter-clockwise.

Young Wil, sensing her mood—even hearing the words her heart was speaking, it seemed—smiled a bit crookedly. "We have grown by the experience, my dearest," he said as he helped her aboard the waiting train. "We need make no decisions now; just (and his eyes regained their twinkle) enjoy this honeymoon!"

True's mood changed. She grew more and more excited as the train's wheels ground out the miles between Slippery Elm and Portland. One by one she shed her concerns, concentrating on the fun of seeing city lights again, reuniting with family, and discussing the challenges of decisions regarding their future. After all, God would guide them. Hadn't He always? And before decisions, a honeymoon!

Even the ramshackle train station failed to depress her, although it was smoke-filled and crowded by unsavory men, only a few of whom dragged off their hats in the presence of a lady. Young Wil's strong, sure arm guided her through. Outside the world was clean and fresh as only the Pacific Northwest knew how to make it—a secret formula of wind and rain and sunshine. True unknowingly blended in with it all perfectly—so perfectly that all who passed turned to look with admiration at the girl in a dainty pink-and-white frock, the style of which suggested an inverted morning glory as its ruffled hemline swept the newly constructed boardwalk.

Familiar salt air tickled the nostrils, and hawking calls of "Tax-*eee*, tax-*eee*!" by drivers licensed to transport passengers for hire by carriage rose above the scream of white-winged gulls wheeling in for a landing and the never-ending stutter of engines as ships put out to sea. "I had forgotten how noisy cities could be," True reflected to herself as Young Wil whistled for a cab. But he overheard.

It was good to hear him laugh boyishly. "Let us hope that we don't draw a buffoon driver who serenades us country folk in Italian! Things have changed so much."

Things had changed as well in the old hotel where twice Mr. and Mrs. Wilson North had begun a honeymoon, only to be interrupted. The basic architecture was of choice quality, bulging and looming in unexpected places, begging to be preserved. The additions to accommodate a more discriminating clientele had taken nothing away. Alterations scarcely showed beneath a new coat of shining white paint. Somehow True felt relieved. She liked change while needing permanence, branching out while retaining roots. *Concentrate on your surroundings, not your philosophy,* True cautioned herself.

Inside, the changes were more visible. Thick red carpets made it difficult to wade through the pile. Chandeliers sparkled with a million prisms, overdone but hypnotic in their faulty beauty. True glanced from the great entrance hall into the diningroom and noted that the family-style tables had been replaced with alcoves which whispered an audible invitation to intimate dining. But the corner alcove boasted a long window which picked up the shimmer of the river and the tree-lined street beyond. Following her gaze, Young Wil arranged a reservation for the table of her choice.

"Happy?" he leaned across that table half an hour later, after they had freshened up and True had donned the best dress she had with her, a periwinkle-blue silk she had taken to the ranch and never worn.

"Deliriously," she said with the blush of a new bride. The truth was that she felt like one—shy, dreaming dreams, with eyes only for her husband. Alone, just the two of them, for the first time. Certainly the cardboard walls of the ranch cabin offered no privacy. The memory spun her mind backward and forward in spite of her resolutions.

"I—I do wish I could lift the curtain on the next act—"

"None of that, Mrs. North," Wil admonished. "Only God knows the end from the beginning. We will do according to His will. We have the assurance that wherever our hearts lead, God's love will follow."

"Oh, Wil, darling Wil," she breathed, "you are blessed with the gift of reminding me to 'Consider the lilies.' "

He dropped his head humbly and reached across the table to close his hands over hers. "Our Father which art in heaven..."

True's voice joined his. But before they ask only for their daily bread, repetition of the Lord's prayer was interrupted. A waiter noiselessly padded to their table and laid a yellow envelope near the heliotrope centerpiece.

With an effort, they continued. Then, ripping the flap somewhat nervously, Wil read aloud: "ALL ARRIVING TOMORROW STOP BEST WISHES ON TESTS STOP LOVE STOP THE FAMILY."

For a moment they stared at each other in disbelief. And then, forgetting their audience, the would-be honeymooners burst into a fit of uncontrollable laughter. One night alone. *One.*

Young Wil was first to recover. Wiping his eyes, he managed one word: "Meantime—"

"Our honeymoon," she gasped, feeling almost giddy. "I don't feel like dessert."

Her husband leaped to his feet in a comical fashion. "Nor I!"

Inside their bedroom Wilson North did not turn on a light. "Come here, brat!"

"Wil North," his wife began, then stopped. It would always be like this. Their love begetting love—and more love—ringed by others.

In the protective circle of his arms, her heart soared high above the trill of the bluebird's song, a song telling of dreams which had never happened—but should have. And would! Released from earth's gravity, forever they would follow the invisible footprints of faith. Beyond the farthest star. And God's love would follow.